D0194942

GLORYLAND

GLORYLAND

a novel

Shelton Johnson

SIERRA CLUB BOOKS
SAN FRANCISCO

The Sierra Club, founded in 1892 by author and conservationist John Muir, is the oldest, largest, and most influential grassroots environmental organization in the United States. With more than a million members and supporters—and some sixty chapters across the country—we are working hard to protect our local communities, ensure an enduring legacy for America's wild places, and find smart energy solutions to stop global warming. To learn how you can participate in the Sierra Club's programs to explore, enjoy, and protect the planet, please address inquiries to Sierra Club, 85 Second Street, San Francisco, California 94105, or visit our website at www.sierraclub.org.

The Sierra Club's book publishing division, Sierra Club Books, has been a leading publisher of titles on the natural world and environmental issues for nearly half a century. We offer books to the general public as a nonprofit educational service in the hope that they may enlarge the public's understanding of the Sierra Club's concerns and priorities. The point of view expressed in each book, however, does not necessarily represent that of the Sierra Club. For more information on Sierra Club Books and a complete list of our titles and authors, please visit www.sierraclubbooks.org.

Published by Sierra Club Books,
85 Second Street, San Francisco, CA 94105

Sierra Club Books are published in association with Counterpoint
(www.counterpointpress.com).

SIERRA CLUB, SIERRA CLUB BOOKS, and the Sierra Club design logos
are registered trademarks of the Sierra Club.

Book design by David Bullen

Library of Congress Cataloging-in-Publication Data
Johnson, Shelton, 1958–
Gloryland : a novel / by Shelton Johnson.
p. cm.
ISBN 978-1-57805-144-1 (trade cloth : alk. paper)
1. United States. Army. Cavalry—African American troops—Fiction. 2. United States.
Army. Cavalry, 9th—Fiction. 3. Yosemite National Park (Calif.)—Fiction. I. Title.
PS3610.O383G56 2009
813'.6—dc22   2009020643

Printed in the United States of America on Rolland Enviro 100 acid-free paper,
which contains 100 percent post-consumer waste, processed chlorine free

Distributed by Publishers Group West

13 12 11 10 09
10 9 8 7 6 5 4 3 2 1

To the memory of my father, James O. Johnson, Jr.,
and my grandparents Anna Mae and Gilbert Yancy.
To my mother, Shirley Johnson;
my brother, James, and his children;
my Aunt Marna; my son, Langston;
and especially my wife, Roxann.
And to the spirits of those buffalo soldiers
who found in me their voice.

Do Lord, oh do Lord
Do remember me
Do Lord, oh do Lord
Do remember me
Do Lord, oh do Lord
Do remember me
Goin way beyond the blue

I got a home in Gloryland
That outshines the sun
I got a home in Gloryland
That outshines the sun
I got a home in Gloryland
That outshines the sun
Goin way beyond the blue

Spiritual

GLORYLAND

Instruction to Mount without Saddle, and to Saddle
Manner of Vaulting

Seize the mane with the left hand, hold the reins of the snaffle in the right hand, and place it on the withers, the thumb to the left, the fingers to the right; raise yourself by a spring on the two wrists, the body straight; pass the right leg extended over the croup of the horse, without touching him, and seat yourself on his back.

from *Cavalry Tactics: or Regulations for the Instruction, Formations, and Movements of the Cavalry of the Army and Volunteers of the United States*. Prepared under the Direction of the War Department, and Authorized and Adopted by the Secretary of War, by Philip St. Geo. Cooke, Brig. Gen. U.S. Army.

getting started

Some things you remember. Some things you can't forget. It's like
Big Creek beside my family's home. Sometimes there's water,
sometimes not. In the spring it's flowing fast and hard, muddy and
furious. In the fall it's almost not there at all. "No Creek" is a better
name round then.

In the fall when you come up to Big Creek for a drink, you open
your hands wide, reach down into what's left of that cool, and try to
carry it to your lips, but all you do is wet your hands, the sleeves of
your coat, and your pants. Hardly any gets past your lips to soothe
your throat. What finally gets into you is what you remember.

In the early summer, when the weather's hot and Big Creek's still
big, you reach down like always, but you're a little too eager, a little
too parched, so you get too close and before you know it, what you
were reaching down to has grabbed hold of you, and you're turning
in the air and falling into all that red water, red as clay. So instead
of you getting the creek, the creek has got you, and you ain't where
you were just a moment before. You're moving downstream, but the
only way you can tell is on account of how quick the land is rushing
by—well, that's what you can't forget.

Most of what you try to remember goes right between your fingers
and all it does is get them wet, but you, you're just as thirsty as before,
and angry too. *What you can't forget* is something so big, bigger than
Big Creek, that it got its own mind and decides where you're going
inside, and it takes you, and you ain't got no control of where that
current's going to flow. You just got to ride it and hope you can keep

3

your head above water, and that you got strength left to make it back to dry land.

What you're about to read is not all I remember, but it is most definitely what I can't forget. So if it seems violent and unsteady and turns back on itself for no reason, well, that's the way my mind works, just like Big Creek in the spring. Later, when that creek goes dry and I look down where it used to be, I can see it's different every year, what it done to the earth, always different, so maybe that water is just being remembered by the ground.

I don't think I know any more about myself than Big Creek knows about the ground, but I been moving for a long time too. Not as long as that creek, but maybe just as hazy as to where I been headed and just as confused along the way, wondering what's round the next bend.

You can learn a lot about yourself, about the world, by just watching water when it moves and when it's still. Still water's rare on a creek, but it's only then that you can see yourself in it. Only then can you see your reflection in something that's got a life of its own but still got the grace to show you to yourself.

The Horse's Paces
Walk, Trot, and Canter

Before moving forward, the horse should be light in hand, the head brought home, (not with the nose stuck out,) the neck arched, and he should stand evenly on both hind legs.

from *Cavalry Tactics*

birthday

It was warm and dark, and Grandma Sara was talking.

I knew it was her even before I knew her, and I knew Daddy too.

"Why you comin now?" she asked. "What you goin to do when you get here?"

There was quiet then, and Daddy whispered, "Maybe she's just here to help us."

"Daniel, it ain't a girl in there but a boy," Grandma Sara said. "He's come for a reason, everybody here for a reason, and I think I know what it is."

I wasn't alone. There were other people in there. All those who came before me were there. People that knew me from the beginning, people I would know at the end. So many folks in such a small space, it should've been uncomfortable, but it wasn't.

It was so quiet, so easy to be there in the place that was my mother. I didn't want to go anywhere, but I could feel something pushing me away from what I was holding on to.

"Elijah!" I heard Grandma Sara call.

Her voice sounded close yet very far away.

"Elijah," she spoke again. "Your name's Elijah. That's what we'll call you, but you'll have another name, a name only the Creator knows. That's the name you'll answer to when it calls you in your sleep. The name you had before. The name you'll have after." And I heard that name in my mind as loud as if it had been shouted, and I knew who I was, who I really was.

"You'll bring us to the old ones," Grandma whispered. "You'll take us home, and it won't be in no chariot of fire, no need for that. We'll walk just fine."

It got quiet again, felt so heavy, the quiet.

I finally let go, and it hurt to not hold and not be held.

Light came out of my mouth, my nose, went back inside. I could see it with my eyes, which had never opened before, could hear it with my ears, which had never listened before. I could see fire that was water, hear water that was fire. Where I was going was a dark place, but something was burning that had to be my heart. I drifted round with my eyes closed to the brightness. My hands, my fingers opened up, then closed round a damp shine that was everywhere.

And that's all I remember of the time before I was born.

My name's Elijah Yancy, and I was born on the first day of January 1863 in a cabin outside of Spartanburg, South Carolina. You might recall that President Lincoln signed the Emancipation Proclamation on the very same day. That's right, the day freedom came, or at least news of it. Mostly it was just rumor, cause slaves round here were only free if there were Union soldiers nearby. Union soldiers wore blue uniforms. On the day I was born there weren't no one round wearing such a thing, which meant that white folks in Spartanburg County didn't get the word that we were free.

My daddy's name was Daniel Yancy, but I never called him that cause I had a nice smile, and I was sure to lose it if I started calling my daddy "Daniel," so I didn't. I just called him "Sir," and after a while I thought that was his name. And my mama's name's Lucinda, but I thought her name was "Ma'am," cause that's what I had to call her. Anyway, Daddy called the emancipation "paper freedom" cause the only place you could find freedom was on that piece of paper. You sure couldn't find it in Spartanburg. My daddy'd been all over the county, and if he'd ever run into freedom I know he would've come home and told us about it.

As I got older, I noticed colored people were having parties on my birthday, and that was interesting cause they never invited me to those parties. And yet I'd be walking along those red country roads and I'd pass by the Joneses' place, and they'd be fiddling and laughing and having a good time, and I'd say to myself, How they know it's my birthday? And then I'd hear the same sort of commotion coming from the Washingtons', who I didn't really know that well, so I couldn't figure out why they'd be cheering for my birthday. It took a while for me to realize that they were excited about freedom, about the Emancipation Proclamation, which had nothing to do with my birthday!

I was taken down a bit when I realized that, but the damage had already been done. By the time I was seven or eight I had an attitude that was bound for trouble. That's what my mama told me. She talked a lot about my attitude, in a way that made it seem like it was something separate from me. I can clearly remember her saying, "Elijah, you can stay here as long as you want, boy, but that attitude of yours got to go!"

Like my attitude could rise in the morning, get dressed, put on shoes, open the door, and walk up the road. Sometimes I felt like my parents only saw me in pieces. There were pieces they liked and pieces they didn't like. What they didn't care for was always encouraged to "find a home elsewhere."

All of this came about cause I was born on the day freedom came, or was supposed to come. I came into the world on *that day*, and like it or not, freedom came with me. I've thought a lot about freedom, particularly when I was walking behind a plow, and the plow was peeling back dirt behind a mule, and the mule was leading the way across a field at sunup. I'd be thinking about freedom, but all I could see was the butt and the stiff-legged gait of that animal working so hard and going nowhere. From time to time its tail would go up just to get my attention, and the mule would drop a reminder to not think of freedom too much, or I might regret it.

My father used to say about the Emancipation Proclamation, "Elijah, the only difference between the day before emancipation and the day after is about forty-eight hours."

Before emancipation we were slaves, and after we were share-croppers. If there's someone reading this who knows the difference between a slave and a sharecropper, please send a message to the colored folks in Spartanburg, cause I'm sure they'd be interested, but good news is a lame mule walking toward South Carolina, while bad news is the fastest thoroughbred in the county. Maybe that's why those parties got quieter and quieter. Colored people began to realize that freedom hadn't come, so there was nothing to celebrate.

Patrol report on Yosemite Park stationery

The Adjutant,   Little Jackass Meadows,
Camp A. E. Wood,   3rd July, 1903
Yosemite Natl. Park, Cal.

Sir: I have the honor to report in accordance to instructions received from you that I found on reaching this camp eleven sacks of Barley.

> Very respectfully,
> John H. Mitchell
> Sergt., troop "L", 9th Cavalry
> Commanding Detachment

dreaming

Freedom. It stays in your head and won't bust out or slip away like tears. I've had enough of freedom and I ain't ever had it. When I sleep, there's freedom. I can be whatever I want to be and no one tells me anything different. I ain't no sharecropper when I'm asleep. I don't know what I am, but it's got nothing to do with rice or sorghum or indigo or anything but the light of the sun rising over a place that never heard the word *nigger*.

Maybe it's cause I was born on Emancipation Day, maybe that's why I am what I am. Born the day freedom was supposed to come. That'd change anybody. Maybe it's cause my Grandma Sara is Seminole. Daddy told me the Seminoles were a runaway band of Creek Indians who went down into Florida. That's why the Spanish called them *cimarron*, which means runaway. There were also slaves and free Africans who ran off from South Carolina and Georgia round the same time, down into Florida. They were runaways too. The English called them *maroons*, which is another word hiding in the word *cimarron*, like *cimarron* was giving it shelter. I like that. Africans and Indians, trying to find something better, found each other, found some shelter, and began calling themselves Seminoles. Together they found something they couldn't get on their own.

Somewhere along the way they stopped running from something and began running to something: freedom. They found it in Spanish Florida, for a while. Then the English offered the Seminoles freedom if they'd fight America in the Revolutionary War. Good trade.

Maybe that's where I got such a bad attitude, from those runaway ancestors. My attitude is spoilt like a pail of milk stuck out too long in the sun and gone bad.

I remember Daddy saying to me, "Boy, be easy round Grandma Sara, you know she's Seminole. She's a proud woman, and too much pride is as bad as too little. She's all bunched up inside with it, who she is and what's been done to her and how she come through it, you understand me, boy?"

And I said, "Yessir." I didn't understand, but it was always safer to say "yessir" and not "nossir" when I was talking to Daddy, so that's what I said all the time even if I didn't know what he was saying.

He looked at me then, with the sun shining on the left side of his face from the hole in the wall, which would have been a window someplace else, and he tried again. He said, "Elijah, your grandma is Seminole, and they a proud people, and the government don't like all that pride in colored folks, so they sent the army down into Florida to get at the Seminole on account of they so full of themselves. They kept sendin more soldiers down into those hot swamps that'd suck the boots right off your feet, and it didn't end there, no, they sent even more white boys into that misery.

"After a bit the government noticed that no soldiers ever come out of those swamps, not a single one. It took some time for them to notice, but they did, and somebody decided it might be better to just leave all those Indians alone, cause the government had no use for a swamp. So the Seminole figure they beat the army, they beat America. It kinda got into they heads that they won, and victory, well, it's like drinkin too much whiskey. You get drunk on it, it blurs your vision, and that's Grandma Sara, she sees the U.S. Army beaten and America beaten, and she's proud. Proud of who she is and who her people are or were. Now you understand what I'm sayin, boy?"

"Yessir, yessir, I understand. You sayin Grandma Sara's mean cause she Seminole, is that right?" I asked.

Daddy looked up to heaven, cuffed me upside my head, and then rubbed my scalp like he was sorry. Through the light of the busted sun I was seeing, he said, "No, boy, you ain't listenin at all. Grandma

Sara's just mean, you hear me? She's mean entirely through, and it ain't got nothin to do with her bein Seminole. It's got to do with what's been done to her on account of her bein Indian."

Well, I was confused, cause folks said I took after my grandmother, and I thought that's where my attitude came from, knowing that Grandma Sara's people held off the army. But here's Daddy saying meanness don't come from being Seminole but from being treated like you're Seminole, being treated poorly, that it's got nothing to do with who you are on the inside and more with what you look like on the outside. I'm part Seminole and can feel it on the inside, but I look more African than Indian.

Feeling something on the inside that you can't find anywhere on the outside can't be good for a person. Feeling something on the outside that you can't find anywhere inside will make you just as sick. Someone takes a whip to you, you can explain why you're raw and bleeding, but what if they beat you up on the inside? Who's gonna know that you're hurting? How do you dress a wound you can't see?

Born the day freedom came. Grandchild of some people who wouldn't let freedom be taken away. No wonder I got attitude. I got so much I could sell most of it off and no one would notice. You need attitude if you're colored in Spartanburg. You need it to get up in the morning, just to open your eyes, but too much attitude in the South will put you down by nightfall. It'll close your eyes for sure.

My dreaming began round this time, when Daddy tried to tell me how Grandma Sara got the way she was. It wasn't so much dreams in my sleep, I just started thinking I could be whatever I wanted to be. I could be an engineer or a doctor cause I liked the idea of fixing what's broken, whether it's a plow or something alive. Yeah, a doctor, that'd be better than sharecropping. I thought this at night in a warm wind like God breathing on me, in bed where I felt the most safe. And the thinking turned to dreaming, and it got scary to be dreaming about who I could be.

That's when I began to get sick. Dreaming about becoming

someone I could never be made me sick, but not on the outside. On the outside I was strong and young and could last all day out in the sun, in the field, but inside something was breaking, going dark even under the sun. When it happened I got cold inside like it was winter even when I was working in the fields. I'd be sweating on the outside but all ice inside, like chills and then fever, from dreaming things that could never be, would never be cause I was a nigger, and niggers ain't supposed to dream.

The sickness got real bad after Mama and I had a run-in with some white man in Spartanburg. We had gone into town for supplies and were walking in the road that morning with the sun glaring down, so I could barely make out the people walking close by, up on a wooden sidewalk. I remember Mama was gripping my hand hard like she was worried someone would steal me, and with me being small my hand was higher than my head, which made my arm and shoulder ache. It was hot and my eyes stung with sweat. I felt like a sack of corn being pulled along.

Suddenly a shadow came across the sun and a white man stepped off the sidewalk and down into the road, right down onto my foot.

"Damn!" I yelled in pain.

"Elijah!" Mama hissed. "You better watch your mouth!"

"Nigger!" the man spat. "Why don't you watch where you're goin, boy?"

I thought the pain in my arm and shoulder was bad, but it was nothing compared to what I felt in my gut. I spent most of my time at home, where nobody ever used that word, and this was the first time I remembered hearing it. But the way he said it cut like a knife, deep inside so you couldn't see the hurt. I felt hot tears on my cheeks, and everything got blurry.

Mama's grip got even tighter. She spun me around and we walked back the way we'd come. When we got to the wagon and got in, Mama reached down, and with a hard flick of her wrists and the snap of the reins the mules woke up. She turned us round and got us out of town, never saying a word along the way, but there was a stiffness to her body like she used too much starch in her dress and it had gone into her bones.

What I can't forget is Mama talking to me when we got home. When we got inside where there was shelter, her holding my face in her rough warm hands like she was praying, I felt how warm it was and safe to be there in her hands. Nothing could hurt me in that shelter that was hands and love, and she said, "Elijah, you forget that man, he nothin to you or to me or your daddy. But you ain't nothin, cause I didn't work a day and a half bringin nothin into this world. I didn't bleed tears or sweat blood bringin nothin into my life. You could never be nothin, you could never be anyone's nigger. You my boy Elijah, you my son, and my son ain't a nigger, and your daddy ain't a nigger, and I ain't a nigger, and it don't matter how much it get said, don't make it true.

"That man's cussin somethin inside him, somethin he hates inside him, but not you cause he don't even know who you are, Elijah. Cause what I'm holdin in my hands is somethin good and kind, and I know you'll never be a nigger unless you forget who you are!"

That's what Mama said, so I never try to be something I ain't, and I ain't ever been a nigger. But I'm Seminole and I'm colored, just like sundown I'm colored, like dirt that's warm and black and red too, like the sun's been shining so long the dirt remembers all that light and holds on to it. It takes a lot of sunsets to turn the ground red down deep, but I guess there's been plenty of sunsets since the beginning, and there weren't no niggers then. Niggers came later.

But knowing I wasn't a nigger made me sick, cause white folks treated me like something I wasn't. When I got older I corrected them, I told them who I was. I said, "Elijah Yancy's my name, what's your name?" I didn't really care if they told me. What mattered was that they knew who I was. I could've been saying I was God, I said it with such pride. I believed my mama when she said Elijah Yancy is God's child, her child, a boy who's got a mother and a father, people who love him, and love ain't nothing. It matters like water matters, or the sun.

So I held on to my dreams even though they hurt my hands, my mind, my soul. It would have been easier to let go, but I was stronger than the pain, love made me stronger, and so I held on even tighter. Deep down there was bleeding I never let anyone see, and maybe it don't matter how much you bleed in the night if the blood's all gone by sunup. But the sheets would be cold with my sweat cause that fever had taken me. Dreams are fire and they'll burn you dry.

The Horse's Paces
Walk, Trot, and Canter

Close the legs and communicate a sufficient impulse to carry him forward without giving the hand; for if you do, the head and neck may relapse into a position which will defy the control of the hand.

from *Cavalry Tactics*

sundays

If there's a good day in the week, I remember it being Sunday. Sunday meant just a few chores, like chopping wood for the fire and bathing. Mama said she liked to be able to see me at least once a week, and she figured if I bathed it might be easier for God to recognize me in church.

Sunday meant sleeping a little bit longer, but not too much. Long enough that when you got up, your bed was so warm it just pulled you back down again, and you went without a struggle.

And Sunday usually meant Mama's fried chicken. That fried chicken convinced me that chickens were created by God so they could be cooked by my mama for me to eat. I could eat her chicken for breakfast, lunch, and dinner every day, but it was only for Sunday cause Sunday was different.

My daddy never really relaxed, but there was a shadow of relaxation about him on Sundays. He looked different, and something about him felt different. He seemed to know deep in his body that he wouldn't be in the field that day. All of him just sagged, but in a good way, on Sundays.

Sunday wasn't so much a time but a feeling inside, a feeling you could only get on that day, leastways for me. Mama used to say that life was just what happened leading up to Sunday, and the things that happened after. For her it was all about Sunday, even when it wasn't Sunday. She said, "Elijah, Sunday's not a day of the week, it's somethin in your heart, and as long as you know that, then you don't have to die and go to heaven to find God, cause God is always waitin for you right here." And she'd gently touch my chest with her hand.

As the time would get closer for going to church, Mama would begin to hum a little, and I don't remember her ever singing except on Sunday mornings. There was just a calm about her all day that you couldn't even find an echo of any other time.

Sunday meant washing, though, washing till my skin felt like it was going to peel off. And the water had to be hot, which is why I was chopping wood in the first place. Even when I was little, Mama would wash me so hard I thought she was trying to polish my bones, she pressed down so hard, scrubbing and scrubbing. No child could ever be that dirty, but Mama said I tried all week to be that dirty and generally succeeded.

After we were all clean, "clean enough to be before God" is how Mama put it, we'd put one more log in the woodstove if it was wintertime, to keep the cabin warm for Grandma Sara. She never went to church, even though she'd raised my mama to love God and to be faithful. Grandma Sara had her own way of talking to God.

I can still see us in our Sunday finery, which meant clothes that were clean and without patches. Daddy would always wear his one "good" hat and Mama had white cotton gloves she only wore then. If it was hot she'd have her little umbrella to keep the sun off. On a cold winter day, she'd be huddled under a thick wool blanket. Either way she'd be sitting tall and straight in the wagon, Daddy next to her happy as he could be. He was always in a better mood when he was next to Mama. I spent a lot of my childhood trying to figure out ways to get them together so he could be in a better mood.

The church where colored folks went wasn't in Spartanburg but a bit outside, so you had to leave the main road into town and follow a little dirt road off to one side. The church was just a wooden shack but it was clean and neat, and everyone going inside it was clean and neat. I remember the deacon sounded like what I thought God must sound like, and the deacon's wife was as close to the word *elegant* as my young self ever saw. It wasn't what she was wearing, it was something inside her that wasn't touched by the rest of the week. She was Sunday come to life.

When the deacon gave his sermon, he seemed to be telling us he could feel what we'd been feeling the week before, but all that pain and struggle was gone now and the struggle and pain ahead hadn't got here yet, cause this was the Lord's day and a time to rejoice. I don't really remember anything in particular that was said in church, but I can't forget how I felt listening to what was said, and watching people I only ever saw on Sunday.

The girls always acted like they was all grown up, wearing dresses like their mamas but smaller, and they sat just as straight, behaving respectfully like they should, but the boys were usually squirming on those hard oak benches, struggling for freedom under ironed white collars and shirts buttoned to breathless. Most of them couldn't wait to get back outside and play. We could play on Sunday afternoons after church, cause usually there would be food people brought to share, and the adults would start talking about news and such. There was no way they could talk and mind where the children were at the same time, so we'd run around like there was no tomorrow, no having to get back to everyday hard work starting before dawn.

There were Goodloes and Andersons and Browns and Joneses and Washingtons and McCarthys and Smiths, more folks than I can remember the names of, just families having a good time. And it didn't matter if it was cloudy or rainy, Sunday afternoons were always the one bright time of the week.

But Sunday mornings we spent indoors. The women with their fans waving at the hot stuffy air, white dresses crackling like a fire when they moved. The fathers stiff as wet sheets left out all night in January, sitting next to their women, their heads bobbing up and down in rhythm to the deacon's words. I remember the singing . . .

> Do Lord, oh do Lord
> Do remember me
> Do Lord, oh do Lord

Do remember me
Do Lord, oh do Lord
Do remember me
Goin way beyond the blue

I got a home in Gloryland
That outshines the sun
I got a home in Gloryland
That outshines the sun
I got a home in Gloryland
That Outshines the sun
Goin way beyond the blue

While we were singing we weren't there no more, not in South Carolina, not in Spartanburg, not even in that church. We were someplace bigger than anywhere else, someplace safe and warm and peaceful. The singing went on and on, and sometimes I'd run out of breath for it. Sitting there trying to get my breath back, I could feel I was part of something bigger than my family, bigger than anything I knew. It was a good feeling, how a forest tree must feel being rooted in the ground and all its roots touching other roots, but they all hidden in the ground, and their touching hidden too.

Daddy once said, "Elijah, you can learn a lot by learnin from plants. They rooted, so you should be that way too. If you know the names of everything that's green and rooted around you, then you always home and you always belong. When some plants is young, they green and move easy in the air, so they don't break in a storm, and that's another thing you can learn. No matter how big a wind is on you, just remember to bend so you don't break, you hear me, boy?"

And I would say "yessir!" like always. But Daddy was right, cause I remembered what he said and I always tried to learn the names of what was growing round me and let the plants be my teachers. When I was older and a soldier in Yosemite, I would see the young red firs doubled over with the weight of snow, but not broken, and

I'd think about what Daddy said, how to bend under the pressure, give in to it, knowing that the burden would lift one day. You gotta outlast the weight so you can rise like those fir trees rise when the snow has melted.

All those colored people, my family and our neighbors, they were using Sundays like trees use the sun. Letting their burdens melt away under the heat of the deacon's sermon, so they could walk out of that building taller than they walked in. Letting their roots tangle up with their neighbors'. Letting the wind of their singing carry their hearts home. Sundays weren't about heaven at all, they were about learning how to be right here on this earth. They were more necessary than air or food. You can live weeks without food and days without water, but we couldn't live at all without Sundays.

The hard thing is to take Sunday with you if you end up going to a place without Sunday.

✒

Patrol report on Yosemite Park stationery,
under "Remarks," Wawona, Cal., July 14, 1903

A party of (4) men and (4) horses from San Francisco passed through as tourists. No arms of any kind.

Very Respectfully,
William Alexander,
Sgt. "L", 9 Cavy.
Commanding Detachment

✒

voting

I remember Daddy getting up before the sun, or the sound of him getting up, the sound of him breathing and speaking to himself or someone besides Mama, and I remember thinking, Who could that be? There's just the four of us, and you couldn't really have a conversation with Grandma Sara. You just nodded and listened to what she had to say, and then she'd say afterward, "I'm glad we had ourselves this little talk!" Like someone else had been talking besides her.

But now it was just Daddy breathing hard in the dark of the cabin, the cotton outside making a noise in the wind like a running creek. I could hear him getting his shoes, putting on the cold like it was overalls, and him saying under his breath, "Man got a right, got a right to . . ." He said it over and over, as if the room was big enough to have an echo, but it wasn't so he made one up. Like that would give him some room for an idea of his that was too big for our little cabin. Freedom can't fit in here, no room for it, but that's what he wants. Only he couldn't tell me about it cause he never had it.

Then in that blue cold he said, "Elijah, boy, you better get on up and get those mules ready, cause sure to God it won't happen with you lyin there."

And I moved in the warmth of my blankets like I was swimming in Big Creek after the sun been on it all day, and it was hard to pull up out of it and get my breath. I could see my breath coming up in the cabin, and I knew without asking that I had to make the fire in our raggedy old stove.

I swung my bare feet down onto the dirt that covered the wood floor cause the walls didn't come all the way down to the floor in some places. No matter how often Mama told me to sweep it up, it just kept coming back. I got up onto it naked and found my overalls. There was just the wind, the sound of my mama breathing, and now my daddy complaining how the dawn always come too quick. Daddy's always saying something unkind about daylight. I think he got problems with the sun cause it showed him how much work was left to do. When it's dark you can't see nothing, which is all right when your fingers is raw and your back is telling you how poorly you treated it all day. I don't know, I just gotta get up, get moving, get that wood.

I did and the fire got going good. The fire was the first nice thing that happened that morning and I wanted to stay a little longer inside the heat, but I wanted to live a little longer too, so I knew I better get on with the mules cause daddy wouldn't find it funny, me standing over the stove like a mule at a trough. I opened the cabin door and stepped out into the morning, so black with just a bit of red through the trees, sunup having as hard a time as me getting out into the world.

I got the mules fed and watered and harnessed up to the wagon, which didn't take much time. The cold made it longer, but by the time I finished it was lightening up good and a breeze with a little fire in it was starting to flow at my back, and when all was ready, I went back up the step into the warm room. Daddy was standing there, taller than his shadow, which was stooped against the wall like it was too tired to stand up alongside him. He was looking at me like I was supposed to say something, so I thought it best to start talking.

"Wagon's ready, sir," was all I said, but it must've been the right thing, cause he just nodded and then sat down in his chair for a bit, like this was one of those times you might need to sit and think about something before you did it. The way he was sitting there made me think of fog on a hill, how it covers up trees and ground but it ain't really there at all, cause you can walk through it, breathe it in and out, nothing much in your way but cold damp air.

Mama said it's God's breath when you get that low fog on the ground. "God's close now, so you better be thinkin good thoughts, boy, cause he can hear you now!"

"Daniel," I heard Mama say from the back of the cabin. "Daniel, you still goin through with this?" Her voice seemed to be saying that Daddy was planning on setting himself on fire or walking stark naked through Spartanburg.

"Sure as this sunup, I'm goin to that courthouse," he said, and his voice was hard as anger and coiled tighter than a rattler before it strikes.

"Then," Mama went on, "you better take Elijah with you. A boy should be there to see his daddy when he's so sure of himself, cause I ain't so sure, you hear me, Daniel? I ain't sure at all!"

"We talked bout this last night," Daddy said, "and I told you I was goin round sunup, and it's sunup and I'm goin."

"Oh yeah, that's right," said Mama, "you goin all right, and here you are gettin ready all right, and you goin to get in that wagon all right, and you goin to head to that courthouse, and I guess that's right. But I'm goin too, and Elijah's goin, we all goin to see you make your mark on that piece of paper, for all the good it'll do, yes, Lord!"

My daddy got up from his chair and walked back to the dark part of the cabin where Mama was, and I could hear him making whispering and soothing noises like a pigeon, but she wasn't being soothed at all. She was crying, and I could feel her tears scalding my cheeks, running hot down my chin, yeah, it must've been her tears coming out of me.

"Why now, Daniel?" she asked soft. "Why now?" she said again.

"No better time, Lucy." He called her Lucy instead of Lucinda when he was being sweet or "trying" to be sweet, Mama said.

"I know it's been hard, Daniel," she said, "so hard that hard don't mean nothin no more, but at least you alive, with us, but you go on to that courthouse and maybe that goin to change!"

Daddy said nothing, but I could see him thinking. His eyelids always closed up when he did that, like they was trying to keep something from getting in. He was going to go no matter what Mama said, I could feel it in the room and hear it when he talked.

"Lucy," he told her, "even you can't convince the sun to not get up this mornin, even you can't do that. I'm tired of it. If I never do anythin else, I'm gonna do this, and this is the mornin, not tomorrow or the next day or next week, but right now, or it won't happen at all. And then I'll be dead, and you'll be sleepin the rest of your life next to a dead man, cold through and through. Oh yeah, I'll be gettin up same as usual, but it'll be a dead man gettin up and workin those fields!"

There was quiet after he said that, and I was trying not to breathe cause I wanted to listen, but they kept speaking softer and softer, as if they were already on the wagon and I'm running along behind and can't keep up, their voices getting faint. Then I heard Mama say, "You don't think I get tired too? We all tired every day, every single day, and there'll be plenty of rest by and by, but not now, Daniel. Not now when our boy's still a boy, and you not here to teach him bout bein a man!"

And Daddy said, "Can't teach Elijah nothin bout bein a man if I ain't one myself. Lucy, that law say we got the right to vote, but no one's votin cause they scared!"

That's when I heard Mama get up off her bed sudden, and though she's not a big woman, I could feel her feet hit the floor. "Daniel!" she said, and her voice was stronger now, "honey, colored people round here got a right to be scared, that's the only right we do have. We got lots of fear and not much of anythin else. Fear of speakin up too much, fear of sayin the right thing or the wrong thing. Fear of wakin up and fear of goin to sleep. Fear's the one thing we got plenty of, and I bustin up inside from my fear that you goin to die today, and maybe us right along with you, cause you got a fear of not bein a man!"

And again it got real quiet, a quiet that made you hold your breath cause you weren't certain the air would still be there once you decided to open your mouth.

"Lucinda," Daddy answered finally, "we ain't walkin a road we walked before. It's done. I'm goin to that courthouse, and I'm goin to vote. And you say you comin, so tell me what you goin to do." He spoke so soft, like maybe the walls would hear and tell the mules outside.

Mama said nothing more, but she got up from the dark back there, passed Daddy, and walked out into the stovelight. She opened the door, stepped down to the yard, and got up into the wagon. I saw she was wearing the dress she had on last night. She never even changed before going to bed.

Daddy walked slowly after her, turned a bit, and said to me, "Come on, boy!" I followed after him and climbed into the back of the wagon. All the way to town, Mama and Daddy didn't look at each other at all, just sat there staring ahead. I can't forget looking at the backs of their heads so straight and unmoving, but their bodies swaying with the motion of the wagon. No one spoke the whole way. I sat in the back watching them stare at nothing at all. After a while I looked down, cause it didn't feel good to look at them.

It might've gotten better, but the wagon bouncing over that rutted road seemed to keep things just below boiling even though no one was talking. The road to town was always bad after the winter rains. It seemed like we spent as much time going from side to side as going forward.

Then we got to town, and right near the center of all those buildings and stores and houses was the courthouse where the white folks came to vote.

Standing in front of the courthouse was the sheriff. Sheriff Reynolds was a big man who always rolled up his sleeves no matter how cold it was. He had a wicked-looking pistol tucked into a leather belt, and he carried an oak walking stick though I never saw him limp. I think the stick was to make other people limp after he hit them with it. He never smiled, and if he had, it probably would've killed him, or at least cut up his face, making it move in a way nature never intended. He ain't the meanest man in the world, but he's probably kin to whoever that man is.

Daddy stopped the wagon in front of the courthouse, which meant he stopped right in front of the sheriff. Sheriff Reynolds wasn't paying any attention to us till then. Colored people had the right to ride a wagon and use the road, but we weren't expected to stop in front of the courthouse. Ever.

"How do, Daniel," said the sheriff softly, but only his voice was soft. His body stiffened up and his face got harder.

"Good mornin, Sheriff," said my daddy.

"Well, Daniel, it was a mighty fine mornin till just a moment ago. Now maybe that was just an accident, maybe your mules are tired and they thought this might be a good place to rest. Maybe that explains why you're blockin the courthouse, keepin the good people of this community from engagin in county business, at least I hope so. Well, you better explain to these mules of yours how they're creatin a misunderstandin here, how some of those good people might start thinkin it was *you* stopped in front of this courthouse. And you wouldn't want that, would you, boy?"

Daddy said nothing at first, but I could see his back straightening up like a tree at the first tug of a storm.

"I don't want no one to get upset with me, Sheriff," Daddy began. "I didn't come here to cause no trouble, I just come to vote, like the law say I got a right to. And I'm goin to vote, sir, if that's all right with you."

I thought it had been quiet back in the cabin, but this was a quiet not used to air or sunlight, and it was out in the open for the first time, naked, cold, and pale as a bass gasping for breath.

Sheriff Reynolds did smile then. His teeth were yellow, stained with tobacco. It seemed to hurt him to smile. I hoped he would stop soon cause I was starting to feel bad, looking at something that was more like a wound gaping on his face than a grin.

"Daniel," he finally said, slow as molasses easing out of an upturned bottle, "I always thought of you as a reasonable nigger, and now it appears you're tryin to change my opinion. I'd rather pretend you didn't say what you just said. So tell those mules of yours to move along and rest somewheres else. You hear me, boy?"

Sheriff Reynolds' voice sounded easy and sincere, but it was like sleeping on a mattress full of razors and nails. No matter how carefully you move, the hard sharpness you can't see on the inside of the bed keeps cutting through to the outside, and you can't see clearly what's tearing you up.

"I'm sorry, Sheriff," said Daddy, "but there ain't nothin wrong with my mules. I stopped them right here, and it wasn't no mistake. I'm here to vote!"

By this time, other white folks had gathered. White and colored folks in town didn't usually have long talks, and very few people had conversations with the sheriff. Those that did were probably going to jail or coming from jail. But I wouldn't call them conversations cause the sheriff was usually the only one talking.

"No, no," said Sheriff Reynolds, with a sour look on his face, and he cocked his head to one side like he was trying to get a better view of my daddy. "You most definitely are not here to vote. And I am gonna arrest you, Daniel, for bein intoxicated in public, cause it's plainly obvious to everyone here that you've been drinkin, and I believe a night in my jail may do you some good. We can sit up all night and talk about your problems, cause I care about you, boy. Believe you me, I'm intent on takin care of you the best way I know how, and before the night is done we will surely come to an understandin."

"I appreciate that, Sheriff," said Daddy. "I know you want to do what's right, and I appreciate your hospitality, invitin me to stay with you and all, but I slept plenty last night. I'm rested and I got somethin to do right here, somethin I been meanin to do for a long time."

And right then Daddy jumped down from the wagon, landing not two feet from the sheriff. Sheriff Reynolds jumped back a little and gripped his stick harder and put his left hand on his pistol, but he didn't seem scared. If anything he seemed anxious for something to start.

"Daniel," said the sheriff, louder now so the people around could hear, "it would be a pity to leave this fine boy of yours without a father, or such a good-lookin woman here without a husband.

Course, me bein the sheriff, I'd be derelict in my duty if I didn't check on 'em from time to time, just to see if they all right. But we can avoid all that if you come with me to jail right now, or turn that wagon round and get yourself home, cause you sure as hell not goin up these courthouse steps."

Daddy took a step toward the courthouse. The crowd stepped back a bit, but Sheriff Reynolds didn't move, standing less than a foot away from Daddy. The sheriff was an inch or so shorter, but he was even heavier. I noticed my father's hands at his sides. They were opening and closing but there was nothing inside them. I could see the veins on his hands slipping round under the skin, and the veins in his neck were full as he bent toward the sheriff like a big old tree leaning into the wind.

"Nigger, you take one more step, I'll bust yo head wide open!" Sheriff Reynolds announced. He was done pretending to be Daddy's friend.

I thought my daddy would explode like a bucket of water left out in the night when the temperature drops below freezing. It wasn't heat he was giving off no more but cold, cold like I ain't never seen in a living man before. The coldness of death must've been inside him trying to get out, and the sheriff had the key in the door, turning it this way and that.

I watched Daddy slowly shift from his right foot to his left. He was about to walk and I couldn't think of any way to stop him, and I didn't know for sure if I should stop him. That's when Mama got down from the wagon. Nobody seemed to see her do it, but somehow she was standing next to my father. She looked so small beside him.

Mama paid no attention to the sheriff. As Daddy leaned his body forward to start walking, Mama hooked the little finger of her right hand squarely into the crook of his left elbow. That's all. No strain, no sweat. Just her little finger on Daddy's arm.

And I watched my daddy, all six foot six inches and two hundred and fifty pounds of him, stop completely under the weight of that finger. I mean, he was moving toward the sheriff till he felt a pressure on him that no one could see but me, and no one could feel but him.

Then my father broke somewhere inside. It was a break you couldn't see on the outside, but he was like an old tree that's finally tired of bending, knows it's been done in by the wind and is just marking time till the next breeze comes up, and down it goes. I watched him die some right there, even though he was still standing, still breathing. I don't know if the sheriff or my mother killed him, or if it was suicide, but a man died in front of that courthouse and the killer got away.

What was left of Daddy turned and got up into the wagon. Mama followed him, but then she stopped and looked back at Sheriff Reynolds. I couldn't clearly see her face, but I could see the sheriff's. It was red like a tomato. The sheriff scratched his neck and looked away. Mama climbed up and sat down next to Daddy, who sat stiff as a corpse. It shocked me to see him shake the reins and get the mules moving away down the street. The crowd that had gathered parted to let the wagon through. Those white people were whispering but saying nothing out loud, and their silence was more frightening than any yelled curses. I lay my head in my mother's lap and tried to forget their eyes.

After the wagon had pulled away, I raised my head and looked back at the sheriff, who was looking down at the ground where my father had stood, as if something should have been there, something he could've picked up and carried away. I couldn't see anything except the strength that had been my daddy lying there in the road. Sheriff Reynolds never moved, like he wasn't even breathing. But then I saw his chest begin to go out and in as we rode away. It must've been hard for that man to go so long without taking a breath.

I didn't breathe too much either till we got home.

Later I found out that even if Daddy had been allowed into that courthouse, it wouldn't have mattered. He didn't have the money to pay the poll tax or the book learning to pass the literacy test.

The sheriff knew that. All those white people gathered on the steps of the courthouse knew it. For Daddy it wasn't about paying for something. He figured he'd already paid. And it wasn't about whether he could read or write. It was about justice. He once told me that if you had to ask for something that was already yours, then you'd given it up. Up to that day Daddy behaved as if he believed he had rights, but he died outside that courthouse trying to claim what nobody should have to ask for.

There's one thing colored people in the South have in common with the dead. The dead have no rights. Maybe Daddy knew that all along.

The Horse's Paces
Walk, Trot, and Canter

The rider should always have a light feeling of the reins; and when
the horse bears hard on the bit, keep the hand steady, use both legs,
which, by bringing his haunches under him, will oblige the horse
to take his weight off your hand.

from *Cavalry Tactics*

grandma sara

Old. Young. The way a river is old and young. Grandma Sara had eyes like that. Eyes that looked through you like you were a window and she could plainly see what was on the other side, even if you couldn't see a thing. You had to ask her about yourself, cause sooner or later you realized you didn't know yourself till she began talking to you. You were a language she used to speak to the dead. How far away her eyes, like stars at night, like the moon in daylight. Always smoking tobacco, I remember smoke round her head. She was always in a cloud sitting there in her rocking chair.

I got so's I knew what was coming when she chose to talk to me, and it was never easy. She was old and bent like an oak's old and bent. She still had grit enough to kill me dead, but she said she loved me, which was why she so hard. Like one time when I was maybe fifteen years old, and she woke up to find me sitting on the floor a few feet away from her chair. My chin was buried in my hands, and I probably looked like I was praying. Anyone talking to God was bound to raise Grandma Sara's interest.

When I peered up at her, the morning sun shone behind her head. She looked like God, if God had been a Black Seminole woman, but when Grandma asked you a question, well, there wasn't much difference between the two.

"What you doin, boy?" she said.

"Nothin, ma'am," I murmured.

"Don't 'nothin' me, boy," she spat back. "You fifteen years old now, and that's old enough for all kinds of trouble." She paused briefly. "Maybe you workin yourself up to go back to that courthouse and finish what your daddy started?"

I wondered how that woman could see my heart so clearly when sometimes I couldn't even feel it.

"No, ma'am," I muttered through my fingers. "I mean, I know I should get that out of my head, but I can't forget how that sheriff looked at Daddy. What he did should be against the law, and Sheriff Reynolds oughtta throw himself in jail for breakin the law!" My voice dropped down then like a bird that forgot what it was singing. I was also thinking bout Grandma Sara, how she'd been around even longer than Daddy and what kinda things must've happened to her, but I didn't know how to say that.

Grandma Sara peered down at me with the look you get when you're eyeing a worm you just put on a hook, wondering if that worm is just the right worm to catch that fish you're after.

"So what else you thinkin bout, young as you is?" she kept on.

I paused before answering cause I didn't want to sound like a fool, but I knew it was hopeless.

"I'm thinkin bout how old you must be," I said then. "How old are you, Grandma Sara?"

She laughed, though there was nothing funny in her eyes. "I'm old enough to remember way back to the beginnin of things, when children knew their manners and were respectful!"

I felt cold like ice had been dropped down my back.

"I'm sorry, Grandma, I didn't mean to be—"

"Course you didn't *mean*," she broke in. "Children nowadays never mean nothin, that's why I don't listen to you most of the time, cause you ain't sayin nothin!"

I squeezed up into myself and got so small that I was gone, right there in front of her, scared to gone like gone was a place on a map. My grandma could make me go there even quicker than my daddy.

"Why you always so mean to me?" I finally asked.

"I figure you might as well get used to it." She looked sad then, like she'd been wanting to cry all her life and finally had the chance but wouldn't take it. Instead, she raised up in her chair, leaned her forearms on her knees, and bent toward me like a tree in the wind.

"Build up callus on your soul, just like on your hands," she said. "Come over here and let me see your hands, boy!"

I was afraid to move but I didn't have a choice. I got up and went over to where she was sitting in her tobacco cloud, and sat down by her feet, so close I could smell the lye soap in her dress.

I reached out my hands and she took them in hers. Her hands felt like something you use to polish wood or stone. They were reddish brown, like sun was in them or too many wood fires. Her hands held memories of fierce daylight and pain. The palms were creased the way ground gets creased by creeks and gullies. Something flowed there that wasn't water, too dry to have ever been touched by rain. She was so dry, maybe the cloud was a part of her turning into air, and me there breathing her in.

"Boy," she said, staring at my hands, "some people work like dogs and you can see it in their hands. If it's good work it's just in the hands, but if it's bad work then it gets in the eyes, and you can see what's rotten when they's lookin at you. Some people, the work they do ain't in the hands or the eyes, it's in the breath, and if it's sweet then they doin somethin right, but if it's sour you can smell the rot.

"You ain't got nothin in you but sweet right now, and I'm tellin you to hold on to it like a secret and don't let the sweet out. You hear what I'm sayin, boy?"

"Yes, ma'am," I said, but she came back, "Don't 'yes ma'am' me, boy, you ain't understood a word I say. But that don't matter, cause I'm puttin it all into your hands right now."

She spat in my hands and said something soft and squeezed them so hard I thought my fingers would snap like kindling. When she let go, there wasn't any spit in my hands. She pressed that spittle into me, into my hands, as if what she was whispering wasn't meant for my ears but for my hands, like hands were supposed to be talked to. She was talking all right, by holding, squeezing, and pressing what she knew about the world into me, like she was kneading bread and I was the dough.

Sometimes Grandma Sara didn't have no use for words at all.

"Don't trust what people say, boy," she'd tell me. "Folks'll say any-thin if they want somethin from you, so pay more mind to what they do with their hands. Hands don't lie."

Now she started talking again so I could hear. "Hands don't lie," she said again. "Everything been done to someone is in their hands, so you got to learn how to read hands, cause the truth is in scars and scabs, not in words. Words are nothin but lies, but hands speak truth. You hear me, Elijah?"

"Yes'm," I said, cause it was the only thing I could say to Grandma Sara if I didn't want to hear something all over again.

She took a deep breath then, so deep I wondered if the room would run out of air. When she exhaled there was a calm about her that hadn't been there before. Then she said, "Boy, I'm just gettin you ready, don't take it personal. I love you, but you soft and the world ain't, so I'm just gettin you ready for what's out there." She paused. "I've seen things and felt things no one should, and I've lost things no one should, but I remember everything ever happened to me. I remember too good, and no one should have so much done to them and remember it all.

"Maybe I should've taken up drinkin, cause I want to forget it all, but I can't. I remember all of it, my people and what the soldiers did to my people, but we killed 'em all and kept killin 'em, and I'm killin 'em right now in my heart. They fallin dead right now, Elijah, I'm killin 'em right now. You hear 'em, boy, you hear 'em cryin out?"

"Yes, ma'am," I lied, my hands twisted round each other like roots. "I hear 'em plenty."

"Then you won't ever forget," she said, like she was relieved. "You won't forget what no one should remember, and then you can sit with Death and be comfortable, maybe ask Death if he wants some-thin to eat, you know, be polite with that thing that's takin away everything you love, try to make him happy somehow.

"Yes, Lord, I've sat with Death a long time now, and I'm so tired of somebody who can't laugh. It ain't natural to never laugh. He just sit there next to me, waitin for me, but I ain't in no hurry." She was getting more and more agitated, until she was just about hollering to the dark of the cabin. "He just gonna have to wait some more, cause I ain't goin nowhere till I'm ready!"

It was quiet after she yelled, and I thought the shadows moved a bit, maybe they were as uncomfortable as I was. But it was me that moved.

"Grandma," I said, cause it was all I could think of, "are you ever goin to die?"

She looked at me and she wasn't smiling.

"No, boy," she said. "I ain't ever gonna die, cause I do what I want when I want to do it, and no one can tell me anythin unless I want to hear it. You remember this, boy, Death's a coward who sneaks up on you in the night, but if you ready and you face him down, he'll crawl away like a worm. No need to fear a worm, and Death's just a worm."

That was Grandma Sara talking. I can still hear her talking in the dark of the room where I was born, and Death in there with her, and Death is frightened of Grandma Sara.

I never met another person without any trace of fear. It was all beat out of her so there was none left. She wasn't brave, she just didn't fear anything cause she had so much pain in her there was no room for anything else. She was busting with pain trying to get out, her seams were wailing. Whatever it was inside her ain't ever been given no name or no proper burial. It can't be killed, and it can't live either, it's just fierce eyes. Eyes you can't turn away from, eyes that held Death when I was a boy. I was more scared of them than I was of Death.

But I loved her too. I loved her strength. She looked frail and brittle like dried grass, but she was more like an old oak that holds on and never lets go. Maybe Grandma Sara was Death. Maybe Death was an old Seminole Indian who was a colored woman who was a grandmother who was a shadow in the corner of a room who was a light in the back of my mind, a fire that won't go out cause there's too much left to burn, and a wind blowing on that fire.

Patrol report on Yosemite Park stationery,
under "Remarks," Wawona, Cal., July 14, 1903

A party of (2) men and (2) horses passed through Return Canyon on route to Soda Springs w/o arms of any kind.

Very Respectfully,
William Alexander,
Sgt. "L", 9 Cavy.
Commanding Detachment

lighting up the woods

I opened my eyes to red light, a soft light against the rough timbers of the house. I remember lying there half asleep, half awake, not really there and nowhere else either, wondering about red shadows flickering on a wall.

It was so cold I could feel it under the sheets like white knives stabbing me through the blankets. I was warm in my little hollow, wandering deep inside, and I didn't want to get up, I wanted to stay away from the night, the wind blowing through it. But that glow wouldn't go away, so I pushed the blankets back away from my nose, down to my chin, and let in a little of that coldness. I wanted to know what was causing the light to play on the far wall, and the only way to find out was to get out of bed.

Sounds easy enough, but it'd been such a struggle to get *into* that bed. Even though it was Sunday, I had chores, and Daddy's memory was pretty good when it came to chores, especially after I turned sixteen a few weeks back. He told me on my birthday that I was almost a man, and a man works harder than a boy. Ever since, my warm bed felt more and more like a stranger, so now that I was finally here it was so hard to get up without being told to. But that light on the wall was getting stronger and I was getting weaker wondering what it was.

Finally I just pushed the covers all the way back and breathed the cold deep, letting it know it couldn't hurt me. Slowly I sat up and swung my legs down to the floor, then stood up. Now I was getting awake, and I could see that the light on the wall was coming from the window on the other side of the cabin. I walked over to the window, pulled the curtains apart, and peered out. It was dark on top of dark with more dark sitting on top of everything that struggled out of the ground, but off in one place there was an angry light, red and yellow, far off in the woods.

I should've gone back to bed. I should've forgotten what I can't forget, but I wanted to know what was lighting up the woods, so I pulled on my overalls and the big wool sweater Mama made for my birthday. It was too big but it covered up the cold.

When I stepped outside I wished that sweater was bigger. I could see my breath in the dim light of a moon that was half eaten. I picked up the old kerosene lamp sitting on the porch and fingered around on the ground for some matches that were usually somewhere round the lamp. Soon I was coaxing a little fire into the world between my hands. I walked off the porch quietly, not wanting to wake my parents or Grandma Sara.

After taking maybe fifty steps, I reached the edge of the woods, my ankles and calves damp with dew. I stopped there and listened, but couldn't hear anything but wind and night sounds, crickets and a great horned owl up high overhead on a branch, telling me over and over that I was a fool and to go to bed.

I ignored it, which is what a fool would do, and started walking toward the light. There wasn't a real path so I had to move round a lot, and soon I was scratched and bleeding from trying to go the most direct way. When I took the way that was easiest I didn't get cut up, but I got nowhere closer to where I wanted to be. When I worked at getting to that light, the woods tore me up. Mama wasn't going to be happy when she saw my sweater.

Every so often, though, I'd notice the light was getting brighter and the moon dimmer. After nearly an hour of bushwhacking, I could see the branches of trees round me where I couldn't before, and I turned down my lamp. Now I went slower and quieter, feeling my heart beating faster. I began to hear voices. And now I was crawling, not even thinking about my sweater getting dirty or tore up. It was dark everywhere except straight ahead, where there were men standing in a circle round something or someone.

White men. I couldn't see their faces cause they'd covered them up with white hoods. They were all in white, wearing white cloth like bedsheets, like the ones I'd left behind where I'd been safe and warm. There was a fire burning at the center of the circle, and some of the white figures standing around it had torches, but I was cold anyhow. I don't remember ever being so cold before or since. The only man whose face I could see clearly, because he was lying near the fire and his head wasn't covered, was a colored man. I could see him cause one of the white men had moved a bit. I recognized him cause I saw him in church that morning. George Washington. His family was sharecroppers, and I knew them.

Mr. Washington was lying on his side with both hands behind his back. He looked really uncomfortable. The Ku Klux was talking to him. I could see one of the white men moving his head and heard a voice hard and cold. I couldn't make out words, just the sound of that white man with the chill of the night in whatever he was saying. There were other voices too, but they weren't having a conversation. They pointed down and laughed, but there was nothing funny in anything I could see.

All the time Mr. Washington lay there like a sack of coal, something just dropped by the side of the road. I felt a stiffness building in my chest, a hardness I'd never felt before. I wanted to run out and tell those men to leave him alone, let him go, but I was tied up too, without any ropes on me, bound to my fear like it was a post in the ground. I couldn't pull myself away either. I could only get closer, till I was just fifty feet away but still in the shadows of trees. But it didn't matter, cause the time for talking was done.

I watched one man reach down and jerk Mr. Washington up. Since his feet were tied, he couldn't get up very well so he kinda slumped back to the ground, and this angered the man who was yanking on him. I heard what sounded like a curse, and I remember thinking it was the first time I'd ever seen a white man help a colored man do anything, but it wasn't really no help at all.

Another Ku Klux hooked his elbow round Mr. Washington's left arm. He seemed unwilling to be freed from the ground, like he'd lost the use of his legs while he was lying there. But finally they had him up, sort of, and he stood there breathing deep and fast, and soon they had a rope round his neck and he breathed even faster; quick, short breaths as if he was running, but he wasn't running. He was just standing there with the noose over his head, and then he turned his head side to side, trying to move away from it, but he could only move so much, and then they brought it down hard round his neck.

His eyes were bright with the light of those torches, seemed brighter than the torches, and he made no sound. No one was talking now, so I could hear the wind in the branches overhead, with the stars so far away in the night, and hear the sound of the men throwing the rope over a branch on the tree behind Mr. Washington. The branch didn't budge as they pulled tight, pulled harder. I wanted the branch to break or at least bend a little, but it was an oak and it was strong, and the weight of Mr. Washington was no weight at all to the oak. It didn't care about a little rope biting into it. It had survived fire and wind, and nothing moved it at all, even when Mr. Washington was off the ground and his body was shaking and his legs dancing round trying to find the earth again, stabbing down, searching for something solid. Even then the oak was still and calm, and I was mad that it would do such a thing. Mad that it wouldn't break but held the man high so his shadow could dance behind him, a crazed black giant leaping up against red flickering in the trees beyond the firelight, dancing to music I hoped to never hear.

That oak had so many other branches, I thought it could stand to lose just one, just let one go, and Mr. Washington would fall to the ground, and maybe he could run away in the confusion of the branch breaking. But the branch held, and the only motion was George Washington hanging from it, moving slower now. But I swear I didn't see cause I was just staring at that damn oak tree that was like me, not moving at all. Then I looked down at the ground where I was lying on my belly, breathing like I was running away, my heart trying to get free from my rib cage. But I couldn't move, so all my heart could do was pound and pound and go nowhere.

Something made me look up, and I saw Mr. Washington was almost still, and I saw one of the men dousing him with something. The smell of it came to me, and I knew what was splashing on him. Kerosene. Then they put their torches into him, and he burst on fire. He tried to scream but it never got out. Fear, shock, and the rope wouldn't let it out. He was blazing, becoming smoke, and then they put their torches out, smothering them real good, until the only light left in the world was the light coming off Mr. Washington's body.

He was lighting up the woods now, casting shadows, moving back and forth, slowly swinging from that oak. The branch was burning hot, and then the branches above him caught fire and the whole tree began to burn, but the branch never let go. I could smell the wood burning and I could smell him, both were in my eyes and my lungs, and smoke was going up into the black sky, moving between the stars till it blacked out the stars and the only light was from the burning tree. It lit up everything I could see and not see, it hurt my eyes to see such a blaze. Everything was visible except the Klan men. They were gone into the dark, and the light couldn't find them.

For a long time, hours maybe, I just stayed where I was, in the coldest shadow I've ever felt. Though there was plenty of heat not too far away, I stayed away from it, curling up round myself like there was a little bit of heat somewhere deep inside me, as if I could curl round my own heart, but it gave me no comfort.

The wind began to blow and the trees started talking. I knew whatever they were saying had nothing to do with what had happened, nothing to do with the life that was taken. And I thought about God and wondered where he was that night, cause it was still Sunday. George Washington had probably talked to God in church that morning. Then I looked at him, yeah, I raised my head and looked at what they'd done to him.

Could this have been the answer to his prayers?

The Horse's Paces
Walk, Trot, and Canter

It is necessary, in order to make the horse handy, to exercise him at trotting out; but it is not enough that he should trot fast; the quickness of the pace should not detract from his lightness in hand, or the ease with which he should be capable of answering all indications of the hand and leg.

from *Cavalry Tactics*

sidewalk

Some months later came a day when I was just too tired to care about what might happen if I began to think of myself as a man. I wasn't a boy anymore, but white people still called me *boy* or *nigger*, and I thought they should know that I was a man, just like Mr. Washington. He was a man, a good man, and that's why they killed him. I could never forget what I'd seen in the woods, Lord knows, I couldn't even talk about it.

Talk? I wanted to scream, but there was a rope round my neck too. I couldn't see it, but I could feel it. That rope made me a nigger. Fear made me a boy, and I didn't want to be a boy or a nigger anymore.

Daddy was a man, a strong man. He wouldn't hide that, so he was bound to have a run-in with Sheriff Reynolds. Yeah, Daddy was still walking round and all, but after that he held his head lower than he used to, let his shoulders slump a bit, so you might've thought that fire was out, but you'd be wrong. He wasn't dead, like I'd been think-ing. He just walked like the dead so he'd be left alone, but if you walk like the dead and can fool someone like the sheriff, it may be just a matter of time before you fool yourself.

Mr. Washington had chosen to walk with his head up, which meant he wasn't a nigger. The Ku Klux don't usually kill niggers. George Washington was a man. That's why he was killed.

For a long time I figured I had just two choices. I could walk the rest of my life with my head down and be sick on the inside. Or I could walk with my head up and be fine on the inside. Course that would attract the notice of the Ku Klux or some kind of attention I didn't want, and I'd be dead soon. But there was a third choice.

Daddy wasn't a nigger either. That's why he stood up to Sheriff Reynolds. He eventually backed down on account of me, on account of Mama, on account of something that was more important than himself, his family. That was the third choice. It's not a question of standing or running, but how long you going to stand or how long you going to run? You got to understand that there's always a third choice even if you can't see it or feel it. Like Daddy. He was busted up inside, and I've seen him busted up on the outside too. That's called sharecropping. Even after winning an argument with a mule, you eventually heal. Daddy would be all right. That's how he got to be strong and old.

But I wasn't there yet, didn't understand. I'd had enough of keeping my head down, and I thought I'd figured out a way to take a stand on something yet live to tell about it. I figured all I had to do was remember to smile with my head up, remember my manners. So I got up one morning when the sky was red with day, put my clothes on, got a fire going in the woodstove, and crept out of the cabin with an idea fixed in my head about walking on a sidewalk.

There was this wooden sidewalk in Spartanburg, running right through town along either side of the main street. The sidewalk lay under the shade trees where white folks walked after church on Sundays. Colored men built it and tended it, but colored folks had to walk in the dirt of the street, and that never made any sense to me. Why build something you could never use?

The path into town from our cabin was kinda overgrown, but you could find it if you knew it was there. I walked without really seeing it, my hands in my pockets trying to keep them warm, and my head held high. Figured I should get some practice before I got to town. I was terrified, but one thing I'd learned from horses and mules was to never let them sense your fear. There had to be no doubt who was in charge and who wasn't.

I had recently turned eighteen, and Daddy had given me a Sunday free of chores as a gift. That was about all we could afford. Since that night in the woods I'd been thinking about what had happened to Mr. Washington and to Daddy and to Grandma Sara in the war against the Seminoles, thinking about all the things in this world I could never change and what I maybe could change. And that's when it come to me to go walk on that sidewalk in town. I remembered watching a group of colored men fixing part of that sidewalk, and when I was younger, I thought it was strange they would do that. Now I felt anger over my fear.

Every abuse I'd ever suffered or seen, every curse, every sour look, every mean gesture or pointed finger or raised eyebrow or jutted chin, every joke that wasn't funny, even the compliments that sat in your gut like a stone, all those were some of the many sick ways of hearing and feeling the word *no*. I started to think that no matter what rule I followed, no matter how many times I smiled or lowered my eyes, I would always be guilty of doing the wrong thing. So I might as well try doing something right, even if it killed me. If I died, I'd at least know what it felt like to be a man, and if I lived I could always remember that I'd once been a man, and all I had to do to get there was go for a walk.

The morning was quiet and getting brighter all the time. Shadows under the elms made the ground look as if it were gone, like I was walking on nothing. It was all right for me to spend my life walking on this nothing, but not on that sidewalk in town.

Pretty soon I could feel the ground getting harder and hear town getting closer. Someone's dog was barking, a door slammed, and somewheres off, a rooster was letting everyone know that I was coming. It's strange how when you're going somewhere you really shouldn't be going, you get there mighty quick. Part of me wished I hadn't got there so fast. But something made me keep walking, keep my feet moving toward that sidewalk up ahead, but I was so afraid that I dropped my head now, and watched my dirty shoes go forward on their own, pulling me along.

People were already walking there cause church had just let out. I could feel the stares, which were empty like the black shadows under elm trees, but colder. I caught the scents of manure and hay from a livery stable to my right, but I didn't look at it. I knew it was there, like the beauty shop on my left that colored women couldn't use.

I kept walking and I knew when I was beside the butcher shop that wouldn't take credit from colored people, no, I didn't need to smell blood to know where death kept a business, or maybe it was the funeral parlor up ahead that only served whites, though Mama once told me we're all the same color to worms. I stared at that shop wondering who would make my coffin on the day I died, and maybe this was the day. I kept looking even after I passed, so I didn't notice I'd turned slightly toward the sidewalk till my right foot bumped up against something hard.

I lifted that foot and put it down squarely on the sidewalk. I leaned forward, pushed off, and brought my left foot up right next to it. Then I was standing on the sidewalk where no colored person was supposed to stand. It was just a few inches off the ground but the sky seemed closer and bluer. I felt if I reached up with my hands, they would turn blue cause the sky was so close. I felt giddy, but I didn't know if it was fear or being up so high. It was just a few inches, the distance between where I'd been and where I was, but it could have been a mountain.

I didn't move right away. Looking down, I could see each sunlit pine plank and how they fit together like they'd always been lined up side by side, like the sidewalk came whole from a mill and colored men had nothing to do with it at all. The sweat of the men who had built it was soaked into the ground under those boards, where eyes couldn't see. There must've been pools of blackness down there, but only insects could taste the salt.

I looked up and saw Spartanburg like it had just come out of the air. The fear hit me again and made my head too heavy to keep up. The trees whispered as I began to walk, head bowed. In front of me and behind me were white people, but they were just bright pieces moving in a fog of perfume, branches, shadows, and light. I could smell them and hear them moving all around me. Eyes were going through me cause I wasn't there, I was a shadow under the magnolias.

I could feel my breath pick up as my feet went up, down, up, down. I was walking on whiteness all broken up under the shade, the trees breaking up the sun and casting it down to silence. I was looking at feet, lots of feet moving toward me or away from me, and a few shoes not moving cause their owners were sitting on benches off to the side, pairs of them just sitting there, nice shoes pointed at me as I walked by. Black trousers, white dresses, scuffing of boots along the sidewalk, tap and scrape of a cane, knees bending, creases on pant legs, dust staining cotton dresses long enough to sweep any darkness off the sidewalk, white enough to bleach any stain out of it.

"Who's that boy?" I heard someone ask behind me.

I didn't turn around, just kept walking. But I looked up quickly then and smiled at the person walking toward me, about to brush past me. He didn't smile back but looked at me the way you look at a stray dog.

"Crazy nigger," someone else said, "probably drunk."

This voice was older, grayer. If I didn't act like I noticed, maybe it would be all right. Just keep walking. If I could tell someone was coming right at me, I moved out of the way. Sometimes I couldn't tell till it was too late and I got shoved aside, violently one time, but I kept going, hands tight as stones in my pockets, sweat slipping down my back like a cold river.

And then something happened in me, and my head, which had been pulled down for so long, was no longer stone, no longer iron. It became so light it began to pull on the rest of me, until my whole self was straight like I'd never bent over before, or ever used my knees to reach down. With my head up, I looked straight ahead and side to side, at everything there was to be seen.

The fear didn't matter anymore. I felt a strength in my blood, and every part of me drank it in like a plant that had gone months without water and suddenly received rain. Something in my body was remembering the reason for blood, the river that joins the living to the dead. All the ancestors in my blood had given me the strength to raise my head and make me smile. It was they who put laughter on my lips, told me to mind my manners and walk like it was the most natural thing on earth.

I remembered to smile, tip my hat, mind my manners as the white folks passed me by. But I couldn't help noticing all the cracks in the wooden planks. Pretty soon, I thought, some colored man will have to fix all those cracks. He'll seal up each one, trapping his own blackness inside with the rot, and when he's done, he won't be allowed back to feel his own work under his feet. Can't use what you make, can't touch what you hold.

How long could this sidewalk be? I didn't know I was breathing hard, but I started to notice how hard it was to breathe, how hot it had become even under those magnolias, the air thick and sweet like the trees were sweating molasses.

Finally the sidewalk ran out. My knee twinged as I stepped off the whiteness into the soft give of ground, and I was all right, but I could hear people whispering even louder than the magnolias. I still had to walk back through town, but now I was afraid, really afraid. I turned and started walking along the sidewalk in the dirt, feeling my shoulders slump, my back begin to ache. Then I remembered why I was there and looked up again, into all of those faces looking down at me, those cold white faces. I looked right back and smiled up at them. It wasn't funny, nothing was funny, but I smiled anyway.

I got back up on the sidewalk like I had every right to, and I didn't even say "pardon" or "excuse me." I walked back through town and people talked, well, it was more like yelling without being loud, but I didn't care what they were saying, cause now I was going home. I was leaving this town, their looks, their words, leaving everything behind me, and when I made it off that sidewalk again, stepping onto dirt was such a relief. It was as close to a blessing as I've ever felt, the feel and give of the dirt on this Sunday. It seemed to welcome me home. The same ground that held those magnolias high above me kept me standing and walking high above the world too. I'd never felt so alive before, and all it took was stepping up just a few inches onto that sidewalk.

As I went out of town on the same road, I could feel people still watching me, so I kept walking where I should. As soon as I thought I was out of sight, I headed off the road and into the shade of trees. I was still breathing hard, but my heart was slowing down. I found a place that looked like someone's old garden, but abandoned. A few bees were droning round roses, lilacs, strawberries. It felt so peaceful and safe that I lay down in the grass and went to sleep almost right away. When I woke up it was the middle of a warm summer night. The moon was almost full. Crickets were chirping, and Big Creek wasn't too far off, cause I could hear frogs singing.

I got up to pee. When I lay back down, I thought how worried Mama and Daddy must be, but I went to sleep anyway. Something pulled me down to the earth and kept me there through the night. At some point there was a clatter of horses cantering by, but since they never stopped, I didn't worry too much. There was no trail to this spot, though it was just off the road.

The sun woke me, coming down through the branches of a live oak, and everything it touched turned yellow. I got up and carefully made my way back to the road. There was no one in sight when I peered up and down, so I headed home, stopping a few times to look back. I expected the sheriff would come after me, or worse, but no one did. Maybe they thought they'd imagined me walking on the sidewalk that bright Sunday morning. Maybe I was just a shadow moving, and they mistook me for a boy named Elijah Yancy. Maybe I never slept in the woods beside the road to Spartanburg.

That's what I was thinking when I got to the place in the road where a narrow lane, barely big enough for a wagon, wound to the left, which was the way to the cabin. The sun was getting high again. Another morning almost done, and I could feel the heat of the day in my clothes. I glanced back again: no one, so I turned onto the road

Daddy had cleared before I was even born. I felt light, light enough to get a lift from the air. Soon my feet found the footpath to our cabin, then the doorstep.

I started up into the cabin, and a shadow fell across me. It was big, but it wasn't no tree.

"Elijah," I heard Daddy say, "where you been, boy?"

I looked up cause I had to. Daddy filled up the doorway, making it look small and uncomfortable. When he moved away from it, closer to me, the doorway looked relieved. I knew how it felt.

"Just walkin, sir," I replied.

He looked through me the way he could when he was angry, like there was something on the other side that was worth looking at but it wasn't me. "Walkin," he said with a grunt. "Where? Greenville? You been gone since yesterday! Your mama and I been worried sick!" There was a vein in Daddy's neck that got big whenever he got angry, and it looked like it was about to burst. "I'd say you were walkin, all right, but in the wrong place. Yeah, we heard about you bein in Spartanburg."

If I'd had any doubt that he was angry, it was gone. But my daddy was good at being angry and not showing it. It was like thunder trying to be polite. You didn't need to hear thunder to know the lightning was close.

"I'm sorry, sir," I said, "but I just got to thinkin bout that sidewalk in town, bout how we're treated, how it ain't fair that even when we go to town we got to walk in the dirt!"

I was looking at him straight on, not afraid or maybe just more foolish than I'd ever been. He looked down at me and I couldn't read him no more. I didn't know what kind of expression he had on cause I'd never seen it before.

"Elijah," he said, in a voice that had all the stiffness hammered out of it. "Boy, you don't need to tell me bout dirt. I seen enough of it, been livin in it, you might even say it keeps me company. Dirt put those clothes on you. Dirt keeps you from gettin hungry. And one day, I hope a long, long time from this day, dirt is gonna put you to sleep." He still had a fire in him, and his voice rose as he talked, got faster, hotter, the words bits of hot iron cast off and too bright to look at without my eyes blurring.

"Just got tired of it, sir," I sputtered. "I believe I had a right to walk there since colored men built that sidewalk. I was just walkin, sir, doin nothin but walkin."

He laughed, low and deep, but there was iron on the edge of that laugh, and I could feel its weight and bite. "Boy, most people when they're tired, they just go to sleep. Lord, I got me a child when he gets too tired, well, he goes walkin where no colored child should ever be walkin."

Then he turned, stooped like he did before going inside, and went in the cabin. He went over to the table that was halfway set for dinner and sat down. I couldn't see Mama anywhere.

"Elijah, come in here," Daddy ordered, with a sigh emptying his chest of air. "Come on in and take a seat." I knew by how he said "Elijah" that I was in trouble. He stretched out the "li" so much I thought my name might snap in two.

"Elijah," he began, "how long you been colored?"

I was taken back a bit. I didn't know what to say and was too afraid to open my mouth.

"Well," he went on, "I been colored most of my life, and in that time I've learned a few things. First is, I know I'm in Spartanburg County, South Carolina, and in Spartanburg, Elijah, colored people know their place if they want to have a place, you understand what I'm sayin?"

"Yessir," I said.

"'Yessir,' you say, so you hear me, but you ain't listenin at all, are you? If you'd been listenin to me every day you been alive in this house, you'd know that only a crazy fool would do what you did."

Now he was standing over me, tall like one of those magnolias in town, but there was just the smell of sweat and mules on him. The chair was lying on the floor behind him. I never heard it hit the floor, but it lay there on its side, still rocking a bit. Except for that sound, it was too quiet for a cabin with two wide-awake people in it.

I tried to open my mouth, tried to speak, but nothing happened. I held in everything I didn't dare say. And then I saw the light in his eyes begin to cool, and Daddy sighed. His shoulders eased closer to his body, and he seemed suddenly sorrowful, as if the weight of all the days he'd spent living in Spartanburg County had suddenly fallen upon him. He bent over, picked up his chair, set it right, and sat down again, letting out another long breath.

He put his hands out for me to see, turning them over so I could see his palms. They were lined with deep creases, cracked and blistered, the hands of a man who had worked hard every day of his grown life. The fields outside our cabin were there because of those hands and their strength. You didn't need to hear him talk about yesterday or last week or last year, all you had to do was look at his hands. My daddy's hands were torn up by something no one should hold for so long, it had opened them up and tilled them like a plow opens the earth, and what was ever put in those rows to grow, those dark lines in my daddy's hands?

"Look at these, boy," he said. "Look hard and long at them."

He raised his hands closer to my face, so close I felt their warmth. Then he dropped them and took my hands in his, their roughness like broke leather. I saw how small I was in his hands, my smooth hands almost nothing in his.

"These," he spoke again, "were the first hands that held you when you was born." He looked at me again like he was remembering that day. "You and your mother are the only things I ever held that were good and sweet to hold. These hands have held things I pray you never have to, and there's nothin I'm afraid to hold if it means keepin you and your mama safe and whole. But . . ." He stopped, looked out the window. Listened.

"There's one thing," he said firmly, "no man should ever have to hold. You see, holdin you when you was born, that's my right as your father, but I got no right to hold you when you die. That's for someone else. And I hope when my time comes it'll be your hands helpin me along to a better place. That's your right."

"I'm sorry," I whispered. "I don't understand."

"Understand this, Elijah," he said, his voice getting hard again. "If you keep on not understandin your place in this world, then these hands will be holdin you, but you won't feel them cause you won't be here no more. You'll be dead. You'll have spoken your mind, you'll get it off your chest, this pain you got, and all you'll get back for it is a rope round your neck. So if death is what you want, well, you keep talkin and walkin, and Death'll find you. But I'll be the one have to put you in the grave, and I've had to carry a load or two in this life, but I'm tellin you that's one load I don't want to carry. Not you in my arms, not my boy, not that way!"

He was breathing heavy now, his eyes looking out at me and somewhere far off all at once. I said nothing, looking away at the walls and floor and table. I was good at saying nothing when Daddy was making a point. I wondered where Mama was, and Grandma Sara. Later I found out they were out looking for me, calling on our neighbors for some word of my whereabouts.

After a while Daddy started again. "I'm hopin," he said, "hopin you remember our conversation today. Don't ever forget who you are and where you are, boy. And don't get that confused with who you think you are, and where you want to be. You hear me, Elijah?"

"Yessir," I said, and that was all that came from my wanting and going to walk on the sidewalk in Spartanburg under the shade trees where the white folks walked after church on Sundays.

Daddy turned and walked out the door, leaving me alone, and I remember thinking I'd hardly ever been alone in that house, and how that felt, and how it must've felt to Mama and Daddy and Grandma Sara. Fearing that someone you love will just walk away one morning and you'll never see them again. In that quiet I remembered something my parents and Grandma Sara could never forget.

Once I had a brother.

꧁

*Patrol report on Yosemite Park stationery,
under "Remarks," Wawona, Cal., July 15, 1903*

A heard of sheep numbering abought 1700, Brand "P".

Very Respectfully,
William Alexander,
Sgt. "L", 9 Cavy.
Commanding Detachment

꧂

daddy's suggestion

I knew the conversation with Daddy about walking wasn't over. I'd opened a door without knowing it and walked through it when I got up onto that sidewalk. And now that door wouldn't close.

When you're a child it's hard to think about leaving home, ever, cause home is so many things. My father's hands, his arms. When I was real young I'd pretend to be too sleepy to walk to my bed, and Daddy would pick me up and carry me. To be lifted off the ground in his strong arms was about the safest place there was. Nothing could ever go wrong there, no hurt could ever get to me. I couldn't imagine being somewhere far from that embrace.

But what you can't imagine is close as the next sunrise. Walking on that sidewalk hadn't been the end of anything, only the beginning. I couldn't forget what it felt like, the day hard as wood below me, and me somewhere up above it. I had never been so high before, not like a bird but still somehow taken by the sky.

But the lightness I was feeling had darkness round the roots, a darkness lit up by George Washington's body. There was always a price to be paid, whether you were walking or standing still. What happened to Mr. Washington should've stopped me from walking on that sidewalk, but it didn't. It encouraged me. No one should die for nothing. Mr. Washington refused to be a nigger. If everybody refused, maybe there wouldn't be any niggers.

Daddy wanted me to never forget my place, but I couldn't go back to the day before. I was stuck right in the middle of *that* day and what it'd done to me. I couldn't forget the day I became a man. When you stand up for the first time, that day you remember. And I couldn't forget Mr. Washington lighting up the woods. I didn't even know how to walk until he showed me what can happen if you remember who you are. So I never really got down from that sidewalk, not in my head.

I remember Mama telling me about how Moses went up the mountain and talked to God, and how the conversation he had with the Almighty changed him, so when he came down from that place it was still burning in him till his face was bright with what God had said. Well, I ain't talked to God, but when I was on that sidewalk maybe I was walking with God. Maybe it was He made my back so straight and put a light in my eyes that others could see, who parted the white folks before me sure as the Red Sea before Moses.

I didn't know that once I got up on that sidewalk I could never get down again. When you carry your head high and look straight out at people, your head becomes light and it ain't a burden at all. Walking the way a man was meant to walk lessens the weight on his heart. I raised my head and found I could never lower it again. I was born at least twice into this world. The first time was through my mother, Lucinda. The second time was right in the middle of that sidewalk.

But if you were to follow that sidewalk out of town, it would lead into the woods and the night, lead to what was left of George Washington. He showed me the way out of the dark by the fire of his own body, and the light of his body still burns in my mind, showing me where I need to go. Am I wrong to make a lantern out of a dead man's body?

Well, it didn't take long for Mama and Daddy to notice their child wasn't a child anymore, and no wonder. The real problem was that others could see what my walking had done to me, more clearly than I could see it myself. I was still too young to realize that a colored man who knew he was a man was dangerous.

I didn't care what most people thought, but I didn't like it when Mama and Daddy started treating me different. They began to look at me like there was someone standing on the other side of me. I didn't know who that person was, and neither did they. I'd become a stranger to them and maybe to myself. If you woke up one day and saw somebody in your home you'd never seen before, that would get your attention. Well, I'd become that somebody, and I guess we were all waiting for an introduction.

One cold morning a few months after my little stroll in town, when the sky was dark with clouds of birds heading south and the sound of them almost too much for air to hold, I heard Grandma Sara talking to my mama. She said, "Don't worry, honey. Elijah's just findin out he's been a boy all these years, and now he ain't."

I was still lying in bed, and they must've thought I was asleep, but I was wide awake and listening to every word. I hate surprises, especially the painful kind, and what's the use of eyes if you don't take the trouble to see or ears if you don't take the time to hear? All those birds singing and squawking, why do they go to all that trouble if people working in fields from sunup to sunset don't bother to listen to what they're saying? Not many do, but it sounds good to hear singing when your body aches and wants to stop.

I was thinking like this one night after dinner, when the dishes had been cleaned and put out of the way, and we were all in the main room by the stove. The time of year it was meant that the night was chilly, so there was a fire burning, and I was sitting there more asleep than awake. I wasn't ready for any surprise, and this one caught me with no defenses.

Even before Daddy spoke, I could feel his stare on my back, and it was hotter than the fire.

Eventually he started up. "Elijah, we been talkin about you, your mama and me." The pause then was so heavy it made me turn completely round in my chair.

Mama and Daddy were looking at me in a way I had never seen before, and Daddy must've got something in his eyes, cause I could see water from them catch the firelight and pull it down his cheeks.

"Well, boy." Another pause. "We think Spartanburg ain't a good place for you no more. As a matter of fact, I'm certain of it. I mean,

it's never been a good place for someone colored, but now it's worse
cause you're grown up."

I was trying hard to follow where he was going. The first thing
he said perplexed me so much, I was having trouble paying good
attention, but the trail he was laying out for me, well, someone born
without eyes could follow that, only I didn't want to.

"See, Elijah," he continued, "you're a man now, and round here
that can get you killed. If you decide it's not safe to be a man, you're
still gonna die, but it'll take a bit longer. Down here we call that
gettin to the next day.

"But you, you startin to have thoughts you ain't supposed to have,
and pretty soon you gonna have dreams you ain't supposed to have,
so something's got to be done quick, and it comes to this."

He stopped again, and I saw there wasn't anything in his eyes
that hadn't been there all along, but held back. Everything that had
ever been done to him, held back till now, and I was the one tipping
the bucket, so what he'd never want to show was spilling out. And
I knew Daddy wasn't talking about just me, he was talking about
himself and Mama and Grandma Sara, all of us sitting there watching him try to hold back.

"Daniel," whispered Grandma Sara, "we talked about doin this
and agreed to it, so you need to just say it. Don't make truth a stranger
in your own home. You know he's truly grown up, and he's just too
big to fit into anything as small as South Carolina."

She paused, then went on. "And you know that if Elijah stays, he's
gonna get noticed, and so are we." She turned her head and swept
the whole room with her gaze, then lifted her right hand with the
fingers out and grabbed the air. "I know it ain't much," she said, "but
it's all we got."

My father nodded heavily, and I could see him trying to find the
right words when no word was strong enough to carry what he was
trying so hard to say, trying so hard not to feel. And I realized Daddy
wasn't just trying to save me, he was trying to save his family. Then
he couldn't hold back anymore.

"Elijah, you gonna have to leave, leave this cabin, leave Spartanburg. Leave this week, and you can't ever come back!"

I felt his words hit me like a blow somewhere deep down where a fist couldn't hope to reach, and I got dizzy from the jarring and the pain. I hadn't been thinking about any doorway right here in my home, but suddenly I saw the hole that opened whenever I pulled open our front door, and on the other side of it someplace I'd never been before. I was having trouble getting my breath.

"Daddy," I whispered somehow without air in me, "why are you tellin me to go away?"

My father shook his head. "No, Elijah," he said softly. "You already gone away. You been gone for weeks, ever since you walked on that sidewalk. Your body's still here hopin you'll come back, but you so far away you can't even hear yourself talk."

He stopped again, and then he talked for some time.

"What I'm sayin, Elijah, is you need to find where you gone off to. You need to get acquainted with who you becomin, but you can't do it here cause it's just not safe for you no more. I don't know if it's safe for you anywhere, but my suggestion is that you walk north, and keep goin that way till you find yourself up North. Seems to me up North is where you can figure out who you are.

"And you gonna need a job. Well, my suggestion is that you join the army. They'll put a uniform on you, and a proud man in a uniform is just a soldier, but round here a proud man is some uppity nigger askin for a lesson. There's plenty of white folks who would love to teach you that lesson, and most of us had to learn it just to live, but it ain't livin, Elijah. It's just gettin to the next day.

"I want you to leave, Elijah, so one day you can write to me and tell me about what happened next week or next month or next year. Never mind the next day, cause here all you got is tomorrow and the tomorrow after that and all the tomorrows that'll ever be, and they all the same till you dead. But if you leave, maybe you can learn how to really put words down on paper, words that mean something, words like the deacon uses on Sunday, maybe even better than the deacon, but you'll need more schoolin than a bunch of Sundays. You'll need this year and next year too. I could've used some of that myself."

And then he smiled, which I wasn't expecting, and said, "Now, next year, that sure does sound like a good place. You got to plan on gettin to next year, figure it out some before you go, yeah. Ain't everyone who can get to next year.

"So one day, young man, you gonna write to me from someplace I never heard of, tell me bout what you doin weeks and months and years down a road I'll never see. But I can see you on it, walkin it, breathin the air there, just like you walked on that sidewalk I ain't ever touched.

"You let me know, Elijah, where you goin and when you get there and where you been, and you'll be the first person of my blood who got past tomorrow."

I sat there like stone, my head hung low, and if it hadn't been for my backbone my head would've been rolling on the floor. What could I say? Leave home? It was one thing to think it, and I'm not saying I never thought it, but it was something else to hear it out loud. It was clear Daddy'd been thinking about it a lot, but the way he talked bout a life I ain't even lived yet, everything just coming out all neat and tidy, well, that scared me. Joining the army, that was something too crazy to imagine.

"Daddy," I choked out, forgetting to call him "Sir." "Daddy, if I go and join the army, people are goin to shoot at me! I could get killed!"

He said, "That's possible, Elijah."

Then I went crazy and I was yelling at my daddy. "Possible!" I shouted. "That's possible?" I yelled again. "I'm the only child you got—"

I stopped cold cause I couldn't believe I said it out loud. Something I was never supposed to say.

I wasn't Mama and Daddy's only child.

I looked over at Grandma Sara, and she was looking at me and whispering something under her breath, like she was waiting for me to take back the words. I ain't her, I can't pull hurtful things out of the air. But I had to say something.

"Daddy," I said. "Mama," I whispered, seeing that her head was down in her hands, "if I leave Spartanburg, what'll happen to you without me, what'll happen to me without you? Put a uniform on me? Daddy, if I put on a uniform, it's certain before God someone's gonna take a shot at me!"

I heard my voice ring in that little cabin like struck iron, like an anvil splattered with hot metal. Then my father stood up again like it was him I'd struck, and the hot iron of his own words started flowing like it could never stop.

"Elijah," he said, "yeah, if you join up with the army, you gonna get yourself a uniform, that's true. And one day you gonna find yourself at one end of a field, not that different from the one outside our door, and there gonna be other soldiers, like you and not like you, at the other end of that field, and you gonna be shootin at them and they shootin at you. And it'll be hell, boy, I know it'll be hell, but those boys won't know you, Elijah. They won't know or care who you are, whose family you are, you just another soldier they takin aim at. It won't be personal, and they might miss."

He stopped and I thought he was done, cause he looked over at Mama until she raised her head and told him something, told him without even moving her eyes or opening her mouth. But then he started again.

"And yeah . . . you had a brother way before you was even born, and he escaped from the plantation we was on cause he couldn't be a slave, and yeah, he went north and joined the army and got killed in the war."

The ground beneath me dropped away and my stomach fell into the hole. I'd known I had a brother somehow, but I didn't know how I knew. It never seemed real cause I didn't know hardly anything about him, except that he wasn't here. It was just a hundred half-remembered little looks between my father and mother, or how Grandma Sara would sometimes sigh for no reason when she looked at me—all that went through my head in an instant. I finally knew what they meant, heard the sound of what never got said and the quiet that covered up every day since that day. The day my brother left home and done exactly what I was about to do.

Meanwhile, Daddy hadn't stopped talking. ". . . it wasn't personal, his luck just run out. But if you stay here in Spartanburg, Elijah, and you keep walkin where you can't be walkin and talkin what you can't be talkin, some white man round here will take aim at you.

"And then it'll be personal, cause he gonna know who you are and what you done, and when it's personal, people aim a whole lot better. That man's gonna shoot you down. Luck won't play into it at all. They gonna bring you to me and I'm gonna pick you up with these hands—"

And he stopped talking and moved his big old hands up and down right in front of my face, and then they were fists, and I kept waiting to feel the blow come down hard, but it never did. He opened his hands up again, and they were yellow and brown inside and open to God like the field outside.

I remembered how his hands felt when they held me, and all the other things they held in his life, and what he'd said about hands, about me, but he didn't talk about that now. He said, "Elijah, you nearly killed your mama gettin here, and you'll probably do the same by goin away, but you gotta go away. I just want to tell you that it was a blessin as a father to hold you while you was here.

"And I want you to remember what we told you, your mama and Grandma Sara and me, cause we won't be there to remind you. What you can do for us is remember how to be a good person, and if you do that, then we'll always be together."

He paused.

"I ain't finished, Elijah. About your walk." He thought for a minute. "I'd steer clear of the main roads and move mostly at night. You can take my Lefever. You always was a better shot with it, so you can get some meat when you think it's safe to shoot and not draw too much notice. Your mama and Grandma Sara taught you plenty bout findin plants you can eat. And you strong, so when you can't find any food, you can work for it. You'll be all right, but be careful."

Then Mama came up to me and held me the way that took me out of myself, and she started to cry, but there were no tears, no water, just her face and her eyes so deep you'd fall into them if you weren't careful.

"Elijah," she said, "you didn't nearly kill me when you came into this world. I was just so happy bout you bein here that your daddy thought I was dyin. You know how I am. I don't talk as much as he do, but that don't mean I ain't got somethin to say.

"Elijah Yancy, I'm happy you leavin us now, cause it means you won't die, at least not here. And it won't kill me, you leavin. I'm happy cause you got a chance to be you, the you God meant you to be and not half a man like you'd end up here in Spartanburg. And I ain't sayin your daddy is half a man, cause he always standin up for this or that, likely to get himself killed. He just lucky so far, and so am I. I won't say don't worry bout us cause it's only human if you do, but I'm goin to smile a long time, knowin that you round somewhere in this world causin trouble!"

Then Mama put her hands on my head and softly rubbed it, like she used to when I was a little boy.

"Elijah," she said, "your brother Oliver—" she paused, "my son, he was a good boy like you, always smilin and laughin," and Mama smiled too, and then she was looking at me no more but at someone else. "But when he got older, he didn't laugh so much and then he hardly spoke, and when he did, it was always questions bout . . ."

She stopped, like there was something she hadn't thought about in a long time. "Bout why things was the way they was, and I could never give him an answer that satisfied him. Such a pretty smile on that boy, but he stopped smilin and acted angry at everyone and everything and started talkin foolishness. We tried to talk to him, but nothin we said seem to do any good, and one day he was gone."

Mama held one hand balled up in the palm of the other, squeezing her fingers and hand, massaging them like they'd been in the cold too long and had lost all feeling.

"He was gone," she whispered. "My baby . . ."

She started to cry and her body got all slack, like a rag draped over a hook. Daddy just looked at her, and Grandma Sara had her eyes closed off from something she didn't want to see. I couldn't tell what it was cause my eyes weren't working too well either.

By then we were all crying, talking or trying to talk through something that was too strong for words, even Mama and Daddy's words. I remember us standing and holding on to each other, holding each other up, and Grandma Sara was in the middle cause she couldn't move much.

She looked at me and winked. I ain't ever seen her do that before, and it was kind of scary. She pulled me closer and whispered in my ears, whispered something she said one time when I was younger.

"Remember this, Elijah. Hands don't lie!" Her hands gripped me with a strength that pushed all the air out of my body, and I had to stop crying cause you need air to make tears.

I left a few days later, but Daddy was wrong about one thing. He thought me leaving was about catching up with myself someplace else, but part of me could never leave that cabin. Hell, I'm there right now, where and when I used to be a little boy named Elijah Yancy.

I left when I became a man.

To Accustom Horses to Military Noises and Firing

The horse, broken to obedience to the hand and legs can be brought to face most things with little trouble. Encouraged gradually to approach anything which he fears, as a drum being beaten, until he feels it with his lip, he will then cease to be alarmed. The field music should be practiced at the exercise grounds or riding house.

from *Cavalry Tactics*

blood memory

I had a dream the night before I left home, before all that walking, before the road began to eat into me with every step, and me becoming just like those roads out of the South, dry or muddy, hot or cold, always empty of something gone so long you couldn't even remember what name it had.

What I dreamed was my mama's doing. I remember her telling me about the slave ships that brought her people to this place, and how so many of them never even made it to America, how they was lucky to never know nothing but Africa. Remembering the sadness in Mama's eyes when she was talking about my brother and saying good-bye made me think about those mothers and fathers she spoke about when I was barely a child, women and men whose brothers and sisters and children did not walk away and become lost, but were stolen.

Before I went to bed the night before leaving, I started thinking about the last night of those colored people from Africa, my people, their last night before they were caught and taken and put deep into the stink of a slave ship, no more sunrise ever again for those who went down into that hold, no more moonlight ever, no more wind, no more anything that was Africa. I was thinking about all that as I fell asleep and woke, or thought I was waking, by the edge of the sea.

I knew it was the Atlantic Ocean without anyone saying, just knew it. It was angry, full of noise, and there was foam coming up from the waves like the water was heaving up something it didn't want no more, like the ocean giving birth to something that didn't want to get born.

And then I saw them, just their heads first, a few here and there and then hundreds, thousands, bobbing up and down, and their bodies beginning to push them up into air, into sound. It was people, colored people, all of them naked and crying. I could hear no sound come out of their lips, but they were yelling plenty cause I could see it in the veins in their necks and the jut of their jaws, how skin hung tight to the bones of their faces. They were crying, all right, or screaming.

They were coming back. They were being born right in front of me. They were walking out of the Atlantic up onto the beach where I was standing. And they were so silent, thousands of them coming out of the water, walking up on the beach dripping with salt and tears, pulling themselves free from what had killed them or was keeping them quiet.

Still I couldn't hear them. Thousands and thousands of men who were boys and women who were girls, all slowly getting free of whatever it was that held them down, that was keeping them back, and it looked like water and sounded like water, and there was salt in the air and black clouds heaving over like an ocean wave in the dead of night.

Then I knew who they were and why there were so many. They were all the Africans who had been ambushed, caught, stolen, trapped, and robbed of those things that couldn't be held in your hand but only in your heart. They were the ones tossed over when they were sick, the ones buried by water before they were even dead. They were the proud ones, the angry ones who spoke up, spit back, curled bones into fists. The ones who had fire for eyes, the ones who set ships ablaze with their tears, who didn't survive the journey, warriors who jumped into the sea, who breathed deep the sweat of sharks that took them to the next world one by one.

Now the ocean was giving them back, whole and no mark on them I could see, nothing to make you think a shadow had ever fallen on them. Nothing but their eyes, which gave back the light of here but also the paleness of there, the *there* that had swallowed them up. Eyes that were too full to ever cry again cause no amount of crying could empty the pain, unless there was room for another ocean right here, pushing this one to the side of the sky.

They kept walking out of the ocean, freeing themselves from water, being born here on a different shore, on the other side of the loves they lost, that were taken from them, their families. Their families, my God, they could never let go of what was taken till the day they died, their fathers' hands, mothers' hands, brothers' hands, sisters' hands all straining to grip through the water, the tears, the blue.

And then it began to change. At first they all were alone, and then one saw a face it remembered, and then another and another. I saw hands grabbing hands, and people seeing people they didn't expect to see ever again, people they hadn't known were gone. It kept happening, and it was beginning to be a sound. That sound grew and grew till it overtook the booming of wave after wave hitting the shore, a sound high like a gull cry but easier to take, a sound like laughter but not laughter, cause it wasn't an easy place for laughter to be.

But whatever it was, the sound started to break up the black clouds over the water. They began to loosen and squirm, and a brightness showed on the ragged edge of the dark. A flicker, a hole in a night barely big enough for a star, but any fool could see that day was coming, even the dead could see day breaking.

Wherever those people were walking to, it was better than the place they'd left behind. All that time walking on the bottom of the sea, through mountains we can't see and canyons we can't reach and flats we got no name for, such a long walk, and only now getting to the other side, rising up to a place without a name.

As I stood there staring out to sea, watching the slave-ship dead come ashore, I could feel something in the wind at my back, and I could see something ablaze in their faces. But when I turned round to see what they saw, what moved them to rise up out of death and cold water, that's when I woke up, and I never had a view of the place they were heading, all those people Mama said were lost and gone. All I could see was them arriving and then passing by me.

I wanted to have that dream again, wanted to have it so I could turn round and see what was pulling them free, find the light that brought them to where they were meant to be, that made every slave, every human being, every mother, father, son, daughter that was thrown or jumped to the waves wake up and know where to go and begin that walk to freedom. But all I could ever dream again was just a dream of water, of a beach, and me all alone on it.

So the dead didn't ever rise again from the sea.

Patrol report on Yosemite Park stationery,
under "Remarks," Wawona, Cal., July 16, 1903

A heard of Sheep abought 1½ mile from the Park line.
Brand "P" Abought 1700.

> Very Respectfully,
> William Alexander,
> Sgt. "L", 9 Cavy.
> Commanding Detachment

walking

It took me nearly two years to walk from South Carolina to Nebraska. Course I had no idea that a place called Nebraska was at the end of the road.

Most of what happened I don't want to talk about, and the rest I'm working real hard on forgetting, but some things you can't forget, like how fear and joy became more than just words. They became a place, all the places besides our cabin. They were all fear. They were all joy. I trusted nobody, cause they were all strangers. I didn't even trust the sun cause the sun lights you up for all to see. But there was joy in moving, seeing a world I'd never seen before.

The moon's a good thing because it lets you see where you're going in the dark. I remember how the moon got broken up by branches and leaves overhead, but when I came out of the shadows, it almost hurt my eyes, the brightness whole and cool around me instead of torn apart by branches and wind.

I was cold plenty, but every step took me closer to the end of the road. I made fires at night where there were no eyes, and the fires kept me warm and spoke to me bout old things, but I've lost the memory of what they said. I was away from people in my head and in my heart because of fear, fear of being alone, of not having my family close by, but in the night when I was closed up in my blanket beside a tree or whatever the road had put before me, I could feel Mama's hand on my head, and the wind on my forehead would be her breath, and the sighing in the branches would be her singing to me, no, I was never alone, so why be afraid?

Sometimes the road was like a river moving back on itself, then going forward, spinning me round. I wasn't always sure which way was west till afternoon, when the sun fell from the sky, wasn't always sure which way was north till the North Star shone above me. Other times, everything would be spinning round in my mind, the names of places and the places without names. Grandma Sara'd taught me you don't need a map if you can read the sky.

The road I followed wasn't plain to see but was plain to me. I felt I was being led, and most always seemed to know to turn here or turn there. Who took my hand in the dark and showed me the way? Something inside me I couldn't name. I wasn't following directions, I was being guided out of the South, west and north. It was as if the ground itself was showing me the way. Sometimes the forest closed in so I had to go round, but only because I wasn't supposed to go in there.

When you're afraid, everything is clear, too clear, and the fear seems like something living, the shadow of everything you're seeing and feeling. I felt like a deer, like whatever gets hunted. When I was moving on the road, my heart was always beating hard, my breath came fast, and I'd be sweating even if it wasn't hot. I got tired before I had a right to be tired, I stopped and looked hard before stepping out of the shade of trees, looking for something or someone that hadn't come yet, listening for sounds that hadn't been made yet. I was afraid of everything and nothing, especially the nothing that's a hole inside when you got no one near who cares if you live or die.

But when you're afraid, your eyes are open wide and you hear more, and you taste the wind for what might be around. Fear wakes you up to what's around you. It can clear your mind so you see that squirrel in the elm overhead or hear a quail bolting out of the bushes, and I always kept Daddy's Lefever ready to fire. Because I was afraid, it was harder to surprise me and easier to get food.

I remembered Grandma Sara saying, "Elijah, plants got homes just like you. Some live by a creek, some live in a meadow or a forest, but some like the edges of things, the space that ain't meadow or forest. You gotta learn to see the line between where one kind of tree grows and another don't. What I'm sayin, boy, is when you find where a plant lives, then you'll find that plant. You do that, and you'll never be hungry."

What Grandma Sara said kept me alive. When I got past the places where there were orchards full of apples, peaches, pears, or plums, and I had to look elsewhere, well, I didn't have to look all that hard to find wild carrots growing right at my feet or spot the wild sweet potatoes, with their heart-shaped leaves and big white flowers, by the edge of an abandoned field.

Because there were so many oaks, I got plenty of acorns in the fall. Other times I could find sour cranberries, wild currants, sweet blackberries or raspberries, mulberries, persimmons, or black walnuts. Another mile down the road would bring me sunflowers or wild lettuce or turnips. I found mushrooms too, under logs or on wet earth after it rained. Food was everywhere. Most of it I could just eat raw, but some I had to prepare, like the acorns.

If I caught cold, I made sassafras tea out of the roots and leaves, or chewed the bark of a holly root. I used flint and steel to start fires at night, and if I needed a fire during the day, I used a pair of eyeglasses I'd found in the woods near our cabin to focus the sun. But fire is a good way to get noticed, so I had to be careful. If I had a fever I'd look for thoroughwort or dogwood. If my stomach bothered me I'd find blackberry root and it would help me.

I made soap from myrtle berries and bathed as often as I could, because the water made me strong and washed a little of my scent away, which made it easier for me to hunt and actually catch something. The thunder of Daddy's gun brought down squirrels, birds, and other small game. But I was careful not to use it too close to people. Eating plants and catching fish was a quieter way of getting food.

It didn't matter that I was always in new country, cause I knew where different kinds of plants lived, knew if they liked running water, thickets or dry open groves or fir woods, wet meadows or farm fields. Everything's got to live somewhere, and it lives there for a reason. You just got to know why.

On a day after days of walking, I was watching the sun lowering west behind the Smokies, and I walked right off the ridgeline path I was on. I dropped down with the sun, my feet sliding in muddy soil and through sweet grass, the smell of it in my head, my hands grasping at the trunks and roots of great trees as I slid by. I could feel the wet ground soak my pants, my legs, feel the plants tearing at my hands as they tried to hold on. I wondered if I'd ever find someplace flat again. But then some ground in a hollow that wanted my acquaintance rose up suddenly out of the woods and stung my rear, while dust settled in a cold breeze about me.

I looked up to find a hole in the forest. I got up, found there was nothing broken, brushed the dirt off me, and walked deeper into that hollow of light and high branches. It was so pretty it made me forget how my hands still stung and my knees ached.

I'd fallen into a place where the ground was covered with tall grass that made the wind sing. I remember the mound there, making the ground look pregnant or swollen from a wound, and the quiet coldness made by a sky losing light. I rested there, lying in the grass by that high mound, and had a dream, or maybe I was awake and listening to a music that was trees and wind and grass.

and the singing coming out of the ground, soft at first, like birds at dawn, quiet but clearing the air of night, singing getting louder and the ground rising and falling as if God was under me breathing, pushing me up and dropping me again, and the song getting louder and louder.

I woke up, or thought I did, and felt the earth giving way beneath me, crumbling away into a hole that something was getting out of, and I was scared it was a bear clawing back to life right under me, but then I saw its hand, her hand, it had to be a woman's hand cause the fingers were long, slender like a woman's, and dusk colored like they held twilight once too often and could never fade like dusk was supposed to. Now there were two hands, and they held fists of dirt, and they opened pouring dirt onto the grass, the hands could never stop bringing out fists of dirt onto the grass.

It wasn't like she was being born cause she was birthing herself, opening up herself so she could get out and be free, for the ground wasn't any different from her. It was her and not her. I could see roots tangled round her calves, her thighs, tangled with blackness, some of it shadow, some not, so you couldn't tell where she ended and the ground began. It was all moving round and round, heaving up and opening till she was mostly free, crawling out on her hands and knees, the dirt falling off of her, her skin like copper beaten to a softness that moved over bone, and her hair long black roots catching the ground. She was still bound to what she was working so hard to get clear of.

Or was she? I couldn't tell, I could only watch her stand up like the first woman who ever stood, like she was just figuring out how knees and thighs and hips were supposed to work. This woman was no baby, but it seemed wrong to feel what I was feeling, wrong to hold her so close with my eyes. So I looked down at the ground, which was gaping like it was surprised at what it had done, giving birth to the first woman, cause that's what she was. And there was no man around but me, and I couldn't even look at her though all I wanted to do was look at her, and more, and then my eyes closed again, and I could hear a voice

I remember the grass speaking softly like it was shy over who might be listening. All I could make out was one word over and over again: "Kituwah," and again, "Kituwah." I didn't know what it meant, then or now, but I know what it felt like. It was peace, like the first day, like when you're held for the first time by your mother. You're naked, but it don't matter. You're helpless, but it don't matter. You're loved and that love holds you up, keeps you safe.

I remember this because it was the only time on the road that eventually led to Fort Robinson that I wasn't afraid. I couldn't be afraid because I felt in the presence of something that was older than fear. Fear hadn't been born yet, but beauty was already old, older than Grandma Sara. It was everywhere and in everything, but stronger in that place the grass called Kituwah.

Everything that happened and didn't happen on the road from Spartanburg moved like water round the memory of Kituwah. The night sounds of Bryson City, North Carolina, when I was lying outside it against a tree. The coldness of a waterfall on my face near Spencer, Tennessee. The tall pole with a white flag that made me cry, near a town called Hopkinsville. What's so sad bout a flag the color of a cloud? Don't know. Empty fields of harvested corn, and an orchard picked clean of all its fruit.

I remember the summer heat and mosquitoes, one becoming the other till the heat was a drone that stung, and the insects were a fire burning my face and neck and arms. And then the winter rain seeping in past every button and fold till I was miserable, and then too numb to care. Only the names of where I walked stayed dry and warm in my head: Port Royal, Princeton, Green's Ferry, Springfield, Fayetteville, Tahlequah, and Fort Gibson. Places filled with people but dead to me.

It was the mountains, forests, and rivers that were alive.

When I was dirty I bathed in a stream. When I was lonely I bathed in a stream. When I was afraid I bathed in a stream. The water was always familiar at dawn. Always the same coldness, the same sweetness at the edge of the grass, the delicious singing in the ground that woke up your mouth, your skin. Big Creek was always with me no matter how far I walked, the waters near our cabin flowing everywhere I went, and when I cried at night it was from the joy of knowing that home was as close as any mountain stream or drop of rain.

Ross's Landing. The Tennessee River. The Mississippi. The Arkansas. It was night and a river, don't matter the name, it was big and cold and I had to get across. I couldn't swim that far, so I had to take the ferry from that man. He was tall and to me he looked big with a wickedness stolen from an oak that was used to hang *niggers*, that kind of tree, and he wanted money to cross the river, money I didn't have, so I pleaded with him long after the sun had gone down to take me across. But he wanted what I didn't have, and it made no sense cause he lived on the other side, so to get home he had to cross the water. So I argued with that white man to bend a bit and take me with him, but oaks don't bend, they only break if the wind is stronger.

I said to him, "I'll just be a shadow by your side, that's all, a shadow, so it don't matter that I got no money! You just goin home, you got to go, and I need to go with you!"

He just looked at me and laughed, if whiskey could laugh and not stink, and showed his yellow teeth like they could bite right through the fear in me, the fear of not getting across to the other side. All I could think of was, I gotta get past this man, I gotta get over there, else I can't keep moving, and only a dead man doesn't move. So I pleaded and pleaded.

Finally he must've got tired of me pleading, cause he grabbed the bow of his big canoe and began to drag it toward the water, running dark and silent a few feet away. When he got there, he went in a couple of steps, then walked back onto the land, went round to the rear and pushed the canoe mostly into the water. He held it steady and looked back at me. It looked enough like an invitation that I stepped in, and moved awkwardly toward the bow of the canoe, rocking it back and forth. He gave a big push and then jumped in at the stern.

The boat began to drift downstream, so he told me to grab the paddle at my feet and use it. I did. He sat down in the back, and began to paddle himself. I could feel his eyes on me.

After a bit I said, "Thank you, sir."

All he said was, "You talk a lot for a shadow, boy."

So I kept quiet all the way cross that river, but he made me paddle all the way. I could only see blackness except for the lantern in the bottom of the boat. I paddled till my arms almost fell off from the aching, but after about a half hour there was a bump that shook the canoe, and we were at the other side. I got out, and he said nothing, and I said nothing, and I walked some more till my legs were as tired as my arms. When I couldn't stand up no more, I drifted off the road, just a shadow boy, lay down, and slept.

I slept well, with a heaviness that came from walking, using my body day and night for months just to put some country between me and South Carolina. Every river meant a crossing, and every crossing meant a ferry or someone like this man on the Tennessee. Afterward there would be the Mississippi, the Arkansas, Oklahoma Territory, and Kansas.

Fear was the road I was following. It wound round through this and that place, past what I remember and what I can't forget. I walked. I killed for meat if I was lucky. I worked for meals sometimes, but always found some food growing where there was no work. As the country opened up, so did the people, mostly, so I found it easier to be out in the open under sun and stars.

It all left me cold inside, but the fires warmed me, the streams rinsed away the mud and dirt, and I slowly made my way west, into a country that got darker with every step. Daddy used to say that going west was asking for trouble. He said that his mother called it the "Darkening Land" because that's where the sun went to die, but that's where I was being led, so maybe there was some light on the other side of that dark? His mother, Artana, my other grandmother, was Cherokee, and she died when I was little. She looked at things different than Grandma Sara, but they came from different people with different stories to tell.

I remember how my grandmother Artana smiled with the sunrise but sighed at sunset. She would have told me I was heading west toward my own death. We all are, I guess, but I hoped there was still a lot of road between me and my final resting place.

You know, there are thousands of places I ain't ever heard of, or even imagined, and I could've ended up in any of those places, but eventually the one I got to was called Nebraska.

To Accustom Horses to Military Noises and Firing

In all lessons, if one or more horses are so restless or unmanageable as to excite and throw the others into confusion, they should be sent off and separately dealt with; they require more pains, and much caressing and other encouragement.

from *Cavalry Tactics*

fort robinson, nebraska

You could tell that one day it would be a town, but the day hadn't come yet. Even though it was just a few miles from Fort Robinson, there wasn't much to it but a dirty street with dirty buildings, and a cold wind that never seemed to stop.

It was April, and the people looked as cold as the land, but if you looked closer there was something inside them smoldering. The fire wasn't completely out. They were settlers, pioneers, the people walking this street or riding in wagons and on horses. Daddy used to say a pioneer was someone who went looking for a place just like what they left behind, but with fewer people, or, better, none at all.

I remember walking down the main street, which seemed to be the only street worth walking on, when I saw out of the corner of my eye a table with a man in a uniform behind it. I paid him no mind and was just walking by when he said, "Excuse me, young man, do you have a moment?"

And I remember being surprised by a white man calling me "young man." *That* got my attention.

I turned to face him and said, "How can I help you, sir?"

He looked at me fully now, and I seemed to meet with his approval. He said to me, "You look like a strong fellow, and the army could always use strong men." He glanced down and gestured to some papers on the table. I walked over to get a better look.

"If you sign your name," he pointed, "or put your mark on this paper, you can become a soldier in the United States Army. You'll get meals paid for and the honor of serving your country. What could be better than that?"

I thought about what Daddy had told me about joining the army, how my attitude, which had gotten me in this situation, could actually help me if I was wearing a uniform, or at least it couldn't hurt.

Besides, what else was I going to do? Nothing had really changed since I left South Carolina. Whether I was there or in Nebraska, if I did nothing to improve myself, I'd be a sharecropper, a farmer who doesn't even own the land he's working. If I worked hard every day to build a better life for myself, I'd be a farmer. If I prayed to God every night for a better world, I'd still be a farmer.

"How much does soldierin pay?" I asked.

"Son," said the man, slow and easy, "if you join now, you'll get thirteen dollars a month, like any white man. You work hard and do your duty, you may even get some stripes, and that means respect. All you got to remember is to be respectful of your superiors and do your duty, and . . ."

He stopped and smiled a little, not much, and finished up with, "You'll even get a pension if you make it through to retirement."

"If I make it through?" I asked with a catch in my throat.

"That's right," he said, "if you make it through. This is the army we're talking about. Being a soldier is honorable but dangerous work. Not every man is suited for it, but if you can listen, learn, follow orders, and trust in those above you, you may spend your days making a contribution to your country, and even get to that retirement."

I laughed a little and said, "So what you're tellin me, sir, all I gotta do to get to that retirement is not get myself killed. Is that right?"

He smiled again. "Getting killed would pose a problem with regard to securing your pension, so certainly I can understand if you were to choose another way of getting on in the world."

He looked down and began sorting through the stack of papers on his desk.

He knew there weren't any other ways. He knew me even though he didn't know my name. Even though I might write it down in front of him, it didn't matter. Sure, the deacon back home had taught me bout the alphabet, how to write my name, but those letters that made up *Elijah Yancy* were no different from the letters some other colored man had put down. However you mix them up, we were all the same. It didn't matter if we were from Mississippi, Alabama, Georgia, Louisiana, or South Carolina, we might as well all have the same name as far as he was concerned.

Colored or white, the military don't care who you really are, you're just a body in a uniform and a name written down to make it easier for the government to notify kin, in case you don't survive. Now I'd *be* the government, the same government that made soldiers of some men and sent them down into the swamps of Florida to hunt Grandma Sara's people. My people. Maybe those soldiers hated Indians, but maybe their choices were no different from mine. They were poor. I'm poor. What choices do poor folks have?

Getting on in the world always meant doing what I was told. If I didn't, my daddy would soon enough let me know how things were. And he didn't have that many choices himself. I couldn't see how the army was going to be much different. It was still sharecropping, only the crop was different. I still didn't own the land, but I had to work it.

Working in the army, though, I wouldn't be planting seeds, I'd be uprooting plants that were native to the soil. Some people called them weeds, but weeds are just plants folks don't got a use for.

Out on the Great Plains, those weeds were called Indians.

I'd heard plenty bout the Indian Wars along the road to Nebraska. Once I got out of the South, it seemed a little safer to move out in the open, so I did. It felt good to be out under the sun, just a stranger looking for work, instead of going the long way round everything and everyone. Strange to say, but I fit in. There were a lot of other people on the road, and they all had something to say.

Particularly about Indians. About every time I got hungry enough to find work, people would be talking bout Indians. Farmers wondering if some Crow raiding party would put their crops to the torch, ranchers afraid that Cheyennes would run off with their cattle, townspeople fearing that the Sioux might attack someday, even if those particular Indians weren't anyplace nearby. Everybody talking, lots of folks just scared, and their voices getting louder and louder the farther I headed west.

I was used to seeing colored people afraid, but not white people. When I thought about it now, the white folks back home were probably just as afraid of the colored people around them, but they hid their fear under white sheets while they were torching a colored family's home, or lynching someone. Out here there was a different threat, and it didn't look like me.

It seemed to me those Indians had something my daddy always wanted more than anything. They had their own land, even if they didn't see the land as something they owned but something that owned them, and "own" ain't even the right word for it. English doesn't have a word for living as if everything matters as much as you do. Ain't it peculiar that the first time someone offered me a real job, I'd be helping to steal land from other Indians? What would Grandma Sara say? My daddy was back home right now working land that didn't belong to him, so I know how he'd feel about it.

Seems like to get something in this world, you gotta take it from someone else. God knows I was tired and hungry, I barely owned the air in my lungs for a few seconds, but there must be a way to get rest without kicking someone out of their bed, and eat without stealing food off another person's plate.

I remember thinking: if I sign my name and put that uniform on, maybe I'll die straight off, cause Grandma Sara will know, just know, and she'll kill me in her heart like she killed those other soldiers. Maybe I won't make it to retirement. But if I don't sign, I may not make it to the end of the week.

I'd been standing in front of that officer for some time, but he was still looking through the papers on his table. No hurry. He had all the time in the world. He knew my decision before I did. Finally he looked up at me.

"So," he asked, "do you have something else in mind? If that's the case, I'm a very busy man . . ."

"No sir," I said. "I'll sign your paper."

I bent over that table and saw where I should leave my mark. I picked up the pen and began to write "Elijah Yancy," nice and clear like the deacon showed me. But as I began to write, I thought of something else and stopped.

I thought of my older brother, Oliver. Like Daddy said, he escaped from the plantation that used to be part of the land we worked. He left before I was even born. He must've had an attitude problem too, but he was a slave, not a sharecropper, so it was an even bigger problem.

You can't have a little bit of freedom. You either got it or you don't. My brother left home to find it, going up North before the war, and when the war came on, he joined some kind of militia and got killed at a place called Fort Wagner. A colored man who knew him in the army came and found us one day and told my mother and father as much as he knew about Oliver.

It took a bit of time for him to find us, and once he did, how could he say what no one would feel comfortable saying to a mother and a father? There ain't no good way to tell people their own flesh and blood ain't here no more. If you're the one getting the news, you can whisper to yourself that the dead are with Jesus, but if you had a choice, you'd decide it'd be all right if Jesus was lonely for a change and you had your son back in your arms.

That soldier who brought us the news didn't have it easy. He made it through all right, though, and they held him like he was their little boy come home. I heard about it later from Grandma Sara cause I was too little to remember much, and Mama and Daddy never talked about it at all. They fixed the man a good dinner, and he told some stories about Oliver, even got my parents to laugh a little. Grandma Sara said laughter was something she never expected to hear that night in our cabin. For a few hours, my brother was alive and with us again, all because of a stranger telling stories, a man we'd never seen before and would never see again.

I thought about this when I went to sign that paper, because I was doing the same thing my brother had done. The same as that colored soldier who lived through the Civil War, lived long enough to tell my parents how their son had died. Both men had stood before a white officer and listened to that soldier talk. It was years ago, but their choices were the same as mine.

All you got to do is not get yourself killed.

As I continued writing my name, I began to hear the words of a tune we used to sing in church. The words came through me and I filled up with tears for the brother I never knew, and for my parents who never talked about him. This is what I heard.

> There's a man goin round takin names
> There's a man goin round takin names
> He has taken my brother's name
> And he's left my heart in pain
> There's a man goin round takin names

I finished writing and handed the paper to the man taking names. He was still smiling, and to this day I've never met another officer in the United States Army who had a bigger, more genuine smile than the officer who took my name.

But when he glanced down at the paper and saw my signature, he frowned. "Son," he said, "an army chaplain will help you learn how to write properly. Some orders are spoken, but some are written down. One day you may even be giving orders. Consequently, you have to be able to read and write in order to be a good soldier."

He added my paper to his pile, put a stone on top of it, then wrote something down on another slip of paper and handed it to me. He said I was to give it to a Sergeant Henry at Fort Robinson, out a ways past town. He jerked his head to his left, as if to point out a dusty road full of wagon ruts and still caked with ice.

"Thank you, sir!" I said.

He just smiled. I reached out my hand for him to shake, but it was obvious the conversation was done. I looked at that scrap of paper fluttering like a wounded bird under that stone, and wondered if it was me trying to get out. I could feel the weight of it on my chest.

I glanced at the officer again. Who was he? He never told me his name. It might've been Death, I don't know. Death probably don't need to ever give his name. The business of giving belongs to other folks. Death's in the business of taking. Whoever that officer was, he took me that day, and I been a soldier ever since.

Most soldiers when they're awake are worrying bout living, but maybe when they sleep they dream a little, like me, wondering who it was that took their names. Back then I thought, Whatever happens, wherever I get sent and whoever I run into, I hope it won't be personal. Cause if Daddy's right, and it ain't personal, some farm boy might miss and make it a little easier for me to get that pension.

All you got to do is not get yourself killed.

I don't think that it was war got my brother killed, or others like him. Like Daddy said, probably his luck run out and he found himself at the wrong end of some field, but I don't think it was iron that killed him. It was freedom. He didn't have it, and he wanted it. He was willing to die for it, and he did. And when he died, he was finally free. But he could've stayed a slave in South Carolina and got that kind of freedom.

If it's true that there are different kinds of freedom, then there must be different kinds of slavery. One kind means somebody chases you, catches you, and puts you in chains. Then there's the kind they got in Nebraska. It's the kind you gotta sign up for.

> Oh, Death is that man takin names
> Death is that man takin names
> He has taken my brother's name
> And he's left my heart in pain
> There's a man goin round takin names

To Accustom Horses to Military Noises and Firing

A few trained horses are mixed with the new ones, and toward the close of a lesson separated a little, and the troopers who ride them fire their pistols, the riding being continued without change.

from *Cavalry Tactics*

ninth cavalryman

I had enlisted the day before, and I had the uniform on now, that bit of blue. I remember the sun being hot on the heavy wool, and I remember feeling different somehow. The difference wasn't just how the new clothes felt on my skin but how I felt in them, which surprised me. I had to admit, that uniform was different from any set of clothes I'd ever worn.

Maybe this feeling showed, or maybe it was just that blue respectability stiff with too much starch, but the townspeople of Fort Robinson seemed to see something that was new, too. They looked at me now like they really saw me, not like yesterday. Then I was just a drifter, a colored one at that.

Everything before seemed like a dream someone else was dreaming, and right now I was waking up into a life I never knew I had. I walked slow and uncertain down the dusty main street of that dusty town in the hot sun. All the towns in Nebraska seemed like they were eager to go to dust. I was just walking, and people were watching me, but it wasn't bad. It was good. I was wearing a soldier's uniform and felt like it tied me to every other man wearing the same uniform, and that all of us represented something bigger than any of us alone.

So the walking I did that day was different from any I'd done before, even on the sidewalk in Spartanburg. I was now a private in the Ninth Cavalry, and I had been ordered to town by Sergeant Henry to get supplies for the barracks. We'd taken a wagon into town, and the sergeant told me to start walking back to the fort because he and the others needed more time. They would pick me up on the road.

"Don't worry, Private!" Sergeant Henry had laughed. "We won't forget you, but after all that walkin you've done, this won't seem like nothin at all!"

I had a feeling I wouldn't see that wagon anywhere on the road back to Fort Robinson, and I was right. At first I was angry, but then I started to find it funny that my first duty for the army involved walking. I was so lost in those thoughts, you know I was bound for trouble, and trouble found me. He was heading out as I was heading in, and I walked into him right in the shadows of the Fort Robinson gate. As I stood there on the doorstep to my new life, dazed and my head smarting, Trouble was glaring at me and rubbing his chin. He was a big colored man, about six foot five, in a blue uniform with three yellow stripes on his sleeve. He was around the size of my father.

"Sorry, sir!" I said, like I would have said to Daddy.

"Sorry!" spat Trouble. "Sorry!" he said again. "Private, is that all you say to a sergeant when you walk into him?"

"No sir," I coughed, "no sir, I just, I mean, I'm *really* sorry, sir, I just wasn't payin attention."

Sergeant Trouble didn't say anything for a while, just looked me over good, and then something in his look seemed to soften a bit.

"When did you enlist, boy?" he asked.

I answered promptly, "Yesterday, sir. Yesterday afternoon."

"Well, well," the sergeant said, "it shows, boy, it shows. But I'm a forgiving man, so I won't hold it against you. What's your name, Private?"

"Yancy, sir," I answered.

"Yancy," he echoed. "What kind of name is that?"

I'd never been asked that, so I thought before answering.

"It's my name, sir," I stated flatly, "and the name of my family."

"Don't mean no offense," he offered, "but knowing your name is the beginning of knowing you better. It tells me something."

He paused and then asked, "So what was that tune you were humming when you walked into me?"

I blinked. "Sir," I asked, "what tune?"

He looked at me, his eyes getting bigger. "You were humming something, son," he said, "and whatever it was I couldn't recognize it, which means you need help. A soldier who can't properly carry a tune probably can't carry other things either."

I'd never heard that before either.

Then a thought seemed to come to him, and he added, "As a matter of fact, I have something for you."

Now I was more surprised. I had just acted like a fool with this man, so what could he have for me that was any good? Trouble reached down into a bag he had on with "U.S." stamped on the outside. It had a worn leather shoulder strap that looked busted in too many places to hold up, but the bag was still holding on, probably terrified of letting go.

"Yancy," he continued, "you're just the sort that should have something like this, so I'm goin to give it to you!"

Trouble was holding some kind of musical instrument. It looked like a flute. It was made of wood and straight, with an opening at both ends, the mouthpiece tapered and very worn, while the other end was just a hollow tube. The end that was tapered had a carved figure on top of it that looked like a buffalo.

"That's real nice of you, sir!" I managed to say. "I only enlisted yesterday, and to be honest, I wasn't expectin any favors, especially a gift on my first day as a soldier. No sir. Why me?"

Sergeant Trouble didn't answer at first. He looked round as if he was doing something he wasn't supposed to. He seemed uncomfortable, like his uniform didn't fit and he was trying to squirm out of it, but at the same time trying to behave like nothing was out of place.

"Well," Trouble said very slowly, his eyes narrowed as he leaned in toward me, squinting slightly, "you look musical." He just about whispered it.

Now that was the strangest thing I'd ever heard. To tell a complete stranger he looks musical . . . it sounded like the beginning of a conversation I once had with a scoundrel from Mississippi, a colored man who also offered something he didn't own but wanted me to have.

"Are you from Mississippi, sir?" I asked.

That simple question took the wind out of Trouble so sudden that all he could say was one word, "Jackson." Then he asked, "How did you know I was from Mississippi?" He seemed suspicious now.

"Just a guess, sir. No offense meant. But go ahead, please tell me bout that flute." I thought it was best to change the subject.

"I'll do that," he said after a bit, "but why don't we move away from this gate and sit for a bit under that tree over there?" He indicated which tree with a nod of his head and began to walk in that direction, and I followed him. I was curious bout where this was heading.

He didn't start talking right off, but seemed to gather his thoughts, and as he did, his eyes seemed to lose focus. Then he began talking in a slower, quieter voice, clenching and unclenching his right hand. Talking like he couldn't help himself.

"It began at sunup. I was riding behind the second lieutenant, and the rest of the men were behind me as we moved down the slope toward the river. It was almost cold enough to see the horses' breath, and they were breathing so loud, I knew we'd wake up the village before it was time. I remember the sun seemed far away, and the heat of it even farther. I heard *Draw saber!* and then the ring of steel sliding out of steel. It seemed louder than the river.

"When the bugle blared out it startled me, even after all these years. The horses had been bunched up cause they knew what was coming, and then, well, we let them loose and followed the crying of that bugle down to the river, through the reeds there, and then we were heaving up, down, up, down, through the water. It was so cold it bit my legs like fire. Then rising out of it, out and up, leaning forward as we rose up in a line, and I heard *Charge!*

"And then it got real still, like back home when a hurricane comes over and the wind blows round you but doesn't touch you ... anyway, in the middle of all that I could hear a flute playing off somewhere, the notes rising and falling like our sabers, high enough so's we could hear it through the firing of our carbines and the yelling of the children looking for their parents and the screams of the parents looking for their children. That flute sound just riding over everything, clean and pure, the only thing clean that day.

"The sound got louder when everything else stopped, and then I couldn't hear it no more. That flute just died away until you couldn't tell it from the wind. There ain't no noise like the sound of a battlefield when the battle is over, but the noise ain't out there, it's in your head, the other side of that hurricane finally catching up to you. And the smell of burning, I can still taste it in my clothes. I can't get the smell out. I wear the smell of that day, put it on in the mornin and sleep in it at night.

"This flute was lying on the ground for anyone fool enough to take it, next to the old man, that Indian who died holding it. I took it, and after a while I started playing it. I figured if he could play it through all that, then I could play it after. Here it is . . ."

And now he was plainly holding it out to me.

"I play it," he continued, "and even when I don't try to remember, hell, *it* does, it can never forget the music it made on that day, but I don't want to hear that day no more, so you can have it, boy. It's yours. You ain't got to that day yet, you're still green. I bet you sleep fine! So you'd be doin me a favor by taking it away."

I didn't say anything, just reached out my hand and took the flute. Sergeant Trouble nodded and slowly turned and walked out of the fort, down the dusty road. He never looked back. I guess that was one thing the army taught him, to not look back.

Trouble never told me his name. He didn't have to. It was all about getting rid of something that hurt too much to hold. I never knew you could give away your pain so easy, hand over to a stranger what's been eating at you from the inside.

The sergeant gave me the pain of that day on the river, and I took it. What could I do, he outranked me. I couldn't just say, sorry, sir, got enough pain of my own, don't need more, try someone else, please. I took it in silence and walked with the flute in my hand back to the barracks of Fort Robinson. I was a soldier now.

The officers say that the negroes make good soldiers and fight like fiends. They certainly manage to stick on their horses like monkeys. The Indians call them "buffalo soldiers," because their woolly heads are so much like the matted cushion that is between the horns of the buffalo.

from *Army Letters from an Officer's Wife*, Camp Supply, Indian Territory, June 1872, Frances M. A. Roe

buffalo soldier

That's what the Indians called us. All of them, Cheyenne, Lakota, Dakota, Kiowa, they called us buffalo soldiers because our hair was just like the hair between the horns of the buffalo.

It's the most respectful of all the names we were called, and it's interesting that it came from people we were fighting. Folks don't usually say kind things bout the people they're in a war with. Yeah, the Indians respected us, at least some of them did, maybe not the Absaroka, but the Absaroka didn't take to anyone who wasn't Absaroka, which means "children of the large beaked bird," and that's what those folks called themselves, but people who weren't part of that tribe called them Crow. The Absaroka, like most of those Indians on the Great Plains, are pretty fierce people, and some of them speak and read English, so if any of them read this and get upset cause I got something wrong, I meant no offense.

Grandma Sara used to say that wars are started by people who ain't got any manners. If the government ever said it was sorry for taking the Indians' land, maybe a lot of what was bad wouldn't have happened. Maybe a war is just a bunch of people all being rude at the same time, and it keeps on getting worse cause no one ever apologizes.

It was hard for me being mixed up in it, cause I'm part Seminole, and even though those Indians weren't Seminole, I felt something in common with them that I didn't feel with most white people. But many of the colored soldiers I served with hated Indians, and the hate was hot, you could feel it. It was strange cause a lot of those soldiers had Indian blood in them, too.

Maybe it was just a relief to them that the violence was against strangers and not their own families back in South Carolina, Georgia, Alabama, Mississippi, Louisiana, Texas. Instead of a white sheriff putting on a hood and joining a lynching party, the law was going after someone else, and they were part of the law, and it might've felt good to not be the victim. But if you weren't the victim, then you were probably the man wearing the white hood, or the blue uniform.

I don't know. It made sense at the time to hate Indians. Otherwise, how could you kill them? Looking back, I don't think I ever actually killed an Indian. At least not directly. There weren't many left to kill by the time I enlisted, and it always seemed like Troop K arrived a few hours late or a few days late.

But I know I was responsible for killing a few, sort of. We got orders to shoot buffalo whenever we came across them, and I knew even then that every good shot was bringing down more than just an animal. I felt bad bout that, still do. You see, to understand those Plains Indians, you got to understand that the buffalo was the heart of them. They ate it, almost all of it. It clothed them, kept them warm, and made it easier for them to see what's hard for a human being to see, that you can't go it alone, you need something out there in the world to help you.

That was the buffalo. It was a church, a shelter, a two-thousand-pound storehouse packed with goods, running round on four hoofs. And there we were, the Ninth, trying to take it all away, take food out of some child's mouth, take away what was keeping her warm in the winter. All that and more you can't say in English. I guess you can only say it in Dakota or dream it in Cheyenne or pray it in Kiowa, but I don't know the words, and even if I did, the meaning would be lost on me. I wish I knew it in Seminole, but Grandma Sara felt it was tough enough being colored, so why would I want to be an Indian too?

What was it all about? Land. The land you were born on. The land you die on. The land you want your children to live and die on. The land that was given to you. How can you let that go without putting up a fight? Just like the colored men and women on those slave ships, refusing to go along, fighting back, even jumping into the sea rather than living as a slave, cause you just can't let go of what you had.

And the people coming in, the settlers, they couldn't let go of what they wanted. They got children too, and some of their boys and girls were born on the way out. Those pioneers didn't know or care that they were traveling through someone's country, bringing cattle onto it or digging for gold in it, or breaking up the prairie for farms, because passing through someone's country is not the same as building a house on it and putting up a fence.

I get angry thinking about it, and I ain't Kiowa or Cheyenne, but I remember Grandma Sara raging bout how no respect was shown to the Seminole when white people came down into Florida, how none of them ever said, "Excuse me, I'd like to live here too." They saw colored people and Indians living and working together, and that didn't set too well with the white people cause they were outnumbered, so it made sense just to kill them all.

It'd be like a stranger walking into your house, sitting in your chair, drinking your whiskey, eating your food, sleeping in your bed, and then treating you like you're just the furniture that come with the place, furniture he don't particularly care for. How mad would you be? Yeah, I understand Seminole anger. So maybe I understand Cheyenne anger too, even if I don't know the words they use to say it.

But I know that for an Indian to call me a buffalo soldier was being bout as respectful as he could, cause the buffalo was right there next to God. And it sure as hell sounded better than "nigger cavalry" or "brunette" or "darkey policeman," no, I think buffalo soldier sounds just fine.

Being a buffalo soldier meant a bugle getting you up before the sun, meant feeding the horses, watering them, and drills for everything you might do on that horse. Drills taught you how to keep your seat if you suddenly had to speed up to a canter or come to a stop, drills

taught you how to turn your horse, back your horse, go at the walk or
the trot, to sidestep, to do everything but dance. And the bugle would
sound another day, and it'd be something new, firing from horseback
or using the saber, riding in formation, learning to move as one unit
and think as one unit, doing it again and again so you wouldn't have
to think because that was the point of drills, to not think but simply
do, because it's hard to think when other people are trying to kill you,
when you're afraid that you're going to die, so the army puts you in
that situation and they drill how you should act, over and over, so
hopefully when you're having that bad day you can survive it by just
slipping into reflex, into the drill. Because crying or praying to God
when bullets are flying don't prepare you for the battlefield, but it
does get you ready for what comes after, and a soldier's duty is to
fight so well that the man on the other side is the one with his hands
pressed together, sobbing and praying for deliverance, the man no
longer holding his rifle, the man who is already dead.

It meant the chaplain with the quiet voice who drilled you with
letters of the alphabet, who made you string letters into words and
words into sentences and sentences into paragraphs and paragraphs
into stories and stories into reports, reports about patrols through
country that was being emptied and filled up at the same time,
patrols that brought Indians and belligerents into custody, warriors
into custody, old men, women, and children into custody, into wagons, into corrals like stock, where they'd be standing round like dead
people.

And that meant I could write letters too, letters home, like Daddy
wanted me to do.

December, 1887

Dear Mama and Daddy and Grandma Sara,
I'm writing to you from Ft. Robinson, Nebraska, where I am serving as
a private with Troop K, Ninth Cavalry. The winters are very cold, but
there are good men here and I guess army life suits me and my attitude. It's
hard seeing what war has done to the Indians, but I know, Grandma, that

doesn't surprise you. Your Elijah is wearing the uniform of the country that made war on your people. I think about this all the time and wish there was something that would've made things turn out different, but I'm a soldier now. I chose to enlist, but circumstances were such that I had very few other choices that would have allowed me to be a man. I'm a warrior and warriors should not feel shame at what they do because war is the job. The shame is on those who give us the work. But the men don't talk much about war. They talk about their families, they tell stories about the people they love.

One day we will be together again. We will all sit together and tell each other everything that's happened since I left. That will be a long night! Daddy, I hope the deacon helped you with the alphabet so you can now write back to me. Mama, don't worry about me. Everyone dies, and if I die a soldier I will be wearing this uniform, and it looks good on me, so maybe Death will think I'm too pretty to leave this world and he'll leave me alone.

Grandma Sara, what you taught me helped get me here, so you only have yourself to blame that I'm a soldier. I know you're yelling at me as you read this so I'm glad I'm a thousand miles away. It would really hurt if I was there with you in Spartanburg. It hurts right now. Take the best of care, all of you.

Your Elijah

Of course, in those first months and years after I left Fort Robinson, I didn't think of myself as a buffalo soldier. We were Ninth Cavalry, and I tell you that meant something, and it still does. Most of my life I've been a soldier, a cavalryman. I'm proud of my regiment, proud of the Ninth because we look so damn good. And because all of us feel like we're more than soldiers, we're representing our families back home, even families that aren't our own.

I may die in this uniform, and if that's my fate, then I will have died for my country, the same country that enslaved Mama and Daddy, that made war against Grandma Sara's people, but maybe me dying will prove that all of us deserve to be treated like Americans because we are Americans, and that's what it means to be in the Ninth Cavalry.

Sure, other buffalo soldiers served in the Tenth Cavalry, but that's probably cause they didn't get accepted into the Ninth. There were colored soldiers in the Twenty-fourth and Twenty-fifth Infantry regiments too, but those poor men can't even ride mules, let alone horses. They got to walk, though they call it "marching." How sad. If a cavalryman's walking, it means he's had a really bad day cause he's either been bucked off his mule or lost his horse.

Now, I'm not saying an infantryman's not a good soldier. They sweat and bleed and risk their lives just like a cavalryman. It's just that when they come marching over a hill singing their songs, they ain't as pretty.

Cavalry or infantry, for colored soldiers like me, the army was a way to be in the world and feel part of something, a better way than sharecropping anyway. But it wasn't easy cause of how some white soldiers felt about us, especially officers. A lot of officers refused to serve with the colored troops. They thought it was beneath them, or maybe some were angry about how their own career in the army wasn't going so well. Those second lieutenants fresh out of West Point were looking for commissions in the First Cavalry or the Second or the Third or the Fourth, and it's a long way down the list before you get to the Ninth or Tenth.

There was one general in particular, a famous one, who felt that leading colored troops would be a personal disgrace. I think about that officer from time to time, bout his hatred of me, his low opinion of what I was capable of, even though he never met me. And I think about how his hate saved quite a few buffalo soldiers from an early end. It ain't often that race works in our favor, but this officer's contempt saved the lives of people who were beneath his notice.

If that officer had been a better man, a man able to see past the color of skin to what's inside, maybe the Ninth Cavalry would be lying under the ground beside the Little Big Horn, instead of the Seventh Cavalry.

At least that's what I tell my men when they're having a bad day, or think they're having a bad day. "It could be worse," I'd say, "it could be a Custer day." Those words usually pull them out of whatever dark hole they fell into. As long as you're breathing, seeing sky, able to put food in your belly, drinking water or whiskey when you want it, even if you're shivering under a blanket out in the middle of a cold so deep that Old Man Winter himself is chilly, well, you're doing all right. You got nothing to complain about. But if it's a Custer Day, you're done.

That's how I got through my thirteen years at all those lonely forts in Nebraska, the Dakotas, Montana, Kansas, and Arizona, going on all those patrols through country that had been emptied of people but not beauty. It was sad, grinding work, riding out day after day looking for the last Lakota, Crow, Arapaho, Comanche, Apache, Hidatsa, Blackfeet, Kiowa, Navajo, Gros Ventre, Osage, Hopi, Cheyenne, Salish, Pawnee, Havasupai. If you name all those nations, say their names out loud one after the other, it does something to the air and to your mind, you hear the voices of people who were here long before all of this started, people who tell stories about how the world began.

I don't know what it did to the other men, but it wore on me. No matter what direction you looked out from a fort, or from the saddle, the people you were looking for weren't there no more, not the way they were just a few years earlier. They all got herded up, forced to walk hundreds of miles, put on trains, and coralled finally in what the government calls a reservation.

I've seen reservations, and I tell you, you can put people inside them, but they can never hold what's inside the people. I remember eyes staring out from bodies that weren't getting enough food or blankets or shelter, not getting enough of what they needed even more than those things. And what was behind those eyes had nothing to do with the reservation, it was something that couldn't be put in a tent or a cabin or a plot of land that wasn't healthy for a tumbleweed.

At least a tumbleweed is free to drift with the wind, and it was freedom behind those eyes. I know what freedom looks like. It always seems to be something outside of me. I recognize it when it strolls by whistling a song I wasn't meant to hear, but no one ever taught me the words to "Freedom."

I guess you got to teach yourself how to sing that song. The words must be about living with yourself after you let go of everything that meant something to you. How do you do that and keep singing? Some of those Indians did.

Like the old man who looked at me through the fence of a fort in Montana and began to sing, sing so hard his chest was like a bellows taking in all he had lost and giving it back to the wind, his white hair blown back, his mouth open and his eyes closing, but the sound, the high cry of his voice like a wounded hawk. The sound of an old man whose world is gone but he's trying to call it back.

I tried to help him, because I'm a fool. I tried to put what he was saying in my flute. The others shut in there saw me do that, saw the soldier playing a cedar flute while they sang, but I didn't look at them because the old man and I were having a conversation, the flute and the cry, and I felt what was Seminole and Cherokee in me sing, and in that moment I could hear Grandma Sara crying too for what she had lost, and what they had lost and what I had lost.

I could feel the coldness in the looks from the soldiers on guard duty, but they couldn't feel my shame, not shame at myself but at such a world where it was so easy to make the wrong choice and then choose to go on living.

I remember hearing that a Paiute named Wovoka was the one who started the Ghost Dance, sometime in the late eighties. I guess they believed if they sang hard enough and long enough, all the dead buffalo would hear them and come back and fill up the hills and valleys and plains, and everything would be like it was before the white man came. Before there were soldiers. Those Indians kept on dancing and singing as if their voices could reach into the world where the buffalo had gone, and where their dead had gone, a world that used to be right there on the plains.

But everybody knew how it would turn out. Except the officers who kept us on patrols, kept us watching and waiting for what wasn't there no more. Soldiers like me, just watching and waiting for it to end.

When someone takes away what you love most in the world, what would you choose to sing? That's what I wondered at the time, what I'd be singing if it were me and my people. I remember Grandma Sara singing in that language that wasn't African or Indian or Spanish but like a stew of all those simmered down to a different flavor, and you didn't have to understand the words to know it was a sad song.

A soldier's supposed to follow orders, not wonder about why, but a voice in me kept asking what those Ghost Dance Indians were singing, and maybe it was God's voice. God must be plenty confused during a war. Men crying out to Him, praying for their lives while they're pulling a trigger or pushing a bayonet, or swinging a tomahawk or thrusting a knife. If God was confused, then where did that leave me?

I think the part of me that's Seminole, the part buried deep, woke up when it heard the singing from the Indian camps.

The Indian War was a river running fast, like Big Creek in the spring flood. It carried away a lot of my years, like the river carried away some Indians on that morning when Sergeant Trouble and his troop charged. A river that went from silver to brown, getting all cloudy from the dirt it picked up, so that pretty soon I couldn't look through it no more. I couldn't swim against its current neither. I just had to ride it out.

Yeah, I'm a buffalo soldier all right. If you want to call me that, go right ahead. I been called a lot worse.

Skirmishing

The objects of employing skirmishers are, to cover movements and evolutions, to gain time, to watch the movements of the enemy, to keep him in check, to prevent his approaching so close to the main body as to annoy the line of march, and to weaken and harass him by their fire; to prepare the way for the charge on infantry, by rendering them unsteady, or drawing their fire.

from *Cavalry Tactics*

the florida blockade

What became the Spanish-American War began in 1898, when the Spanish blew up the U.S.S. *Maine* in Cuba. I was back in Fort Robinson, Nebraska, when it started.

Almost ten years had passed since the end of the Indian Wars and nothing that interesting had happened in between. In that time Troop K just drifted from fort to fort, and the routine of garrison life didn't change all that much. Only the fort names changed: Huachuca, Davis, Larned, Smith, Reno, Griffin, Lawton, Sill, Bayard, Riley. Oh, yeah, and my rank. First I got promoted to corporal and then to sergeant.

One thing that happened when I got back to Fort Robinson was that I got approval to go home for about two weeks, for the first time. For a long time I wasn't sure if I really wanted to, cause of what Daddy told me when I left, cause South Carolina was still South Carolina, and cause my attitude had only gotten worse since I became a sergeant in the Ninth Cavalry. Even now, I wanted to see my family cause it had been such a long time, but I wasn't dying to see them, if you understand my meaning. It's not like I didn't miss them, but they were always with me.

But I put in for the leave anyway cause I wanted them to see who I was now, and maybe the uniform would keep me out of trouble. I figured my request would be turned down because of the blowing up of the *Maine*, but it wasn't. I ended up taking the train down from Fort Robinson to Atlanta, Georgia, with some of the other cavalrymen, who were on their way to Tampa, Florida, and then to Cuba. I'd switch trains in Atlanta and keep heading east.

At a lot of places along the railroad there were people, white and colored folks standing together on both sides of the station platforms, cheering us on, waving flags, excited about seeing us soldiers. Until we got close to the Mason-Dixon Line. South of that boundary there was silence, and the whites and colored were standing on opposite sides of the tracks. I remember how that made me feel, and the look in the eyes of the men in my troop.

Disappointment followed by Sadness followed by Anger. Those were the names of the towns along the tracks from that point on. And when we got to Atlanta, there was a message from some colonel denying all approved leave.

I couldn't go home. After thirteen years. I was headed for a war now, and it was a good thing, cause I felt like killing somebody. A few days past Atlanta, we got to Tampa, Florida, where army troops from all over were gathering to ship off to Cuba. That's where the war was supposed to be, but meanwhile a different war broke out. The battleground was just off the train tracks in Tampa.

Don't remember the regiment, but white volunteers from Ohio were the cause of it. Maybe it was the liquor they'd been drinking, but I think it was hate, not whiskey, drove those boys to do what they did. They grabbed a two-year-old Negro child from its mother, probably the sweetest thing on this earth to that child's mama and daddy, and they saw fit to use that child as a target just to show the world how well they could shoot. They showed the world all right, and their aim was true, except what hit home was how little they valued the life of a colored child.

And that started the Tampa Riot, which raged all through the night of June 6, 1898. When some colored soldiers heard about the shooting, they went crazy and busted up some white-only saloons. I was stationed in an encampment just outside town, and the commanding officer had forbidden us to leave under any circumstances. There were a few officers from white regiments coming into the camp, enough to give us news of what was happening. Apparently, the blood of colored people didn't stop flowing through the streets till sunup.

And that's about the time, or shortly thereafter, when the Florida Blockade began. At least that's what I call the anger that clouds my sight every time I remember that night.

You see, I was hoping to say something bout colored men fighting in Cuba, bout how the Tenth Cavalry fought at Las Guasimas, or the Twenty-fifth Infantry at El Caney, or the Twenty-fourth Infantry, the Ninth and Tenth Cavalries, and Roosevelt's Rough Riders all charging up San Juan Hill. That's what I was hoping, but the blockade won't let me get there.

I got so much heat in me that I can't see past Florida at all. Cuba just won't come into view no matter how I strain my eyes. And the problem ain't my vision, it's that my anger's so big I can't see to the other side. It's like bad weather filling up sky with white clouds and black lightning, filling you up till you choke and burn.

If Anger is a place to live in, then I think 1898 is the year I moved all the way there. But when you're a good citizen of Anger, you're living alone, and there ain't no church, no God to hear you raging, and no family near enough to get singed by your heat, like I used to get burned sitting beside Grandma Sara.

I'm not living in Anger full-time anymore, but I'm still so mad bout what happened in Florida that I can't feel good bout what happened in Cuba. I just can't get there cause of that blockade in my heart. And it's a shame, cause good men died in Cuba. They fought bravely, even gallantly, no matter what Colonel Roosevelt said later. Roosevelt was wrong to say what he said, and maybe he apologized, but it wasn't good enough.

Colored soldiers running from a fight, he'd said. Colored soldiers who weren't no good unless white officers were leading them. Yeah, he should've been sorry!

Like those white boys who started that riot in Tampa. After the streets "ran red with Negro blood," like a newspaper said, those white soldiers from Ohio could go to any restaurant they wanted, cause you work up an appetite pulling a trigger, or maybe they went to get something cool to drink cause they worked up such a thirst. But no matter where they chose to go, they would've been served like gentlemen, while a colored soldier could only hope to get served round the back, if at all. Do you think those white boys ever said "I'm sorry" for what they done?

So that's why I can't get to Cuba. I want to, believe me. I need to get to Cuba. I want to talk bout the heights of San Juan, bout gallantry under fire. It would be a helluva lot easier to talk bout war and grown men dying than bout some child who was used for target practice in Tampa.

But the blockade's in my way, and until it clears, I won't ever be able to see past Florida.

To Accustom Horses to Military Noises and Firing
If the horses become much excited discontinue the firing
until they become calm.

from *Cavalry Tactics*

philippines

I finally got over Tampa, got past the blockade, and saw what was on the other side.

The Pacific Ocean. The war with Spain ended just a couple months after it started. America won, so on a piece of paper called the Treaty of Paris, we got what had been Spanish property, including the Philippine Islands. The problem was that no one bothered asking the Filipinos how they felt about the deal.

They didn't like it. Which is how Troop K and the rest of the Third Squadron, Ninth U.S. Cavalry, ended up on transport ships to the Philippine Islands, by way of San Francisco. We'd received orders to quell the revolt. I didn't quite understand what *quell* meant till a corporal of mine, who was from Atlanta and had more schooling than me, said it basically meant the same thing as *suppress*.

Well, I knew that word front and back. After that, we all got drunk together, Corporal Bingham, that word, and me. And when it came to me that we'd be quelling people who'd been fighting the Spanish for their freedom, I felt like having another drink.

Freedom. There it was again. That word. And once again I felt like I was on the wrong side of it. Maybe that's why I couldn't get my bearings, couldn't tell which way was north or south. Besides, I was out there in the ocean, and being in that big water without a compass was a bit like being on a battlefield when guns are blazing round you, and people are dying round you, and there's so much commotion you're not certain where the enemy is.

Bingham and I were afraid that *where* was about to be replaced by *who*, and that's what led to the whiskey. It's hard to explain the feeling of going to war. You don't completely know what you're getting into, or if you can get out of it alive. Over that bottle of whiskey, Bingham told me he'd had the same feeling when he got married.

"No sir," he said, when I asked him about it. "I didn't know at all what I was getting into when I got hitched, but so far so good. Maybe cause Helen knows I'm the one with the revolver."

I laughed, and he looked at me, smiled back.

"You're a soldier," he said, "you know as well as me that in war, it's the man holdin the gun who gets to sort things out."

"But Bingham," I argued, still laughing, "in a war every soldier's got a gun!"

"That's right!" he agreed, his eyes bright, "and that's why a cavalryman's got the edge over a woman in a marriage."

Once we landed in the harbor in Luzon, we figured the main enemy might be the climate. Manila was steam and a fiery sun, like a bath of mist, but no water you could drink except what was on your skin, and your clothes were never dry. Inside you were a forest that was underwater, and you were breathing rain, you were breathing clouds, and I felt suffocated. I could never get a breath without feeling like I was drowning.

The people were colored but not South Carolina colored or Mississippi colored, but Philippine colored, and they talked Philippine talk and wore clothes that could handle clouds and had faces that didn't mind water flowing over them. They were sad faces and smiling faces at the same time, and even though they were strangers I felt I knew them, because they were colored. I never felt more like a stranger than when I was in those green mountains trying to find something cool enough to breathe without getting killed. Those Filipinos were fighting hard for their freedom, and I was fighting to take it from them . . . me, Elijah Yancy, who didn't know what freedom tasted or looked or smelled like, but could take it out of the hands of a child.

And I had no choice cause I had enlisted. I had made my mark, signed my name on that piece of paper to get a job, a profession, a pension. A man taking names took mine, and before I knew it I was killing people who could've been my family, but I didn't have any choice cause I didn't want to be a sharecropper.

You understand what I'm saying? I got sent to those islands, and nobody asked me how I felt about it, but it didn't matter what I felt cause I was just supposed to say "Yes sir!" and do what I was told. So the ship took me there, and the islands took me once I was there, and once I saw how beautiful the people were and what they were doing, I knew I had made a mistake. But I couldn't get out of the uniform.

It had me and it was tight, and if I took it off I would be naked and alone, so I kept it on and kept killing people, following orders that said kill the Insurrectos. And then when the Insurrectos were either dead or gone, things slowed down to confusion cause then I could really look round, see what I had done and who I had done it to. I didn't like things being that slow, I didn't like that I could focus clearly on what was before me and behind me, and it got to a point where I stopped looking over my shoulder cause it hurt too much.

My hands were scalded from the heat of my Krag firing, hotter than the sun in my hands, but no hotter than what was in my heart, what was in my throat. And I couldn't say nothing, all I could do was follow orders and give orders and hope at the end that I wasn't to blame, hope that something good happened at the end. I couldn't see how, though, cause there was so much hate heating up a place that was already plenty hot. I'd come all the way across an ocean just to find more hate, mostly. It was hard to see these people fighting for freedom, and then see how they was treated by so many American soldiers, white soldiers, who treated them no different than colored folks back home, and that's what started the war between us.

I can't forget that white sergeant in Manila, his face the color of spoilt cream and his smile with no heat in it, the way he looked at me standing on a street corner, looked me over like I was meat hanging from a hook and he was wondering if I was fresh or rotten, good enough to eat or something to bury quick.

"What they call you, boy?" he asked, and his voice was a knife sticking in and turning.

"My men call me *sir*," I said back to him, "if you want to know, Sergeant." Cause he was a sergeant just like me, we were the same rank except he was white and I was colored, and he wanted me to know the difference, wanted me to feel it deep. He didn't have to try so hard.

"Well, *Sergeant*," he said, like he was spitting out something that tasted awful. Then he stopped and looked round at all the Filipino people that was passing by us in the street, sliding their eyes over us so we wouldn't notice them. He looked at them the same way he looked at me. Then he started talking again, but not really to me, cause he didn't really see me no better than my shadow on the ground.

"I'm from Minnesota, boy, and we got plenty of niggers round there, but I ain't seen niggers like these before. Sure, the women are all right after a while, but they still stink like niggers, they feel the same, and I was wondering when I saw you, what you felt bout them, considering you a nigger too and all. And, well," he paused again, "I consider myself a fair man, so I figure you got an opinion bout that, so I ask you, boy, what do you think of these niggers round here?"

Talk about smell, I hated his smell and his arrogance and his hate most of all, but I didn't hate him cause he was sick, my mama would have said, and people who are sick need help, not curses.

I did want to curse him right there for all to hear, but all I said was, "Well, Sergeant, I been here several months now, and I've seen many interesting things and people who are even more interesting, but in all that time I ain't seen any niggers. Now, seems like you seein something that ain't there, so I'd be careful of drinkin any more of what you been drinkin, cause it's makin you see what ain't there and not see what is, which ain't healthy for a soldier."

He took a step back from me as if I had just jumped up out of the ground, like a dead man who decided to speak up and say things he could never say when he was alive.

"Nigger," he snarled, "if we was back home, you'd be dead now."

"Sergeant," I replied, "maybe I'm already dead and this is heaven, and these are all angels round us, and you got off the train at the wrong stop cause you weren't meant to be here. Maybe none of us was meant to be here, but we got to make the most of it cause we're supposed to be in hell, but somehow we got up to heaven and it's only a matter of time before we're found out. But if you keep raisin your voice, then we'll be found out, so I'd whisper if I was you. If you ain't careful, both of us is goin to end up in hell."

He looked confused by all that, which is what I wanted. Sometimes talking crazy makes more sense than being reasonable. Plenty of colored people been killed in South Carolina trying to be reasonable with people who just wanted them dead. If you have to talk to crazy people, and you act crazier, maybe you can walk away while they're trying to understand what wasn't meant to be understood.

So I walked away from that fool, who just stayed there with his mouth open and didn't do nothing cause he didn't know what to do.

I've seen men out of their minds on a battlefield and no bullet touches them, while men who keep cool and try to reason get all shot up, and they're lying there bleeding trying to figure out what happened to them, as if reason had anything to do with it. If something's crazy, then you got to be crazier if you want to survive.

A lot happened to me in the Philippines. Not all of it was bad, and some of it was beautiful. Now and then I managed to get out of my uniform and breathe a little better. But mostly I was bound up in my uniform and my orders and the hate that came across the ocean with us. That sergeant in Manila, and people like him, was the real cause of the Philippine-American War. Yes, an American ship in the Havana harbor blew up, and President McKinley was assassinated in 1901. But I believe the Philippine Insurrection happened mostly cause of hate no one bothered to hide. When you call someone nigger while you're shaking his hand, you shouldn't be surprised when he gets angry and wants to hurt you as deep as you hurt him.

Just about anywhere I know, that's reason enough for a fight.

꧁꧂

Patrol report on Yosemite Park stationery,
under "Remarks," Wawona, Cal., July 19, 1903

A heard of sheep at Arndt Lake numbering abought 1600.
Brand "M", A Pack train of (2) burrows.

> Very Respectfully,
> William Alexander,
> Sgt. "L", 9 Cavy.
> Commanding Detachment

꧁꧂

two prayers from luzon

Dear God:
    i'm havin a hard time breathin
it's so hot and the air is full of water,
i'm walkin on the ground, but i'm drownin,
my clothes never dry
and neither do i,
i would be so grateful for a wind
to blow over me, a cool wind
off a mesa in arizona at night,
yeah, that would be nice,
just send that cold, dry breeze
into this green weeping filipinos call a forest,
thank you, God!

oh, i forgot,
i do appreciate the sun,
but i wish it were clearer,
i think even the sun
is troubled by all these clouds
so you'd be helpin the sun
as well as me if a wind
would come up and blow
the rain away, and then i could see
clearer who's tryin to kill me,
who i'm tryin to kill,
and all the reasons why,

although i don't know if light can do that
cause seein clear is not always bout
illumination
even when you see how water
washes all the blood away
all the rot away
all the pain away,
well, not all of it cause
lately in my soul nothin is flowin
and no breeze is blowin,
it's just a big dark hole
full of whispers, prayers, curses,
tears, piss, and stagnant water,
so a wind out of arizona
goin right through me
would be sweet.

dear God:
i don't know what to do
no more with a smile
or long black hair down to a waist
my hands were hungry to hold.
what do i do with black eyes
starin at me that way?
and how her dress
come up over hips that way
what do i do with that?
and it wouldn't have mattered
if she hadn't looked at me
like i was the one, the only one
that was meant to hold her
that way, and she smiled at me
as i rode by, lookin up at me,
and i almost fell off a my horse.

i become a deserter right there,
i would've fought for aguinaldo
right there, and every insurrecto in these islands
just for another smile from that sweet young thing,
twistin me in my saddle till the 2nd lieutenant yelled
at me bout breakin formation
as if that mattered, considerin
my heart was busted
by those deep black eyes lookin into me
that way with that smile, God almighty
why she do that to me?

To Accustom Horses to Military Noises and Firing
In firing from the horse's back the pistol shoud
at first be held vertically.

from *Cavalry Tactics*

the *logan* and captain young

What I remember most bout the voyage back to California was how even the sea felt uneasy. It was more restless than I was, rolling and churning. I wondered what was beneath all that commotion struggling to get out. I'd felt like that ever since leaving Manila, and not just my stomach.

It was strange to spend all those months on ground that never moved, and the whole time feeling inside like the water out there, neither one ever quiet. I see now that even when I was in that jungle, I was still on that boat in the stormy water, being tossed round and not knowing why. I can see me hunched over and creeping through all that hot green country, and struggling to stay upright on that ship deck at the same time. If someone introduced me to the self I was then, what would I say?

"Boy, you look like hell, worse than hell, you look like the manure hell is built on top of!" Yeah, that's what I'd say if I could talk to myself, instead of standing by this railing peering down into an ocean just as roiled up as I am.

Listen to it roar. Listen to me roar. Just like water, I am bigger than the world, and nobody knows me even if they know my name. Pacific, that's what they call you, and the lieutenant says that means peace or peaceful, except you're anything but. I've known a few people who were like this water, all loud and scary on the outside, but what are they really like deep down, so far down you'd drown before you got there?

Maybe somewhere at the bottom of all this there's no noise, no movement, just nothing. Maybe nothing wears the ocean like I wear this uniform or my skin. Something to cover up what shouldn't be seen. The water knows I'm naked even though I'm standing here clothed. Though I act all right, this water can feel the lie underneath. It ain't pacific at all, and neither am I. Who moves inside me that's got my name, my voice, my blood, but don't know me?

Then the ship pitched again, and I let go of my insides, but it all got lost in the spray. If I fell in, would the Pacific even know I was there? I wondered how many people and other living things had died in this water, and the water took it all in and still was itself, never became something else. I remembered the dream I had when I was just leaving home, the dream about slaves who jumped or were thrown into the sea. The sea got into them after they fell into the sea. This water can become anything it wants to, but it never forgets what it is.

If it didn't make you so sick, a man could learn something from this water. Even when I was being sick, it made me think.

Then came a long slow deep roll to the other side, and I held on tight to the rail. It was like holding on to ice but it was better than becoming ice. I felt someone next to me and looked down, which was easy since I was already looking down on account of I was throwing up my breakfast all over the deck. And I saw shoes down by my shoes, shoes shiny with spray and polish, too bright to be the shoes of an enlisted man. It was an officer's shoes shining there by my feet, and there were officer's pants rising up above those shoes.

And the view didn't improve as I looked all the way up, into the eyes of Captain Charles Young.

I'd always wanted to meet Captain Young, but not like this. Not with what I'd eaten this morning all over my coat, my pants, my shoes. I wanted to look my best when meeting one of the few colored officers in the army, a colored man who was also a West Point graduate, and who I'd heard had said that "the worst thing I could ever wish on an enemy would be to make him colored and a cadet at West Point." The man every soldier in Troop K looked up to cause of who he was and what he was and what he'd done, the same man who was standing in front of me for the first time.

"Captain Young!" I gasped, so excited I forgot to salute. I stuck out my right hand to shake his, and only then remembered that I was just using that hand to wipe the puke from my mouth, but it was too late to pull it away. I didn't want to offend him, but, hell, I was offending him anyway.

Captain Young looked down at my hand and then in my face, and I saw that what's at the bottom of this ocean was also at the bottom of this man's eyes. And whatever that is, I still ain't got a name for it.

"Sergeant," he said finally, "you're a mess. No, soldier, you're beyond a mess, and I'll take your hand once it's clean, but for the moment I suggest you go below and wash yourself thoroughly."

I stood at attention, stiff as a flag after an ice storm. Here was the man I wanted to meet more than any other man in this world, the man who made me proud to wear the uniform, and I was a disgrace in his eyes.

"Yes sir!" I said to him. "I'm sorry, sir, but ocean-goin don't agree with me, sir. I thought the fresh air up here on deck would be better than bein down below, and it was for a bit, but—" I paused to gather myself and steady my words. "I'm sorry, Captain Young," I said again, as if repeating it would make things better. "It won't happen again, sir!"

He seemed to lose a little iron. His body was still stiff like he had joints missing, but his eyes were warmer. I thought I could see some part of him the army had never touched, somewhere way down at the bottom of his eyes.

"Very good, sergeant, very good," he answered. He started to turn with the motion of the ship, but then turned back to me and asked, "What's your name?"

I stood up even straighter before replying, "Sergeant Elijah Yancy, Troop K, sir!"

And this time I saw just a bit of a smile hiding in the corners of his mouth.

"Yancy," he said. "Well, enjoy the rest of the voyage, Sergeant Yancy. California will be somewhat steadier than the ocean. You'll settle down soon enough."

He saluted, I saluted, and he walked off. The rolling of the ship didn't seem a problem to him at all. Must be something they teach you at West Point, but I think the most important things about him he didn't learn in school.

Of all my time on the *Logan*, meeting Captain Young is what I remember most clearly. I was embarrassed at the time, but no more, cause at least he saw that I was a human being, and every officer needs to be reminded about that once in a while. I remind myself all the time.

Patrol report on Yosemite Park stationery,
under "Remarks," Soda Springs, August 1, 1903

Corpl. Holmes & 1 man Patrol the Bloody Canyon. return
Aug. 2nd. No trespassing what ever. 1 Private patrol the
Alkali Creek. return the same day, no trespassing.

> Corpl. Holmes,
> K. Troop, 9th Cav.,
> Soda Springs

a prayer at sea

I t's strange, not being where you're going and not where you were
either, but somewhere in between. That's what it was like being
on the *Logan*. I've spent most of my life at sea, between one thing and
another, but it wasn't always as violent and perilous as the part of that
voyage a few weeks out of Luzon.

*dear God, don't let me die. it would hurt mama and daddy to lose me, but
it would really upset grandma sara. you know how she is. she would be
sure to rage at you for lettin me get myself killed, and she wouldn't mean
to be disrespectful, but she's bout done with pain.*

I kind of got used to being in between. I was at sea growing up in
Spartanburg. I was at sea serving at Fort Robinson and fighting in
the Philippines.

*no, i think it would be best if you let me live. not for my sake, but you
pretty busy and probably don't have the patience to listen to my grandmother rail at you, especially when she so good at it.*

What does it feel like to cross over? To really get to where you're
going? Maybe when Death finally gets you, he's just letting your
dreams go free cause they've been trapped in your head all your life
and could never open up their wings and fly off.

*and it would probably break mama's heart to lose me cause she's already
lost one child, and i know there's plenty of other mothers who lost children*

and you thinkin why should i save this one? i don't know the answer to that. i just know that daddy don't want to hold me when i'm dead and put my body in the ground.

No one wants to die. No one wants to be forgotten, and to be forgotten is to die. Maybe that's why I pray so much, so God can learn to pick my voice out of the noise he's got to listen to, so he can remember my voice.

i hope you take these words as the prayers of a fearful and chastened man and do not doubt the fierce devotion that was mine when i was a child on sundays in spartanburg, where we had so many conversations bout me being colored, and how that made my life so interestin.

Lots of soldiers pray to God and got good reason for it. I never met most of them, but that don't mean I don't know them or don't care about them. They wore the uniform, and it doesn't matter if it was infantry or cavalry.

and i appreciate the opportunity to fight for my country, but i didn't feel right killin filipinos when all they wanted was freedom, and i'm curious how come colored men got to take away freedom from some other people when we ain't ever had it ourselves?

All my life in the army, and elsewhere, I heard voices other than my own. The army teaches you to work together, to be a unit. Maybe I been in the army too long. Maybe this ain't just my story I been telling.

that's how i feel and i'm not alone cause some of the men in troop k feel like they fightin on the wrong side.

Those Filipino colored people had families just like mine. And those families worried about their men when they were far away.

And prayed for them the last thing before they went to sleep at night.
Just like me, they wanted God's help.

*thank you for listenin and i hope you can hear me cause i'm a long way
from home. in my absence, please take care of mama and daddy and
grandma sara.*

Yeah, most soldiers are strangers to me, but God knows each of
their names and what's in their hearts, cause each soldier sleeps in the
space between a mother's or a father's hands, black hands in prayer.
There are words in that darkness, and they're not all meant for me.

respectfully,

So many voices in the night. How many prayers will get through
to the other side? How many lost at sea?

elijah yancy

To Accustom Horses to Military Noises and Firing

Young horses are in like manner accustomed to the manual of
arms, waving of flags, military music, &c.

from *Cavalry Tactics*

parade

The 12th of May 1903 was sunny but cold. I stood along a sidewalk on Van Ness Avenue with San Franciscans on every side: whites, Chinese, Mexicans, a few colored people, but mostly whites, and lots of schoolchildren in their Sunday best, all waiting to see President Theodore Roosevelt.

When people looked at me, I could tell that some of them had never seen a colored soldier before. It was a strange look, curious but with no hate. They didn't look for long, though, cause folks were there to see the president, who was on a speaking tour of California.

A few anxious policemen were walking down the street with their batons, so no one got too close. Their uniforms fit them well, as the occasion warranted, and looked new even if they weren't. Nothing was frayed or dirty.

It was cold in the shadows and loud from all the talking, but I could see the sun bright on the building opposite where I was standing. I felt something or someone brush against my right side and I looked down. It was a young boy with reddish hair and blue eyes, peering up at me and smiling.

"Can you see President Roosevelt?" he shouted, breathing hard. I wondered how this child could talk without air in his lungs. The excitement of the crowd lit up his face so much he could've been used at night for a lantern.

"Naw," I said. "All I see is people waitin all along Van Ness, and the police havin a devil of a time keepin folks out of the road."

"But the president . . . can you see him? I mean, he should be here soon, he's supposed to be here!" he said. Each word came out of him with no room for the next, so it took a bit for me to make sense of what he was asking.

"All I see," I began, gazing up the street, "is what I told you. No more. But he'll be here, and the Ninth as well," I added.

"Who's the Ninth?" he asked. I couldn't tell if he was really curious or just being polite. He probably didn't have many conversations with colored people, let alone soldiers.

"Young man," I said, "the Ninth means Ninth Regiment of Cavalry. I'm with Troop K. There's quite a few colored soldiers stationed here at the Presidio. Some of us were picked to escort the president at this here parade, and some were not."

The boy did something funny with his mouth as if he'd just put something in it that didn't taste right, and he couldn't make up his mind whether to swallow or spit. He looked me up and down good. I think about then was the first time he'd really seen me, though I was clearly wearing a uniform.

"You're a nigger," he said, "and a soldier?"

He was confused. He could deal with me being a nigger and probably was all right with me being a soldier, but both, well, that was unusual enough to challenge whatever he'd been taught.

"No," I said, "I ain't no nigger, and don't know any either, but I'm African and Seminole Indian, which means I'm part Creek and possibly Muskogee. Might be some Gullah in there, I don't know for sure.

"And I'm not just a soldier. I'm a U.S. cavalryman, a sergeant in the Ninth Regiment, but don't think about it too much right now. You don't want to fall down on this sidewalk, cause what with everyone watchin for the president, you could be lyin here for hours before someone notices you. You could give it some thought when you get older, cause by then you'll be able to handle whiskey. And you might need a drink."

He seemed to be considering whether or not to smile, but he didn't want to get into trouble, and I think he already sensed that the conversation had gone on too long. He smiled anyway as he turned and said, "Thanks, soldier!"

It was so crowded that he was gone just like that behind a jumble of pants, dresses, sleeves, arms pointing, and white hands gesturing up the road. All those white hands like birds, white birds, so many I couldn't see the bodies they were attached to, and the sun making them flutter by themselves. I couldn't see whole people, just pieces of them: faces, heads, hats, parasols, cravats, white shirts, hair in curls, rings, all jumbled up. The only thing keeping it all from spilling out onto Van Ness were the frustrated policemen, who obviously were not enjoying this duty at all. Shaking their heads, shouting to the crowd to keep back, yelling the same things over and over, and no one seemed to be listening.

"Move on back, folks, please!" I heard one officer say. "Please make room! You can't see the president if you don't make room for him to get here!" The officer, a tall fellow with gray hair, red cheeks, and sideburns too long for his face then spat on the ground and kept moving down the line.

So many people together made the air sound like the sea. All those voices, high and low, sounding together like waves rolling down the avenue, a waterless sea, and you could hear and feel the power of it whenever the crowd started moving. That's why the police were so nervous, cause they knew they couldn't stop the crowd if it wanted to move.

Then the mules and horses came. You couldn't hear them till they were up close. I watched their legs move and their hooves strike the ground, but it was silent with all that cheering going on. First there were mounted police, but people didn't pay much attention to them. What caught their eye was what came after: column after column of cavalry swinging into view.

Not just any cavalry, the Ninth was parading down Van Ness, right in front of the presidential entourage. It was most of Troop I, about fifty men in dress uniforms, and they were all staring ahead

down the street as if no one at all was standing alongside, and as they
came it seemed to me that the sea of sound parted, and silence was at
the bottom. Over that silence the tap and click of mules and horses
moving at the walk suddenly could be heard as Troop I forded that
silence, like they'd been drilling for years on the safest way to man-
uever through it.

All their tack was clean and smooth, bridles, reins, saddles, saddle-
bags, stirrups, blankets, all looking like they'd just come out of a
box, and even the horses looked just unpacked, brushed down and
combed, and they moved as one, like they knew President Roosevelt
was riding behind them.

But what got to me were the men on horseback, sitting bolt
upright in their saddles and looking straight ahead. They didn't
wave at the crowd or even look to one side or the other, just rode as
if this was the last time they'd ever ride on this earth. That's what I
can't forget. And they didn't have to say anything about pride, cause
it was in how they held themselves as they rode. A sea of cheers and
cries was breaking on either side of them like waves, but they calmly
rode through and it never touched them.

Thousands of schoolchildren along the edges of the sidewalks
were frantically waving their little flags, and I saw those flags slow
as the cavalry approached, those children just as surprised to see the
Fighting Ninth as that little boy was to see me close up.

I thought I saw the regimental flag borne by a fellow I remembered running into at the Presidio, but I couldn't be sure. The flag
drooped in the shadows for a bit, but just as it came out into the sun,
a breeze picked up and it fully unfurled for all to see. But I had no
trouble at all recognizing Captain Charles Young riding at the head
of the column, even ahead of the flag. He wasn't a big man, but there
was a quiet resolve in the line of his body that made him taller. Back
straight, head pitched slightly forward, heels down in the stirrups, he
gazed coolly down the road at something only he could see.

By the time Roosevelt came by in his carriage, with the Secret
Service walking behind him, well, it was a bit of a letdown. All the

pomp was riding up ahead of him in columns of two, and he was just the circumstance.

I felt something that day I've not felt since, and it wasn't just pride. I still can't put a name to it. I guess the closest thing to what I was feeling would be the sight of Captain Young riding in front of that column of men. He was all alone out in that road, in that parade, in that city, in all the brightness, a West Point graduate and a colored officer, but the weight of that seemed nothing as he rode by sitting tall on his horse, his back as straight as if an iron rod had replaced his spine. That man was a soldier on the inside and a real officer, and he didn't even need a uniform. You can tell when people are in command of themselves, and Captain Young was like that.

Then the parade was over, so fast, but I keep seeing it, the troop of colored soldiers going past and the people watching them, not quite certain what they were really seeing, oh yeah, I remember that part of the day better than the sky or the sunlight or the flags or the cheering. What I can't forget is a few dozen colored men in uniform with Teddy Roosevelt in tow behind them.

They weren't escorting the president, no sir. On that day, President Roosevelt was escorting Captain Young's soldiers. And the silence that followed them down Van Ness Avenue is still there, the same silence they strode over, those mules and horses and men, on that day in May of 1903.

woman at crissy field

I remember another day during that time President Roosevelt came to San Francisco. More of a person than a day. More of a woman staying in my head like a coal that don't know the fire's out.

This time they were marching at a parade ground called Crissy Field. It was a place for horses and noise, officers shouting and movements like razors cutting the air, and the smell of sweat. Once again Troop I was there parading with President Roosevelt. And more thousands of people, old and young, all there to glimpse one man, get close to one man.

Maybe it wasn't the man himself that drew people, but when someone's got power like he did, how can you not look? When you run into a bear up in the mountains, you got to look cause it might be Death coming toward you, and you want to see it coming. Roosevelt had that kind of power.

But there are other kinds of power that pull you even if you don't want to go. There was this woman at Crissy Field on the day when Roosevelt was filling up the view. I was there, off duty, just like other folks who wanted to see the president, and I saw her along the edge of the crowd.

I saw her in pieces at first: an arm, part of a shoulder, her umbrella, her hands moving. That's all, but the pieces made me want to see all of her. I remember moving closer, walking past people who ignored me or were angry cause I got in their view, and I apologized and kept moving closer to that colored woman in a white dress on the edge of the crowd.

She was tall, straight as a tree that never knew the wind, and her long brown fingers were wrapped round the handle of her umbrella in such a way that I began to envy that umbrella. She was as pretty as the statues you see outside public buildings.

There are things you get hungry and thirsty for when you go without, particularly things you can't find in the army. I mean things so pretty you want to pick them up and hold them in your hands, get their scent and taste, and if they tasted all right, bite into them and never regret swallowing, the feel of something real good going down. You can't find those things in the army.

This woman gave so much to the day, to the light from the sky and the air around her, but the people around her never noticed. They were just looking for the president and blind to all else. Maybe what they really needed to find was sitting right beside them the whole time. Maybe it was that little child in a wagon, or the hand of a loved one in their hand. I don't know, I don't even know what I was looking for, or hoping for, but something found me when I saw that woman.

I wanted to get closer without being noticed. I didn't want to be caught, although she had already caught me and didn't even know I was hers. I think I was moving without being aware of moving. All I wanted was to get closer, like a moth dancing round the fire of a candle.

By the time I was only ten feet away, she wasn't even human anymore, gone way past human to something higher. Like when I was a boy in church, walking up to the place where the deacon stood, and I figured that was where God was too. With every step I was getting closer to a place like that, and it started to choke up my heart.

She was so beautiful.

I was right behind her. I could see her chest swell up and fall as she breathed. I could see little drops of sweat on her neck, and how smooth her skin was, shining with moisture, and there was a softness about her that went beyond what you could touch with your hands, a softness you could only feel in your mind.

I wanted to reach out and touch her, but I couldn't. She was a fine woman, a respectable woman. Anyone could see that. She wasn't like the women I was used to seeing and touching and holding in those times when you don't have time to talk, to find out and consider what it means to be close to another human being. That was different, sinful, what the deacon railed against when I was a boy. It was something wrong that felt all right after months or years of not feeling anything that mattered.

This here wasn't lust. It was desire, but more than wanting a body to hold through the night. It was a different kind of hunger and thirst. Until I saw this woman, I didn't know my soul was starved and my heart was parched for something besides the flow of blood. She woke me up from a sleep so deep I didn't even know I'd been dreaming all my life.

What do you do when you wake up for the first time? There I was standing next to the very thing, the very woman, the something without a name that I'd been looking for without knowing I was searching at all, and I was paralyzed at the thought of speaking, struck dumb by even the idea of touching.

I stood a foot or so back from her, close enough to breathe her in, and I breathed so deep of what I thought she might be that my lungs hurt from filling them up. There were flowers coming off her, I could smell them, and they were all kinds, just mixed up and rising off her. I don't remember if my eyes were closed or open. I don't think it mattered. You don't need eyes to see beauty once you've breathed it in. You don't need ears to hear beauty once you got it inside your head. You don't need hands to feel beauty, once it seeps into your bones.

Yeah, I was taking her in all right. I was getting so much of her that I wondered how there could be any left to cast a shadow on the ground.

She went on paying no attention to the man behind her, who could pay no attention to anything but the woman in front of him.

And then I saw her stiffen a bit and tremble like a tree the first time it ever felt a breeze, from a thrill that I couldn't understand. I wondered how this woman could be so excited just to see Roosevelt? He was President of the United States, but I didn't think he had that kind of power.

And then I saw and understood right away.

There were Ninth Cavalrymen escorting the president, and one corporal seemed to be looking and leaning out the same way this woman was looking and leaning in. When their eyes finally met, I mean, I couldn't really see that, but her body vibrated like a banjo string that's been plucked. Something shook in her and in him, they heard it in each other and felt something the whole world round them couldn't feel.

It was just one look, cause he was riding by, but the look was long and full of something I've never had. I don't even know what to call it. But whatever it is, you can't buy it nowhere. It was obvious that each of them belonged to the other in a way words ain't got the power to tell. Being president is one kind of power, and this was another.

Life's got a kick worse than an army mule. It'll knock you over and leave you shaking your head wondering what happened.

All those people crowding round trying to get a glimpse of one man who didn't really care that they were there at all! And right here in front of everybody was something many people never get to see or hear or feel. Yeah, there was something special going on that day at Crissy Field.

After the president passed, the crowd moved into the hole he left behind, and the woman was gone.

I never saw her again.

I went out to Crissy Field hoping to get a glimpse of the President of the United States, but I forgot to look. I did get a good view of something I'd been looking for but didn't know till I saw it. Something I wanted more than anything in this world moved into my life without really touching it, and then moved out. It was a glimpse of a better way to be with someone, and my heart saw it plain.

Rallying

To give the troopers the habit of rallying promptly, after having been dispersed, the Captain places the squadron at the extremity of the ground; and after giving notice to the files on the flanks of platoons to remain upon the line with him, he causes the charge as foragers to be sounded. At this signal the troopers disperse and charge as foragers; when they are at the distance of 150 or 200 paces, the Captain causes the rally to be sounded, which is executed as prescribed, No. 294.

from *Cavalry Tactics*

lombard gate

Sergeant Yancy," said Second Lieutenant Rubottom, "get the stock ready, and inform the men that we're heading out."

"Beg your pardon, sir, but headin where?" I asked.

He swiveled his head away toward the east. "Troop K has been ordered to Yosemite, Sergeant Yancy, and we're going to make the best of a bad assignment."

I thought a minute and then asked, "What's Yosemite?"

"*Yo-sem-i-te*," began Rubottom wearily, stretching out the word till each syllable stood by itself, "is a thing called a national park, bout two hundred miles from here, up in the Sierra Nevada."

Every time Rubottom answered a question, he had a habit of making new ones. It wasn't easy talking to the man. I had no idea what a national park was, but the train that brought us to the Presidio from Florida had taken us through California's Sierra Nevada, a range of big mountains to the east that even now, in May, were all buried in snow.

Rubottom seemed in a hurry, as usual. Being around him made me anxious cause it felt like something was about to happen, even though nothing usually did. Now he looked like he wanted to be gone, but I had another question.

"Lieutenant Rubottom, sir. What's a national park?"

"Yancy," said Rubottom, "a national park is a problem for the United States Army created by the secretary of the Interior. At least that's how General MacArthur sees it, and I agree with the general, but unfortunately the secretary of war feels that Troops I, K, L, and M will provide a suitable solution. Now do you understand?"

"Yes sir!" I said. I didn't, but it seemed best to pretend I did, or I'd just hear more questions dressed up as answers.

"Good," Rubottom continued. "Now, in two hours I will have prepared detailed instructions regarding our departure from the Presidio, and I expect that you will carry out these instructions with your usual zeal. Do you understand?"

"Yes sir!" I said again. Responding with a "no sir!" when an officer's expecting a "yes sir!" usually just led to misery.

"That's fine, Sergeant," said Rubottom, sounding like a mule with colic. "Well, those are our orders, but we must hope that someone like MacArthur can conceive a way to countermand this ridiculous assignment, so we can get to the real work of the military." He walked away muttering what might have been curses. Rubottom had always been short-tempered, with a very low opinion of anything or anyone other than Rubottom.

I still didn't know what a national park was or what I would be doing with the rest of Troop K in Yosemite, but claiming ignorance was not a bad strategy when things went to hell and Rubottom was looking for someone to blame.

In less than two days we were on the move, equipped for extended duty in a place few of us had ever heard of. A farrier at the Presidio told me the army had been in Yosemite since 1891, protecting the park during the summer months. He said this national park wasn't like something you'd find in San Francisco. Apparently Yosemite was more than a grassy area with fountains and shade trees, so I thought it was strange they called it a park. Folks went all that distance just to take in the scenery, but I guess some took a little more than that, like timber or deer, and others had been grazing livestock there illegally. That's why the park needed protecting. I guess winter took over that duty once the soldiers left.

I still didn't know enough to look forward to the destination, but I looked forward to the change. Being away from a garrison with its endless drills and inspections would be a relief, even if Yosemite was, according to Rubottom, "a waste of military time."

I've forgotten most of that farewell day in San Francisco, but I do remember the slow ride out from the Presidio, up the winding road from the stables in columns of two, the hard clatter of hooves on harder ground, the creaking of caissons and wagons as the mules strained to pull them along, and the band playing "The Girl I Left Behind Me." What I can't forget, though, is a short conversation with some sentries when we finally got to the Lombard Gate of the Presidio. As we rode through, a couple of mules ahead of us got into an altercation, so we had to stop while the teamsters calmed them down. I heard the sentries talking.

"How come these niggers get to go to Yosemite?" one asked.

"Yeah," commented the other, "that's a plum duty and it's going to niggers instead of white soldiers. There are days I just don't understand the army."

It was right about then that my opinion of Yosemite began to improve.

"Hey, boys," I shouted to the soldiers, "I hear the fishin is pretty good up in the Sierra. If you're nice, maybe I'll bring you back some catfish or bass or maybe trout. I can't say which cause I just don't know what-all's up there in those mountains, but I figure we'll have plenty of time to find out!"

Some of the boys riding behind me started laughing, but not those sentries. I couldn't hear their comments once we started up again, cause the noise drowned out their voices, but I could see the meaning plainly written on their faces. It was a sight to make you smile.

It felt real nice to be starting the trip with the warm regard of my comrades. I was feeling pretty good bout myself till I turned in the saddle and looked straight into the glare of Second Lieutenant Rubottom, who was looking back at me with contempt. *Contempt* is a word the lieutenant likes using and demonstrating, particularly in regard to me. In this case the translation roughly meant, "Yancy, I'm going to make you wish you'd never been born!"

That's what's so wonderful bout military life. After a while, officers get to know you so well they don't even have to talk anymore, they can just hit you over the head with a look. Must be special training cadets get at West Point, to get their faces to communicate so clearly what ain't proper to say. The second lieutenant must've scored high on that drill.

San Francisco was cold, but the coldness coming off Rubottom was going to give me frostbite if it lasted much longer. Still, it was worth it just to see those sentries choke.

Maybe Yosemite wouldn't be so bad after all.

Practice of Paces for Maneuver

The remount horses must now be carefully practiced, as all the regimental horses must be, at the paces of maneuver.

from *Cavalry Tactics*

trail hazards

Horses and mules, heads rising and falling, clatter of hooves, wagons rolling along, creaking. The wind blows dust and grit into you till you can't tell where you've been from where you're going: Lombard Gate, San Bruno, Mayfield, Santa Clara, Madrone, Wilson's Ranch, Mountain House, Los Banos, Firebaugh, Madera, Raymond, Crooks Ranch, Wawona, Camp A. E. Wood. Just names on a map and signposts in my mind, marking out miles of rolling hills, the Central Valley, foothills, and finally the Sierra Nevada.

There were campfires at night, a bugler putting you to sleep and waking you up, telling you to go to mess and eat, and then "Boots and Saddles." So get the horses ready and assemble in some field you've never seen before, probably won't see again, and a long ride through the heat of the valley, the sun riding high, till the watering call played, like that bugle knew the horses were thirsty and the men parched. We stop, too short, then ride on through the country between sunrise and sunset, but late in the day something's bothering the first sergeant, and the bugle tells us we got to stop so a private from Troop L can help a teamster fix the wheel that came off a Dougherty wagon, and we got to listen to Leo Frye, the cook from Troop I, curse and swear at the mule who did it.

On and on till finally we're in our blankets staring up at the stars. And the next day's the same, the next night, and the day after, a routine of things you do or don't do, the second lieutenant watching the enlisted men but not looking like he's watching, Captain Young breaking from the column to adjust his saddle but then watching us as we ride by, an inspection, no warning, and you hope you get by him without hearing a shout to stop, and when you do you realize there's a God after all. And it all happens without a break in your mind, like water in a creek flowing, until after eleven days we reach the foothills, which ain't the right word for a sea of flowers blooming wherever the ground's never known a plow.

So much color hurts the eyes after the gray fog of the Presidio, but sometimes pain is good when it's a rainbow or the sun going down or your back and legs hurting from being in the saddle, cause that's what it means to be a cavalryman. A Ninth Cavalryman, the sight surprising to a little white boy we passed in a field near Wilson's Ranch, from the look on his face, him pointing at Bingham, who's black as burnt wood, a color the boy wasn't expecting, pointing at him with his mouth open, not expecting Bingham to point back with his mouth open too, and there was laughter on Bingham's face but not the face of the boy who had never seen colored soldiers. I thought it was odd for him to be surprised, in a field of flowers that had so much color you'd think God had swiped that rainbow from the sky to paint the grasses round the boy's feet, cause a boy playing in a field needs more than the color green to get through the day. Growing up in South Carolina, I sure did, but there was probably a law in Spartanburg about having too much of the wrong kind of color when there's work to be done.

I'm working now at trying to remember the ride from and to, and I can't help that it all gets mixed up in my mind so it sounds like this, cause remembering is whiskey with no food in your gut, setting your belly and your mind on fire.

I could handle Firebaugh, just a town, and Madera was no problem at all, just a town, but that sequoia they called the Grizzly Giant, that wasn't just a tree. It had outgrown the word *tree* the way I had outgrown the word *boy*, and busted out in every direction with branches the color of sunset, branches that were trees, busted into my mind so I started wondering, If this was *tree* in Yosemite then what was *mountain* in Yosemite, or *waterfall*?

Nothing here seemed to fit the word they used to describe it, especially the word *park*. Resnick told me there were bears, lions, mule deer, bobcats, wolverines, and coyotes wandering around in what they called a park. If this is what *park* meant, then what did *cliff* mean here or *canyon* or *river*? Yeah, it was pretty all right, the prettiest place I'd ever seen. A knife can be pretty too, but that don't make it any less sharp.

I learned about beauty those early months in Yosemite, and I also learned how death can hide in beauty.

There I was, on patrol in the shadow of mountains like none I'd ever imagined, riding under trees I'd never touched before, looking out into distances I'd never taken in before, and I had so few words to describe not just what I saw but how it made me feel. At those times death is the last thing you'd think of, but it was round every bend in the trail if you forgot for a moment where you were.

It was the path coming out of Bloody Canyon, one place in particular that was kind of falling away, so you had to move your mule close to the uphill side or the trail might give way underneath you. Death was waiting for you to forget that the ground couldn't always be depended on.

It was all the creeks you had to pass in the high country, little streams that flowed into the Merced or the Tuolumne, silent and dry by late summer but hell to cross in the spring when they were violent with snowmelt. I'd turn my mule upstream trying to find a safe place to ford, but each time I got a slightly different view of death compared to the ones downstream.

It was the bear tracks I'd find in my camp in the morning after sleeping soundly, wrapped in blankets to shut out the night. I'd wake up to a beautiful day with no thought of danger, then realize Death had crept up to me in the middle of the night, taken a sniff, decided I wasn't interesting enough, and left.

Death was also people. Like the father and son who'd shot a deer outside the park boundary, they said, and the deer just ran back into the park to die. They didn't shoot it inside the park even if it looked that way, they said, and if I was from around here I would know they's just good people doing what they been doing for a long time, and it ain't their fault the government come into the mountains and start calling it a park, make it hard for a man to feed himself, feed his family. Cause that's all they was doing, and it weren't no crime before the soldiers came.

And he didn't have nothing against no colored soldiers, though he couldn't figure why the government expected people to obey rules in a place where there weren't none before. And put colored soldiers here to enforce the rules when good people aren't used to taking orders from colored people, whether they're in uniform or not. The father smiled saying this, but his eyes had the coldness of death.

So when this kind of death came near, I'd try to take it easy on them, see what it was like for them, though they could've cared less what it was like for me. And I'd tell them not to look at the color of my brownblack skin but at the blue of the uniform I was wearing, ask them if they recognized the color. They'd get all upset cause their eyes were working just fine, they said, they could see that I'm a nigger but not see that I'm a soldier. Nature hadn't prepared them to see both. Then I'd ask them to see not just the uniform I was wearing but the sergeant stripes on my sleeves, which meant I was in charge, not them, the stripes that gave me authority over them and also the right to give orders to the corporal or the private, who were armed with carbines and who would follow my orders without question. I learned that people's vision always improves if there's a weapon brought into view.

And finally this father and son saw that we were bound to do our duty and that we meant no harm by stopping them cause they were poaching, cause they was on the wrong side of the boundary. And it wasn't their fault or ours, the father said, it was whatever officer drew a line on a map through these mountains, a line they couldn't see and neither could this poor deer. He agreed it would help if they chose to hunt well away from the park boundary next time, but we didn't let them take the deer cause it was inside the park now, and they didn't seem like the kind of people who would do anything illegal. They went along with that, sort of, and left, and the entire time it felt like thunder was building up in the sky. Though there were no clouds, I saw plenty of lightning in the eyes of that father not wanting to back down in front of his son, but he knew we'd do what we had to do, and that meant them going home without dinner.

Before leaving, though, he gave me and my men a look that was hard enough and small enough to slip into a pistol.

Death went hungry that day, but I knew we'd run into him again farther down the trail. He'd be a big rock coming down after a rain, or a tree in a part of the forest where there'd been a fire. He'd drop without a sound right in front of us or behind us, to remind us he was never too far away.

It wasn't that I thought about death all the time, cause I didn't. It's just that every second of my life in Yosemite it was clear that things were dying and other things were coming to be. Everything flowing like a current in swift water, and anything not mindful of itself getting pulled in like leaves or twigs or pebbles, and going away. None of that ever comes back.

Something coming into the world may make a little noise, but it don't usually try to kill you. But God Almighty there's a show going on when something's heading out, and it always seems to want company.

It's pretty here all right, so pretty you can get stupid looking at it and forget to pay attention to Death, who walks up wearing Yosemite as if it were a fine suit of clothes, and while you're admiring the cloth and color, there's Death standing in front of you and smiling, considering all the ways he's got to kill you. Yeah, death hides in beauty.

To Accustom Horses to Military Noises and Firing

When the horses are accustomed to the firing, they are formed at
the end of the riding ground and marched abreast slowly toward a
party of dismounted men placed at the other end; these fire several
volleys, until the horses are within forty or fifty yards; when the
firing ceases, the horses are ridden steadily on until they reach the
men, they are then stopped and caressed.

from *Cavalry Tactics*

relaxing at a bar in raymond

I'm not saying it was hatred of colored people that led to what happened on that Saturday in May of 1903, cause a lot of things can make an otherwise good man pick up a firearm and shoot a stranger in the gut. Naw, I don't remember it being color at all. I think it had to do with Ben Bane being a teamster. Some people don't like what other people do for a living. It can irritate them, make them unpleasant to be round.

I'd only been at Camp Wood for a couple of weeks when a group of us were ordered to go to Raymond to pick up some supplies Lieutenant Rubottom had ordered. Raymond, a little town we'd passed through on the way to Wawona, was also the shipping point for any army regiment in Yosemite. It had saloons, which meant whiskey, which meant soldiers. I already missed the saloons in San Francisco, and even the gambling tables. I never gambled myself, but it was interesting to watch other soldiers risk a month's pay on the throw of the dice.

Though it was still early spring, the weather was already hot, so by the time we finished loading up the pack animals, some of the men felt like getting a drink, and I went along.

Just because a man is colored and he gets shot in the belly don't mean there wasn't no call for it. Mr. Bill Dunn was the proprietor of that saloon and a respected citizen of Raymond, so there'd be no reason for him to attack someone unless it was deserved. Ben Bane must've had it coming. He should've known better than to speak rudely to a white man, but I guess he didn't.

After all, Bane wasn't a soldier. He wasn't Ninth Cavalry, he was just a colored worker hired by the Ninth to do a job, and he was good at that job but rough like wood that ain't been worked properly or that's just cross-grained from the start. Ben Bane wasn't smooth enough for Bill Dunn, and Dunn turned him inside out for it. You could see what had been inside Bane on the floor of that saloon. It wasn't pretty, but when is blood beautiful? When it stays inside where it belongs.

He should've seen it coming. California's not Florida or Mississippi, but it ain't the promised land either. Boy should've known better than to speak out that way, but sometimes you get angry, and anger's a wild mustang that don't want a bit in its mouth, so that horse starts bucking, taking you someplace you never intended.

I figure that's what happened in the bar. It wasn't bout a white man who shot a colored man in self-defense. No, it was bout what a word'll do when it's heard at the wrong time by the wrong person. Maybe you can only hear *nigger* so many times in your life before you crack. Like a furnace stoked with too much wood, you get too hot and blow up.

Colored people who blow up in South Carolina get taught a lesson, but it ain't a lesson you can use. You're gone, and you won't be coming back. It would be so much easier if you had a chance to correct your mistake. If that's how things were, I wouldn't have this clear, lasting memory of a colored man lying in a pool of his blood on the dusty floor of a saloon in Raymond, California, where things weren't all that different from South Carolina in some ways. Ain't no plantations round there, but you could still get whipped or called *nigger*.

Ben Bane didn't deserve a bullet. The man just wanted a drink! I think it must've happened cause Bane walked into Dunn's saloon with us. He was in the company of seven soldiers of the Ninth Cavalry. All of us had fought in the Philippines and knew Death personally as a foul-smelling bastard with no sense of humor. Why would we be nervous about entering a saloon? Bane probably figured he was in good company.

But he maybe didn't notice that we were a little on edge when we walked in. We were veterans, been round long enough to know how important it is, walking into a place where you may not be welcome, to look hard but not seem like you're looking, listen but not seem like you're listening, and smell the air for blood that hasn't been spilled yet. Animals that get hunted know this, that violence is a thought before it's a deed, a kind of stink mixed in with sweat that you got to learn to smell. It's what it feels like the second before stacked logs burst into flame. You got to know the fire's coming if you don't want to get burned.

What I'm saying is that all of us were nervous except Ben Bane. Bane was thirsty and he wanted a drink. It was his idea to go inside that saloon. It didn't seem like a bad idea at all.

I remember hearing from a first sergeant bout another group of Ninth Cavalrymen who went into a bar in Texas. Those soldiers were there protecting the town, but it didn't matter. They had a right to a shot of whiskey, but they forgot they had no rights a white man was bound to respect. Some of them died cause of what they forgot.

We walked in. Seven of us remembered who we were and what we were. Ben Bane forgot. He stood at the bar, talking loud, and he couldn't see the smoke coming off Mr. William Dunn, who was already close to exploding, couldn't see how Dunn hated the sight of us colored men, nigger soldiers wearing the uniform of the United States of America. His country. Us walking into his saloon was enough to light his fuse.

When you light a fuse, usually you hold a flame to it and then back away fast once it catches. You don't stand there casually gripping a glass of whiskey while the fire slowly eases up that fuse to the dynamite. But that's what we did, even though we knew an explosion was coming. We sipped fire slow and easy, like it didn't matter that Dunn was behind the bar muttering under his breath, obviously bout us.

And that's all it took. Ben Bane pulled out a long wicked knife from somewhere I couldn't see, pointed it right at Dunn so there was no mistaking who the words were for, and said in a clear loud voice, "I'll carve your heart out!"

It was only then I realized that Bane was just as angry as Dunn. Dunn's clear hate for us had set a fuse burning in Bane, hot as the fire already raging in Dunn.

The sound of "out" had hardly left the air when Dunn reached down and quickly brought up a pistol, aimed, and fired point-blank at Bane.

Bane yelled and clutched at his gut, doubling over as he fell, and then he was down on the floor, his legs pumping up and down like he was running, and rolling from side to side, trying to plug the hole in his gut with his hands. It wasn't working, and through his red fingers I could see what I didn't want to see.

My pistol was still in its holster, and so was everyone else's. Bill Dunn waved his back and forth at us, saying, "Go on, go on, I'll shoot all you sons of bitches, you—!" and he cursed some more, but none of us moved. Each was probably hoping someone else would make a move, take a bullet so the others could get the bastard, but no one made that sacrifice.

We stood there so long that people outside started to come in, thinking it was all over, and that broke the tension. Dunn slowly lowered his weapon as they came in, peeking over shoulders to see what was left of the excitement.

Statements were taken, but no one asked us anything. Bill Dunn told his story. You could read it in the *Gazette* a few days later. We never went back to that saloon, we found other places in town that didn't care what color you were as long as your money was American.

I can't forget that day, but no one asked me my opinion. I guess I didn't have one. Some of the cavalrymen who were there followed the story for a while. Luckily Ben Bane survived his injury, but the criminal charges against Bill Dunn were eventually dropped, as there were no eyewitnesses to the shooting. There was just William Dunn and a saloon full of colored soldiers.

Patrol report on Yosemite Park stationery,
under "Remarks," Soda Springs, August 4, 1903

1 Private Patrol the Tioga Road. return the same day, no trespassing. Corpl. Holmes & 1 man Patrol the Bloody Canyon. return the same day, no trespassing.

> Corpl. Holmes,
> K. Troop, 9th Cav.,
> Soda Springs

on patrol

We had posts up in the high country, wooden shelters lost under the blue of that sky. They were small and seemed way too small when I first saw one. There was grain in a little shed next to the post, and hay too. There were cracks in the walls to let the heat out and the wind in. Those cracks worked pretty well. The floor was packed dirt that didn't want to stay packed. The ceiling was rows of cedar slats with pitch in between to discourage rain and snow.

When you walked in, you saw a table and a lamp on the table and a ledger beside the lamp. You wrote down what had happened before you came inside, things that had gone wrong on that patrol and things that had gone right. If your mule or horse was looking thin, well, you wrote that down. If someone's mount lost a shoe or an animal had colic, you wrote that, or if you were low on grain, or if a red fir had fallen across the trail, you wrote that down too.

There were so many things you wrote down, like a broken halter, a latigo fraying on your saddle, the bit your horse was trying to spit out as if it could spit out what it didn't want to swallow . . . yeah, write it down, write it all down. Prove that you can write, prove that you can follow orders, but don't say that, just write down what the lieutenant wants to hear. Good news, cause bad news makes the man unhappy. Officers like good news. Write it all down. But I remember things that never got on paper, things you couldn't put onto paper, cause it would be asking too much of something so weak as paper.

Should I have put down the anger burning in the eyes of that gentleman from San Francisco who didn't appreciate colored soldiers stopping him from going where he needed to go? No, I didn't write that down. Anyway it wasn't anger, it was what anger sits on top of and keeps hidden. The contempt in his voice, like he was talking to someone who didn't even have the right to talk back, something lower than a mule, only mules ain't low even if some people think they are. How do I put that down in the ledger sitting on a table by a lamp in a one-room shack under a red fir in the cold bright mountains, how could I write that?

You'd think that with tall trees leaning down like giants and speaking in whispers, with the wind blowing all the time and so much sky leaning over the trees leaning over me, with all that, you'd think there wouldn't be room left in my head for that fool in his nice suit looking down on me from a height of more than thirty years. Cause that's how much time has passed since that day and me writing it down. But a man can always make room in his head for foolishness.

That morning was a bright sun, a bitter wind, and trees sounding lonesome. It was the last day of a patrol, and we were just a few miles from Soda Springs, Corporal Bingham and Private McAllister trailing behind me. As we headed down the rocky trail, I saw a horseman below me heading up.

You could tell the man had money by the way he rode. It was strange, putting so much effort into something that didn't matter at all out here. Even his horse, a big shiny bay, had an attitude. I swear that animal was looking down on my mule, which wasn't easy considering we had the higher ground, but when I got a closer look, I could tell right off the horse was just following orders. I hate it when people mistreat their animals.

"Who are you?" the man sputtered, and, "What is the meaning of this?"

We had stopped him right in the middle of the trail just to say hello, just to ask if he was enjoying the country he was riding through and advise that he go cautiously. It was meant to be civil and pleasant, but some people got a manner that whips pleasant right on the butt, so you got to work to get pleasant in the right mood again.

"Well, sir," I must've said, "we're soldiers, as you can see, and we have an obligation to say hello to folks, and you a visitor and all, so it seemed right to—"

"To stop me from my business, is that what you were going to say?" he cut in, and now his face was red, and there were veins in his neck that looked like they didn't want to be in his neck anymore, like they was about to burst any time. I never met anyone, before or since, who looked and sounded like they could be killed by a "hello," but here he was in front of me, and there was no way round him and his problem.

"No sir," I said. "It's just we've had a few fires round here from campfires that haven't been put out proper. So I was only saying hello, and respectfully was going to ask you to take care with your fires, sir." I ended there cause it looked like he was going to die from what was boiling inside him.

"Now you listen to me, *soldier*," and he said *soldier* like it was a curse, like it was the nastiest thing a man could say to another man, a thing you'd say to someone who'd spat on you. It was something hard, cold, and mean the way he said it, but all he did was call me what I was.

"I don't know who you people are or who you think you are, but it's obvious you have never been taught the proper way to address a gentleman!" he said in a rush. The words came out like bullets fired with the intent to maim or kill, but afterward I was still sitting there on my horse, and Corporal Bingham was still there, and the private too.

Then Bingham, who was behind me, did something I've never forgotten. He started to laugh. First it was kind of low, like thunder so far away you imagine it ain't really there, and then it began to grow, and there was no doubt as it rose into peal after peal of genuine hilarity that my trooper was just laughing and laughing at the poor man!

And if that rich man had looked like he was about to bust before, now he was truly giving way in his shoulders and at his neck, yes indeed, he was about to blow. Then Bingham stopped laughing and said softly, "Sir, the sergeant here was just tryin to say hello, but you just actin like he's been pissin on you the whole time, so it seems to me you the one who's behavin poorly."

He said it calm as calm could be, like he always said that sort of thing to white people.

Now the white man did explode.

"What is your name, boy? How . . . how *dare* you speak to me with such a tone!" His voice was like a loud growl, but it held too much contempt for the truthful sound an animal makes. The mix of hate and fear in his voice I'd heard all my life, as a child in Spartanburg and in the army too, but it sounded funny here under the great trees, like it was lost.

I turned around and said, "Bingham," quiet enough that the gentleman couldn't hear but my corporal could. Could hear in my voice that he was on the edge, that we were all on the edge, and considering that none of us could fly, I didn't appreciate him pushing us over on account of this fool here.

Bingham looked at me, and I could tell he was considering his choices, which were few, and then he looked up to the sky as if God had something to say, which he probably did. It's always easier to hear God when you're about to die. I don't know if God spoke to Bingham, but the man came to some kind of decision.

"Sir," Bingham said to the visitor, saying it slow. Even slower, he took out his Colt with his right hand, casually resting his forearm on the pommel of his saddle with the revolver visible, but pointing down. "You don't have a right to call me nigger."

It had been quiet since the white man's outburst, but now I could hear the horses breathing and the red firs around us creaking, and I could see that man seeing us for the first time with the blue hardness he used for eyes, how they looked at Bingham's revolver without focusing on it.

"Soldier," he said carefully, "I didn't call you any such thing. Don't be putting words in my mouth!"

"No sir," Bingham corrected him, still speaking soft and slow. "You called me a nigger, you called us all niggers, and maybe you didn't use that word, but those words you did use, well, they added up to nigger. I may not be an educated man, and I know there's much in this world I'll never understand, but one thing I know is when I been called a nigger—"

I broke in. "Excuse me, mister, what is *your* name, sir?" While Bingham spoke, the man had been looking round at all of us with those cold eyes, but as he turned toward me, he seemed to be considering something he hadn't thought of before. Maybe he was thinking how we were all alone out here in the middle of nowhere.

"My name is unimportant," he answered sourly.

"All right, Mr. Unimportant," I began, "it appears you've mistaken Corporal Bingham and the rest of us for niggers, and to be honest, I can understand how that happened. I mean, the sun is bright and hot, but here we are in the shade of these beautiful trees—you know they're red fir? Well, I guess you just couldn't make out our uniforms with all the glare and shadows, isn't that right? I mean, you couldn't tell we were soldiers, and that we're armed and all, and you probably didn't know that we have the authority to stop anyone at any time for any reason. You couldn't see all that cause of the sun and shade, so you just thought we were men who had no business stoppin such an important man as yourself.

"But now, sir, I think you clearly see your mistake, just as clearly as you see the corporal's desire to use that revolver. And I hope you can discern—now, ain't that a fine word? The chaplain taught me all about *discern*—so I'm hopin you can discern how eagerly the corporal's waitin for me to give the order. Cause that's how the army is, you can't just do somethin without orders.

"So, Mr. Unimportant," I finished up, "I haven't quite decided what order to give the corporal here. Do you have any suggestions?"

Mr. Unimportant fidgeted a bit in his saddle, looked up at the sun as if for advice, then pulled out a red silk handkerchief from the waist pocket of the vest he wore under his coat. Holding it to his face, he cleared his throat before speaking, cleared it of all the words he wanted to say but couldn't get up the nerve to say.

"Sergeant," he said in a low voice, like he was talking to a dog that he suddenly realized had teeth and wasn't friendly, "I think you should ask your corporal to put his gun away because I meant no harm, and I really must be going." And then he added quickly, "With your permission, of course."

I waited a minute, holding his eyes.

"Well, now, Mr. Unimportant," I said, "how can I refuse such courtesy? You may proceed on your way, sir, but remember that Yosemite is under the protection of the Ninth Cavalry. That means colored soldiers, and we have a job, no, a duty that we do our best to fulfill. And that means makin certain everyone understands that huntin's not allowed, and grazin livestock up here's not allowed, and leavin your campfire for the rain and snow to put out is not allowed.

"As a matter of fact, there's a lot of things not allowed, and one of them is somethin you just did, but you admitted your mistake, and I'm happy bout that cause we avoided havin to ride through some rough country. You understand what I'm sayin, sir?"

"I believe I do, Sergeant," was all the man said. Then he put his spurs to his horse, and he was down the trail.

I turned to Bingham, who was still holding his Colt.

"Corporal," I said, "you plannin on puttin that revolver away any time soon?"

Private McAllister laughed, but you could tell he didn't think it was funny. I kept staring at Bingham, who seemed to realize for the first time that he'd drawn his pistol.

"Yes sir!" said Bingham. "I always follow orders, sir. You know that." He smiled a bit as he holstered his weapon, but seemed a little disappointed. I think deep down he'd wanted me to give the order to aim and fire, but just because you feel like killing somebody don't mean you got a right to.

When I was a boy, Grandma Sara told me how she killed the

whole U.S. Army, but only in her heart. She never aimed a rifle or pulled a trigger or went to jail, but inside her soul there was a massacre, and not one soldier got out alive.

Maybe killing someone in your heart ain't illegal cause you can't see the damage, but that don't mean it can't be felt, don't mean that someone or something didn't die. My daddy nearly died on the street outside the courthouse in Spartanburg. There were no wounds on him, no blood, but he almost died. I figure most people know someone who's dead or had something killed in them. And no one ever went to jail for it.

We rode on through sunlight and shade.

After that patrol, when I was writing in the ledger beside the lamp on the table in the post, all I ended up putting down was this: "Encountered gentleman from San Francisco, explained park rules and regulations."

So much of what happens never gets written down, but still you can't forget it. There's a lot between the lines of a ledger, a lot of talking that never got heard, a lot of feeling that never got across. I always wished there was someplace I could put all of that day and all the other days on patrol, someplace that could take it all in.

I particularly wished I could put down what happened to Bingham that day, cause I thought about it a lot afterward. Bingham didn't drink unless he needed to, and he'd never acted crazy before, but he'd been up in these mountains for months, and mountains are like whiskey. A little bit every day can open you up in ways that are hard to imagine, but a lot every day goes down deep and does things to a man. I never realized how deep it had gone down into Bingham.

Patrol report on Yosemite Park stationery,
under "Remarks," Wawona, Cal., August 13, 1903

At the Tuolumne Meadows Station I found Corporal Holmes and two Privates Troop K, 9th Cavalry in Camp and one Private on patrol up Alkali Creek. This detachment has a good camp which, except for the fact that no latrine had been constructed, was in good condition. The grass near this station was excellent and the horses were in good condition. From Corporal Holmes' retained memoranda of scouts, this detachment seems to have properly patrolled its section of the Park.

Very Respectfully,
J. T. Nance,
Capt., 9 Cavy,
Commanding Detachment

blood memory

Some things you remember. Some things you can't forget. Remembering the heat of the sun ain't a dream, but what about the dreams of fire I dreamed in Yosemite?

Something bout the place seeps into you like the cold of a creek or the sun's heat soaking into granite. It gets to you and into you. It was different from South Carolina. I was born into Spartanburg, but I woke up in Yosemite. Some places you can live your life and not pay much attention to what's around you, but those mountains held my eyes and my mind like nothing else I've seen. It didn't happen all at once, it kind of grew in me, this feeling I still have even after those times have gone cold as an evening fire round sunrise.

So many days in the saddle. So many nights looking up at stars or clouds or the moon trying to free herself from weather she couldn't even feel. The light that almost got through was often prettier than what did. The animals moving round the camp that you heard but didn't see. Yellow eyes burning in blackness, little fires drifting over the ground or creeping up close to the campfires.

All of what was around me got into my lungs when I breathed, into my head when I looked, into my heart when I heard, into my bones when I touched, and it stayed there like a stack of wood piled up deep in the dark of me. And there was a spark and it all began to smoke, light started coming out of a place inside me where light had never been, and I started dreaming the same dream over and over.

In the dream I'd wake up and be standing beside Bingham and McAllister, and the fire would be low, smoldering into coals like little orange flowers blooming without a day. The night was round me, the red firs leaning in as if a wind was at their backs, and stars peering over the shoulders of trees, white eyes staring down as if my waking up was somehow indecent.

I would walk off a ways from the fire and begin to undress. It was cold, but the fire in me made up for it, so I didn't need clothes. I was naked like the day I was born, but as a man, not a baby. I could move, and I did.

It always happened the same. I would begin to move, walking or running out from the fire, right out from the safety and the comfort of that fire, out into darkness, into something I should've been avoiding. But I felt different about the night and darkness when I was in this dream.

I was running along a trail, the same trail we'd been following just a few hours earlier, but now I was naked and alone, running on darkness, breathing it in deep like I was stoking a fire, as if the darkness was wood and I was a furnace looking to turn something to ash. I was hungry but I didn't know what food was. I was thirsty but didn't know what there was to drink. There was only the cold mountain air, so I drank that as I ran and ran and ran, and the night didn't care that I was naked. I wasn't cold even though I ran barefoot through drifts of snow, my feet didn't sting at the touch of it, and I wasn't afraid of the darkness. I wasn't afraid of anything.

And there was something else, something I had never felt before. I was free. I could run in any direction, and it was all right cause no one was chasing me. I could run north and that was fine. I could run south and that was all right too. I could run east or west, run in circles round some nameless meadow covered with the night frost, and it didn't matter, it was all right to be running, to be free.

A colored man running in the wild and no one chasing him. Just running for the joy of running and breathing and seeing and hearing and feeling, one foot after the other, right, left, and right again, beating down like rain beats down, in a rhythm that sounded in my heart. And the blood in me was the same blood running through everything round me, and the stillness I ran through was me running through myself, finally unafraid.

Is that what freedom is? To run and yet be still? To sleep and yet be awake? I asked myself those questions in the dream, then ran away from the words in my own head, and it wasn't deceitful or dishonest, it's just that when you're an animal you can't waste your life thinking bout your life. You got to run cause that's what bodies are for, to be used and used up entirely, like how a creek uses up a lake or trees use up the sun or a man and a woman use each other up, but nothing ever gets empty, everything is always full, like this night I'm taking in and letting out, yes, this is what I'm supposed to do.

You can't find answers sitting still. You can only find God if you're running. Only if you're moving can you be moved, and God only talks to those who can be moved by what he's saying, she's saying. And in the dream pretty soon my daddy's running beside me and my mama too, and they're both naked, and I look back and see Grandma Sara running, and a man beside her who must be my grandfather, and someone behind him, someone I should know, whose name I should have bright in me like a fire. And behind my family is more of my family, and behind them more again, great-great-great-great-great-great-great-grandmothers and -grandfathers, all of them running with me in a night that has no sunset and no sunrise but only a dark sky full of stars.

Thousands and thousands of black people and red people, the color of night, the color of fire, my people, running behind me, making no sound but their breathing like a mighty wind, so when I thought I was running alone in the world, I was wrong, cause everyone that made me was right behind me, and every step I took in the world was leading them on into the moment before waking from whatever sleep this was, if it was sleep and the other waking.

It started to rain as we ran, and the rain was all the tears of my family and my ancestors, and it was sweet on the tongue and the body, the coolness of that rain comforting and soothing to all the miles of hurt my people had run.

I saw that we were running in great winding circles that moved like a wind blowing back on itself, and I was lifted up in that wind, looking back down on my people. I saw the path they were following on the black earth, a path that turned back on itself, going nowhere and everywhere, a path like the whirlpools at the tips of fingers, but whose fingerprint? What hand held us, and what was this path that held no fear or pain?

The same dream, night after night, and I would wake up sweaty and tired, my legs and feet aching, and round me Yosemite, listening, knowing something about me that I didn't know. It knew the feel of my naked feet, though I'd slept hard on the cold ground with my shoes on. It knew the part of me that was never still. It was moving like I was moving when both of us looked like we were sleeping.

Waking up, I saw my own hands and fingers in front of my eyes, as if I'd held them pressed together all night praying, and now they were unfolding like a flower opening to the sun. There in the tips of my fingers, I could see the same curving paths I followed in the dream, like the contours of the land I'd run through, and I knew my people were in there, all my relations running round through my fingers, and one day if I ever had a child, I'd be in there too, running in the fingertips of someone who ain't even born yet.

I'm already there, part of a hand that can hold a father and a son and a daughter and everyone that's my blood who's ever been and ever will be, and that was the dream, and it runs like water underground through everything I'm saying. And what's green and rooted in it knows it's there, and can't live without it.

To Accustom Horses to Military Noises and Firing

Especial care should be taken not to alter the feel of the horse's mouth when firing, or suddenly to close the legs; the rider being cool and quiet, his horse will soon follow the example.

from *Cavalry Tactics*

cocked pistol

Something was eating away at Private First Class Bledsoe, something you couldn't see, but it got so's you could feel a bite in the air whenever he was around.

All of us got darkness, holes inside where you don't want light to go, but Bledsoe's was beginning to show on the outside. It was in his attitude, in his voice, the way he moved, how he answered when you called his name, and it was beginning to interfere with his soldiering. It got harder and harder for him to give an order and take one. I guess he'd been taking so much all his life, he just got full up. How much can you take before you start falling apart inside like a house with wood rot or termites, the damage invisible until it all crashes down?

I was taught that pain makes calluses, rough leathery skin spreading over what's tender, but sometimes even that skin can split open and bleed. I still don't really understand what happened to Bledsoe. All I know is that one moment four of us, myself, Bledsoe, McAllister, and Bingham, were standing on the edge of a meadow swatting at mosquitoes in the country north of the Tuolumne River, a place where there were more rocks than trees, with a mild breeze blowing past. And while I was thinking what a beautiful day it was, I was also thinking about how to pull Bledsoe out of the hole he'd put himself into and where he lay silent and raw.

All I'd asked him to do was help dig a latrine for our camp that night, cause we didn't have enough time to make it to the post, and it was a reasonable thing to ask a private to do, should've been expected after all his years in the army. It was just an order like a thousand others I'd given, and even McAllister thought it was wrong for Bledsoe to argue about doing his job, but the whole time he was swelling up to bust, and we couldn't see it cause we were so caught up in being annoyed at him.

One minute I was staring up at the sky, hoping for a little rain to cool me off, pushing the conversation to one side of my head the way you sweep a floor clean. The next minute an arm was round my neck, and I felt something hard and cold pressed against my right temple.

I lost my balance. I couldn't breathe, and my hands went out by themselves trying to find something to grip, but there was only air. I could see McAllister with his lower jaw dropped, and Bingham staring at me like I was Jesus come back. Since I couldn't see Bledsoe, I figured it was his arm round my neck, his stinky breath in my face, and his regulation Colt revolver pressed against my head.

He cocked it. The click was loud, louder than the wind in the trees and the meadow, louder than the creek. Even my heart, which was beginning to pound, was quieter than the cocking of that pistol.

He didn't say nothing, I couldn't get any breath to talk, and McAllister and Bingham were too surprised, I guess. The conversation we'd been having was over, and the next one looked like it would be short. We were way past words anyway. If talk was a country we'd been visiting, we had crossed the border to someplace else. There were only two choices.

Either Bledsoe'd blow my brains out or he wouldn't.

All I heard was breathing and the wind in the grass and the whisper in the red firs, the one that comes from nothing and fades to nothing. There were a few birds singing, not a lot cause it was getting close to twilight. A few clouds were passing over, and I could've sworn they slowed down as they passed, as if they were trying to get a better look at what was happening below.

Except for not getting much air, I wasn't too bad off. In a way it was just like being back in South Carolina. Every day of my life there, something I could only see part of was squeezing my throat and breathing down my neck. This here was just the feel of an arm round my throat cutting off air. It was a feeling of floating in and out of things. It was the knowledge that a cocked pistol was pressed up against my skull, and that my life could end at any time. I was used to this. Bledsoe was just reminding me that this was my life, days and nights of being out of breath, feeling I had no control of anything round me, and Death always right behind me with a gun to my head and his bony finger on the trigger.

Yeah, I'd been here before. And I knew without thinking that if I moved, he'd pull the trigger. If Bingham or McAllister moved, he'd pull the trigger. He had all the power, and that's what all this was about.

Back at Fort Robinson, we did drills that taught you to act and not think, cause thinking just clouds the issue at moments like this, and you were better off acting from instinct. So I did nothing.

And that was what saved my life. It was a lifetime of doing nothing, the longest ten or twenty minutes I ever spent. McAllister didn't move. Bingham didn't move. No one and nothing moved except the Sierra Nevada and everything else in it.

We must've presented a funny picture. Four colored soldiers standing stock-still at the edge of a meadow, surrounded by bare granite hills. Soldiers who weren't talking, only staring at each other.

After a bit, I could feel the muscles in Bledsoe's arm twitch and then begin to relax. I didn't know if this meant he was about to let me go or he was just getting tired. Whatever the reason, all of a sudden I could breathe and my head started to clear.

I still did nothing, but doing nothing was something. Growing up in the South had taught me not to confuse fighting with surviving. Surviving didn't mean backing down or lowering your head like a dog, it meant holding on like an oak in a flood. You put your roots down deep and gripped and let the water come. That's surviving, and it's what I was doing with Bledsoe. It's what we were all doing. All of us knew about living in a world where we had no power. I'm here on this earth cause my family understood that the best way to fight was just to survive. If you were born with a pistol to your head, the only way to fight was to make it to the next second, and that meant knowing what was in the head of the person whose finger was tightening on the trigger.

This gave me an advantage with Bledsoe. I knew and all of us knew what was in his head, cause we weren't any different. The same acid gnawing at his gut was in ours too, we were just holding up better right then. Anyway, we all knew how it would turn out if we did nothing. We'd survive.

And that's what happened.

After a few more minutes, Bledsoe got tired of holding that pistol to my head, and he dropped his arm. I stepped away from him, turned toward him. He was breathing hard, looking at the ground, and then he let the pistol drop. It fell to the ground with a dull thud like a stone.

He sat down next to it and began to cry. I reached down and picked up the Colt and tossed it to McAllister, who caught it and tucked it carefully under his belt. Then I sat down in front of Bledsoe. I didn't touch him. I didn't say anything to him, just sat there inches away, and he knew I was there. He was crying hard now.

McAllister and Bingham sat too, on either side of Bledsoe. They were angry and sad cause they knew he had just left the army by doing what he'd done, left the only real kin he had, and his life was about to get a helluva lot worse.

The last thing that man needed was more words, so we kept on saying nothing. We helped him get up, and to do that we had to put our arms around him. Once he was standing we could've let go, but we didn't, and he didn't seem to mind. We kept holding him up.

We should've been angry. Bledsoe could've killed me. But he didn't. He was just mad and he couldn't hold a pistol to the head of everyone who'd hurt him deeply, make them take notice. We were the only ones in reach. His brothers. His family.

We didn't let go of him for a long time.

Patrol report on Yosemite Park stationery,
under "Remarks," Soda Springs, August 3, 1903

Corpl. Holmes & 1 Man Patrol the Alkali Creek. return the same day, no trespassing whatever.

> Corpl. Holmes,
> K. Troop, 9th Cav.,
> Soda Springs

leaving anger

I'd been in rough country before. The kind of country that leaves
calluses on the bottom of your feet if you walk through it barefoot. The kind of terrain that'll chew up a body and spit it out in the
sun. I'd been there before.

But the worst place I've been in was Anger. Anger is a country
inside, and I lived there so long I thought I'd never get out alive. It's
a place you can wander through asking all sorts of questions and getting very few answers. I built me a house there, and it had windows
that looked out to nowhere and doors that wouldn't swing out but
only in. You couldn't lock anything out, you could only lock yourself
in. And my house was right in the middle of Anger.

Every night while I lived there, I'd lie in bed and pray to God bout
why being colored was my fate in this life. I asked God why he was
so cruel to do this to a little boy, and I yelled and screamed and cried
inside so loud that I got to be like a bell so shaken by its own sound
that it decided to never ring again.

I lived in Anger so long I forgot there were other places you could
live. I didn't notice that I had no neighbors and no friends. I didn't
notice that being alone was a place I'd built with my own hands.
When you're a good citizen of Anger, you're stuck inside you, feeling sorry for yourself cause there ain't nobody around to take up the
slack. Nobody comes round to visit or see how you are. You don't get
no mail. There's no newspaper cause there ain't no news.

When you put down roots in Anger, you don't get older but you
don't get any younger. You don't ever get fat or skinny or sick with a
cold. To catch a cold you got to be open a little, but you're a boarded-up

house with doors and windows that don't work right. Wind can't get to you and the sun been gone so long you can't even say "sun." It's dark all the time, which means no plants growing or animals to eat them. You're the only living thing in the country, if you can call it living.

Kinda looks silly to build a fence round that lone house. Who or what are you keeping out? Or are you just that afraid of something busting down the door you nailed shut and showing you a road out of Anger?

Now that would be really scary. To bring the walls down. To break the windows into pieces. To shatter the door. To strip yourself naked of all the things you put on when you were angry and afraid. To walk out to the road without a stitch of clothing on and no need for modesty, cause there ain't no one around to see you naked. You scared the world away and the sun away and life away, and everyone who ever thought they loved you away, so why not be free of everything and walk out of that country just like it was the day you were born?

I had this kinda argument with God for a lot of years while I was in Anger. For a long time I was yelling and crying so much I couldn't hear what he was trying to say. But more and more I had trouble not hearing it. He was always talking about leaving Anger . . .

Now you're scared, ain't you, Elijah? It takes courage to move out of Anger, don't it, boy? It's easy living there, right? Cause it's always someone else's fault when something goes wrong, it's never your fault, cause you a victim of a white man's hate. You didn't call yourself a nigger, did you? It was always someone else or something else that made you hurt, made you sick, made you want to die. But you were lying to yourself all those days and nights, lying to yourself and calling it prayers or hope or justice, calling it the Ku Klux or bigots or bastards, every curse you could find like stones lying on the ground waiting to be thrown. Lying to yourself, cause it was easier country to walk through than the truth.

If Anger is a flat empty land, and you the emptiest thing in it, then Truth is a country of high mountains that knows the feel of God's feet walking and God's voice talking and God's hands feeling every-thing that's alive and not alive.

What was it made me see that I had to walk straight through Anger to the other side? What was it told me to get up and go away from the dark? What was it that reached inside me and pulled me to the outside and said "Live!" I don't know, but I guess I walked out of Anger to find out.

Fear is the next town over to Anger, and I spent a lot of time there too, but no longer.

When I got to Yosemite, I found the country of Truth. I'm not afraid here, cause there ain't no lies to catch me unawares. There's only what I can see and hear and smell and feel. God don't make lies, he only makes truth. He made this his country, and this is the place where I finally built me another house, in the heart of Truth.

Trees don't lie bout how they feel bout air. Trees don't care that you're colored. A bear or a river or a canyon or a bird don't care that you're colored. It don't even matter to a rattlesnake that you're col-ored. I just don't matter to Yosemite, and that's Truth. It's not about hate here or love, it's only bout how long and how hard you can hold on, and that's Truth. Though it's a hard country, Truth is a place you can live in and die in and have some peace.

There ain't no niggers allowed in Truth, but all *people* can move to Truth and settle and live and raise families there, and grow old and go to sleep forever. Truth is the country I patrol, and my job is to keep out lies. If I find them in Yosemite, I am to escort them to the border and push them back over into their own country.

Mountains can fill your dreams all night long, but they can't hold a lie for even a minute. Have you ever heard a redtail cry in the Sierra on the bluest day in a country of stone? That cry is picked up by the rock, made louder, and the mountains hold on to it and sound it back longer than the hawk could ever do. These mountains hold snow all year long, they grip the roots of trees and feel the feet of every living thing that walks this country, but most of all they hold something that can't melt away or rot or die, and that's Truth.

I will leave Yosemite one day. I will saddle up my mule and follow an order on a piece of paper that don't even have my name written on it, but I will do my duty. That day I will not be happy. It will be a hard thing to leave this country, to let go of what holds me so close, to abandon what was so hard to find.

The long ride back to wherever it says on that paper will be hard enough cause of distance and bad roads, but harder still cause I won't be going home.

Of the Spur

When the troopers employ the spur, the instructor observes that
they do not bear too much upon the reins, which would counter-
act the effect of the spur. He also observes that the troopers do
not use the spur unnecessarily.

from *Cavalry Tactics*

hetch hetchy

Some places you live in, but there're some that live in you, settle in you the way sediment gathers under a stream that's slowed down. As long as you ain't moving too fast, the feel of that place builds up in the dark of you, under your heart while the blood flows over. All you got to do is slow down so it can drop out of the sky and collect.

Hetch Hetchy is a place like that, a place that slows you down to a speed proper for a human being. When you've been in that kind of place for a while, you start moving at the speed of grass coming up or snow falling down, you ain't going no faster than a leaf budding out in the spring, and it just feels right.

It happened to me on my first patrol through that valley in the fall of '03, with Corporal Bingham and Private McAllister. The three of us from Troop K had ridden over on a patrol from the post at Rogers Lake, in the high country north of Mount Hoffman, with orders to check into a report of illegal sheepherders in Hetch Hetchy. As usual, we'd be looking for poachers and other livestock too. It was a long day's ride from Rogers Lake, and by the time we came over the last ridge before Hetch Hetchy, we weren't talking much.

All of us were daydreaming as we rode down from a high ridge on that winding rocky trail, almost as bad as the one into Bloody Canyon, the sort of trail where, when you glance over, you don't see the ground moving under you. All you see is what's a long ways below.

I was in front when we rounded a bend that brought the valley into proper view. It looked like Yosemite Valley but smaller. You could see high granite cliffs rising up on both sides, and on one side was a rock face that looked like El Capitan, only smaller. I say smaller, but it must've been two thousand feet high, with a face God had cut in half, like he'd been using lightning as a saber. On the maps it was called Hetch Hetchy Dome. Opposite, on the southern wall, was Kolana Rock, which on a different map was called Sugar Loaf. I didn't quite understand that name, except maybe meaning a loaf big enough for angels. Anyway, it was enough to stop your thoughts and leave you gaping.

That's what the country was like all over.

In general, we didn't talk much on patrols, cause the mountains and valleys and meadows kept shutting us up. It seemed like God was usually talking in a big voice here and over there and round the bend yonder, and when God's talking, you shut up. So we were quiet as we came down the trail and round the last switchback, into a bit of a draw and then the meadows of Hetch Hetchy.

Yellow pines were growing round the edges of the meadows, and alder and cottonwood along the banks of the Tuolumne River, but like always it was the oaks that drew my eye, standing tall and strong and black without a hope of bending. Lying under them were broken branches from storms that got the upper hand, making me think of bones all busted up under a body that didn't care if the sky was trying to break it in two.

Those oaks reminded me of my daddy. Yeah, Daddy would've felt at home in this country.

Before we even got fully into the meadow, I could already feel that this place had me, like the quiet was a hook and I was a fish dangling from it, grinning, happy to be caught and laid out under the blue of heaven. My mule seemed to like it, too. He kept moving his head from side to side and grabbing mouthfuls of Hetch Hetchy growing on both sides of the trail. After a while there was so much grass hanging from his mouth that Satan looked like he had a long green beard.

Yeah, my mule was named Satan, but he was all right. He didn't much care for people, but he had a hunger for meadows, particularly this one in Hetch Hetchy. Sometimes I had the feeling that where I ended up was mostly bout my mule's appetite, and the fact that we were supposed to be looking for sheepherders or timber thieves or poachers, well, that was secondary.

We were there cause I was following orders, and I was on this exact path through the meadow cause I was following my mule. But when I was out on patrol, I was also following my own heart, and most of the time it wanted to be in someplace like Hetch Hetchy. I'd been hearing about this valley since I got to Yosemite. There weren't any officers around, and who's to say how long it would take us to do our job here properly? So I gave my men to understand that we wouldn't be hurrying back. We had supplies enough to camp for a few days, and I already had my eye on a spot by the river near the welcoming shade of some large black oaks.

I mean, what's wrong with granite rising up like gray church walls thousands of feet high, a ceiling of blue sky and clouds, and a floor covered with wildflowers? Nothing wrong that I could see, so what if we lingered a bit longer than we should have? Seems to me it should be a crime if you're in a hurry to get away from a place like this. Sundays back in Spartanburg, I remember how if anyone in the congregation got up too quick after the service ended, the deacon would give that person a meaningful look. God don't take it too kindly when people he's spending time with just get up all of a sudden and leave.

Hetch Hetchy was a church too, and the deacon was the Almighty himself. In Yosemite I was in church every day, and I didn't want to offend the Creator by being in too much of a hurry. So that was why, three mornings after coming into the Hetch Hetchy meadows, we were still there and had only just gotten packed up to head back, having found no sheepherders. We hadn't seen another human soul in the valley all that time, but I couldn't consider the time wasted.

One thing bout slowing down is you start seeing things you otherwise might've missed. Unless we were on an urgent mission where speed was required, I always encouraged my men to move no faster than the country round them. That way they were more likely to see what was there in front of them.

Maybe that was how I saw those two figures in a distant grove of oaks, south of the river on the other side of the valley. They were so small in the valley's bigness, at first I wasn't sure I'd seen them at all. Just two little specks in a big green space with oaks standing alongside them and blackness under the trees, as if shadows that had lost their way in the world had finally found a safe place to rest. Then I thought the specks might be deer, hunched over like they were, until they moved in a way that set them apart from the land round them.

We changed our course, riding toward the Tuolumne River and toward them, and as we got closer, I saw they were Indians, an old woman and a girl around ten or eleven. They were bent over because they were picking up acorns off the ground and putting them in baskets. I looked around again but still saw just the two women, which was surprising. I was used to coming across Indians in Yosemite Valley, members of a tribe called Ahwahneechee who lived in cedar cabins, the children peering out when soldiers rode by or playing outside near the chukkas, raised wooden structures where the Indians stored acorns. Close by would be a roundhouse where they held ceremonies, a low building that was bigger inside than outside on account of it being mostly a hole in the ground with earth and cedar for walls.

But there were no cabins here, and no other people I could see. I wondered if these two were living here all on their own, at the heart of clouds and sky, granite cliffs and tall grass. They seemed so alone in a valley big enough to hold a city.

They saw us too, and didn't seem happy at the sight. I couldn't blame them much. I've seen very few Indians who enjoyed the company of soldiers, particularly soldiers in the U.S. Cavalry.

As we crossed the river I could feel Satan tense and then ease into the coldness. It was already a hot day, and not yet past noon. We gained the opposite bank and wheeled to the left, but not too sudden. I signaled to Bingham and McAllister to fall into single file instead of three abreast. I was really working on not presenting myself as an enemy, but then again, it's just like an enemy to not act like one when they're closing in.

The woman and the girl stopped their gathering as we came up, and the girl began to cringe and cry a little. Both of them watched us the way you eye a rattlesnake that's about to strike. I heard the girl say something to the woman, but the only words I could make out sounded like *suntati* and *tuma' asi*. She kept repeating those words while pointing at my uniform and gesturing at me.

About ten feet from them we halted our mules. The old woman slowly backed away, and the little girl screamed and ran off a bit, but stopped and edged back when the old woman shouted at her. They were both wearing long calico dresses, which seemed out of place in the wilderness of Hetch Hetchy. Like they were wearing their Sunday best, only they were in church all the time, so why dress up for it?

Then I remembered what First Lieutenant Resnick told me about the Indians that lived in Yosemite back before the settlers and the army came, and what happened to them. There were a bunch of tribes with names like Miwok, Ahwahneechee, Paiute, Chukchansi, Yokut, Mono, and Karuk. Most of them just traveled through the mountains to hunt or trade, and some lived here. But around fifty years ago, the Gold Rush brought so many new people into the Sierra foothills that game got scarce. It got harder and harder for the Indians to find food, so they got desperate, and some of them began to raid the mining camps. The miners fought back, mustering up a battalion to hunt down the Indians. They found them, all right, and found Yosemite Valley at the same time, and there was a skirmish. The troops burned the Ahwahneechee homes and graneries, and the Indians got sent to a reservation but eventually scattered in the mountains without food or shelter.

The lieutenant didn't seem at all upset by any of this, but I felt bad hearing it. It made me think of Grandma Sara and the Seminole. Well, the Indians who survived those times seemed to figure that resisting anymore would just get them killed, so they tried to get along with the strangers who'd invaded their lands.

The lieutenant also told me, with a wolf's smile, that most of the Indians hereabouts used to go almost naked in the summer, when it could hit 100 degrees in the valleys. Being from South Carolina, I could understand that just fine. But some of the white folks considered it improper and made the Indians cover themselves. So the women got used to wearing those calico dresses, I guess.

Now this old woman was standing in front of us, her knees bent, arching back with one arm shielding her eyes as if she was blinded by what she was seeing or recoiling from a blow that hadn't fallen yet.

We didn't do anything. We just sat there, listening to insects feeding in the meadow, the bees droning, the wind. After a long spell, her arm went down and she stood up almost straight. Then she surprised the hell out of me by saying loudly, "What you want?"

It wasn't that I'd never heard an Indian speak English before. Some of the ones living in Yosemite Valley or around the outskirts of the park worked for stock packers or traded skins for food or dug latrines for the army. But here we were in a place that seemed like it had been the same since the beginning of time.

I finally found my own tongue. "Hello, ma'am," I said with a nod. "We don't want anything at all. We're just on patrol in this part of the park." I stopped, not knowing how much she understood, but also on account of how hard she was looking at me. It was a bit unsettling.

"Well," I went ahead, "we had a report of sheep grazin over here, and we got orders to find out if that was true."

There was a long pause, which the river filled nicely, otherwise it would have been quieter than a grave.

"No sheep here, soldier." The old woman spoke quickly when she did respond. She jerked her head toward the southeast. "You go away now." She understood a fair amount, it seemed. But now I could feel the fear in her, even stronger than the fear that was so obvious in the girl. The old woman had kept it hidden till now. Along with the fear was anger, too.

I had to do something, so I dismounted slowly. A cavalryman is always at a disadvantage if he's dismounted. I figured she might know that if she'd spent any time around soldiers. Before I got down, I looked back and smiled at McAllister and Bingham, not saying anything but telling them to stay on their horses. They understood and smiled back.

So we were all smiling when I turned to face the old woman again. I thought about the people in history who'd been killed by men who were smiling. How do you tell someone you ain't a threat when you're a soldier wearing a uniform and carrying weapons, and they're Indian?

I decided it was best not to talk anymore just then, but to behave as if I was an invited guest. So I yawned and sat down with my back to Kolana Rock, facing the old woman. There were lots of things I wanted to know, like what tribe was she from and how did she come to speak any English. But I figured that just being still might settle things down right then.

"Ma'am," I said softly, "we been ridin a long time, so you don't mind if I sit a bit?"

She looked back with just a sly hint of a smile herself.

"Soldier," she said, "you sitting now."

I nodded again and said in as clear and as level a tone as I could find, "Yes, ma'am, I guess I am, but I meant no offense, and I'm sorry if I offended you or the girl."

The old woman was small but had a power in her. She didn't answer right away but looked at me steady. Then her eyes went inside, and she started talking. "When I . . ." she pointed to the girl, "was like her, soldiers come. They kill, but not all. They chase. The people . . ." she bent over and reached down, grabbing some dirt with her right hand. Then she straightened and opened it to the wind, "go away, many places. Most never come back. Cold. No food."

She stopped talking and her eyes looked away, then came right back at me. "Soldiers burn everything, *everything*." Her voice rose higher as she spoke, but she whispered the second "everything" much softer than the first. "The people not killed," she continued, words emptying out of her, "much sickness."

The little girl urgently pulled on the woman's arm, making her lower her head so she could whisper something to her. The woman said something back just as quick, and her body seemed to give off a coldness as she spoke. The girl lowered her head then and turned to stone.

The old woman carefully sat down a few feet from me.

"Why you here?" she asked again, calmer this time.

"Like I said, ma'am, we're just on a patrol, and we don't mean you or anyone here any harm." I was trying my best to sound reassuring. "We're not that Mariposa Battalion came through here years back, we don't soldier for the state of California. We're Ninth Cavalry, United States Army, and we're here patrollin the park, that's all, lookin for sheep or cattle grazin where they shouldn't be, lookin for poachers, ma'am, lookin for timber thieves and fires that weren't put out proper. We're just doin a lotta lookin, ma'am, but one thing we ain't lookin for is families like yours here, cause there ain't no Indian war I know of goin on in Yosemite."

She looked at me and smiled a little, but her eyes were small and cold like two stars barely lit in a winter sky.

"Good speech, soldier," she said. "You say no killing people, but I think long time about soldiers killing my relations, there." She pointed toward the east, and I wondered if that meant she was Paiute. I knew they came from the east side of the Sierra. She hesitated. "Maybe you the same?"

My shoulders slumped a bit at that, and I got frustrated and sad cause she wasn't understanding at all. But I couldn't fault her opinion. How would my mama and daddy have responded if a group of Klansmen had come knocking on our cabin door, offering to help us out?

"Ma'am," I started again, "look at me. You ain't the only one who's seen bad times. My men here and myself, our people were slaves once, and when that ended, they were beaten and whipped and strung up under trees just so they'd never forget who was who, so I understand how—"

"You know nothing!" she choked out. "Nothing about us, understand nothing. You not white, but not our people . . ." Her voice trailed off.

I let a little quiet get in before I tried again.

"Ma'am, I'm not going to hurt you. I'm just a colored soldier from South Carolina, a soldier who's African and Seminole and who knows what else. So I guess when you look at me you could just as easily be seein a friend as an enemy, and right now I'm under orders to be a friend."

I paused, knowing how that must've sounded, then added, "I'm a soldier and I follow orders, that's true, but I got a heart, ma'am, and I got family like you, and I wouldn't want anything to happen to my people. So I appreciate why you don't trust a word I'm sayin, and I appreciate you talkin to me at all, but please watch our actions, ma'am, before you decide.

"We're headin out now, and I'm sorry for comin in here and scarin you and the girl, but we got a job to do, and our job is takin care of the park. And maybe we can't do that like you, but that don't mean we don't care bout it, cause we do."

I was a bit out of breath after that. The girl still looked scared but now wondering too. That woman smiled that little smile again, and spoke to me like I was a child.

"Soldier," she said, "your park a new thing, but my people live many lives in these mountains." She spread her arms wide and said a name I couldn't understand. "I born in Ah-wah-nee." Now, I knew that was the name the Indians called Yosemite Valley. "Ran away when those soldiers came. Long time after, I come back, work in hotel, speak American.

"Now new soldiers come but not stay. You go away, but we stay. Maybe you come back, we talk. Maybe not. Go away, soldier. Bye bye."

I got up and so did she, and at least she was still smiling.

"My name's Elijah," I said to her.

"My name not for you," she responded with a small shake of her head. "Name of this place not for you. You don't know where you are. You lost, soldier, you lost."

She paused as I mounted Satan again.

"Maybe you come back, Elijah," she went on, "maybe I tell where you are, and you get off that mule. Stay off, stay on ground."

"That'd be nice, ma'am," I said back. "I hate not knowin where I am, so I'd appreciate hearin that bit of information."

I nodded to my men and we rode off. But as we started to get some distance between us and those two, I kept on thinking bout them. Did the old woman and the girl live there all the time or move from place to place? It made sense that these folks would head down to the foothills before winter and return to Hetch Hetchy in the spring.

One question in particular had been gnawing at me since we first came upon them, and it finally got clear in my head. I sat back deep in the saddle and pulled gently on the reins, stopping my mule. Bingham and McAllister were riding ahead and didn't notice, went on cantering toward the trail out of the valley.

I rode slowly up to the old woman, who had already gone back to her work.

"Excuse me, ma'am," I called out, "but you're all alone out here. Where are the rest of your people?"

Then her eyes got a look in them that cut and stung. In a voice halfway between a sob and a cry, she answered, "All dead, all gone, you go away too!" And she put her back to me and kept gathering her acorns. I sat there for a bit, but that was all. Then I put spurs to Satan and rode away to the others.

It didn't take long to catch up with Bingham and McAllister, who had waited for me just around the first bend. They never asked for an explanation, and I was done talking for that day. From halfway back up the trail, the old woman and the girl had shrunk to almost nothing, or maybe they were just such a part of the place that you couldn't really pick them out. I never saw them again.

That old woman of Hetch Hetchy reminded me of my grandmother, both full of pride and anger and fear all mixed in. Grandma Sara and this woman, they had the same defiance, the same fire, but the Indian woman was still in her home and Grandma Sara had been torn away from the place she loved. This old woman and her grandchild hadn't been taken from their home, at least not yet. They were what made Hetch Hetchy a place that lives in my head even after so many years have passed.

When we got to the patrol cabin back at Rogers Lake, I wrote in the ledger about the day's patrol. After the date, I wrote: "Entered Hetch Hetchy. Found Indians, inquired about sheep in area, none found, continued patrol."

What I didn't write was how quiet the valley was when we left, quiet the way a lake rides over something you can't see or touch, something that's drifted down slow through water. And the weight of coldness keeps it down so you never see it again unless you jump into it and pull yourself to the bottom.

Some might call that suicide. But what did the old woman and the girl call it? I don't know if it had a proper English name, but it felt like a kind of sadness so deep that it would make you want to die and never stop praying for the deaths of others.

Or maybe it would make you want to live, and never stop praying for the lives of others. Yeah, I been there too.

Practice of Paces for Maneuver

Nothing can be more important to the regularity and order, and often the success, of large bodies of cavalry than uniformity in the gaits. The walk should be at the rate of three and three-fourths miles an hour, the trot seven and a half miles an hour, and the gallop ten miles an hour. To confirm the horses in these uniform rates, measure off a half mile and practice the horses to walk it in eight minutes, trot it in four minutes, and gallop it in three minutes.

from *Cavalry Tactics*

right there at heaven's gate

I met God during the summer of '03, a time when clouds like black anvils were stacked high over the mountains and a cold wind was coming down hard. I was in the country just east of the Minarets, high up along a creek where there'd been reports of herders grazing sheep, though there wasn't much to chew on up here but rock. All that rock did make me feel sorry for the sheepherders. Most of them were Indian or Mexican or Basque, the kind of people who couldn't run their sheep down in the Central Valley. They'd been run out, or run up would be closer to the truth.

Because I was close to timberline, it was a chilly night. Because I was sleeping so close to the sky, I knew the night wouldn't be long. I was by myself this time. No patrol. Lieutenant Rubottom had asked me to take a new ledger to the patrol cabin near Devil's Postpile. It was on the sunrise side of the range, and night caught me before I could get there. After taking care of my mule, I just spread my blanket on the ground and fell asleep with no dinner, cause I had no need for food just then.

I fully expected rain or snow to find me, but the clouds went away late in the night, leaving a hole big enough to fall into, if you could fall up instead of down. The stars were close enough that you could almost feel their heat, almost. I could feel the frost beginning, so after getting up to pee off in the bushes, I went back under my blanket. I remember feeling happy before falling back to sleep, happy cause I was by myself. No one to give orders to. No one giving me orders. No one complaining. Just me, Satan, and mountains.

Come to think of it, I was beyond happy. If Happy is a country you can find on this earth, I'd already walked through it to the other side. That's how I was feeling when I went back to sleep.

Sunrise in the Sierra is always pretty, but this one was different, or I was different. I recall how ice grew in the wool of my blanket right before sunup, and how that ice figured out a way to get into my right knee bout the same time it was dampening the blanket. I must've opened my eyes, cold and in a little bit of pain, to see the sky not getting brighter but losing a little blackness.

I wondered what that would be like, to lose a little blackness. I appreciate what God's done for me, but I might not mind losing a little blackness, kind of how the sky was doing it. Sky don't appear guilty for not being black no more. Guess I was feeling sort of tired from being black, and here was this black sky turning blue with a little red and then some yellow mixing in, till the whole world seemed colorful and a bit confused.

Lying there, I started remembering how the sun came up when I was a boy, watching how light filled the doorway of our cabin. That made me think of my grandmother, not Grandma Sara but Daddy's mother, a Cherokee woman red as Georgia clay. Her name was Artana, and I only knew her when I was still little.

When someone you know dies when you're real young, it's hard to tell later on if you're remembering a real person or someone you made up. But I thought I remembered how, when I was five or so, I'd wake and hear her getting up in the darkest part of the morning and walking out the front door. Every morning she'd stand there on the front porch, stand there in the cold singing, in that black squeezed outta the bellies of stones as they're waiting for the world to end. She was like that, hunched over like a red fir sapling under the snow.

She'd sing softly at first, and then a wind would come up from somewhere close and far away, and the wind would blow more of her voice out of her throat, as if encouraging a whisper to be more, and as she sang louder the sky got lighter and lighter, like smoke in a stove slowly becoming fire.

As the bodies of trees got clearer, so did her voice. Her body rose up straight, and her song rose up and brought the sun with it. I thought it was her making the sun rise, making the light that filled everything. I didn't know no better, still don't, cause here I was now watching it happen all over again, and I could feel her song in me, like when you touch a piano someone's playing and you can feel the music shaking in your fingers.

Who's shaking this sky now? Who's shaking me? Is it my grandma Artana singing? How can there be so much music in so much quiet? Those were the kinda thoughts I was having when I noticed what I might've missed.

Looking east toward the Sierra crest, I could see a ridgeline with a few trees along it and the sun slowly coming up behind them. Sunlight was growing round them, through every branch and twig, till it seemed like the trees were on fire. I think they were some sort of juniper, the kind that can take in so much of the morning light you'd expect them to shine even in the middle of the night. I couldn't see the sun, but I could plainly see the sun's influence on those trees. Day was still on the other side of the ridge, but it was coming out of the junipers, as if that was where the sun went at night.

Then the trees began to disappear. They got so bright with the sun that they must've caught fire, and they were hot with it. I wasn't expecting wood to turn into glass, but I was looking clear through those trees and seeing the other side of where they were rooted. Trees had become windowpanes with sunrise just beyond, and I was alone with no one to point it out to.

That's when I heard Artana's song in me, singing like she used to when she was welcoming the sun.

Wen day yah ho
Wen day yah ho
Wen day yah
Wen day yah

Ho, ho, ho, ho
Heya ho, heya ho
Yah yah yah

Over and over, the words sounding in me like I was a church or open to the sky like these mountains. It kept going out and back, out and back, till I lost what was sound and what was echo.

Sunrise was taking so long to happen, I started thinking maybe this wasn't sunrise, maybe it was still the middle of the night and God was dropping by. But I could tell by the feel of the air that it was just another day breaking, and as soon as I had that thought, everything began to change. The cloudfire on the ridge slowly melted back into trees, and the trees became only junipers, and the light became just sunlight again.

But for a moment or two, it was like cathedral doors swinging wide. Heaven was just beyond the doorway, God was holding up a lantern so bright it lit up all of paradise, and I was standing beside Satan, gaping on the doorstep. I was struck dumb by the light of God, right there at heaven's gate, and I couldn't open my mouth to pray or even whisper *thank you*, I swear, that's what dawn was like on that day.

I don't know what miracles are, but if you get a chance to glimpse heaven without having to die first, well, that's a miracle if you ask me.

Lieutenant Resnick told me the Sierra Nevada are the tallest mountains in America. I knew I was high up, but never dreamt I was that high. I'd been riding long and hard for a few days before getting here, but I had no idea that a mule could take you most of the way to the next world, or that the next world was so close to Yosemite. I'd gone way beyond the blue, for sure.

God is everywhere, but I'm thinking he prefers some places more than others. I'm thinking he spends a lot of time in these mountains. That means my mama's bound to be happy, cause I'm finally a churchgoing man. Every day in Yosemite is like Sunday, and I don't have to dress right or mind my manners. All I gotta do to be in church is open my eyes in the morning. Every day here is a kind of prayer, and every night the prayer is answered. I can hear a sermon in the leaves whenever the wind blows. I can hear an *amen* when the rivers answer. When it rains, the world is singing what was sung at the beginning of creation, and at night before I close my eyes again I can hear it sounding in the ground under my head, in the rocks, the trees, the creeks, and deep in my bones, the same thing sung softly all night long.

I can never quite make out the words, and I'm afraid I'll have to leave Yosemite before I understand what God is saying to me, and what I should be saying back.

If we do finally talk, I think it'll be a conversation about what happens to junipers at daybreak, and why I can never forget that ordinary things touched by God become miracles, and that absolutely everything at one time or another is touched by God.

Before sunrise ended, while the trees were still on fire, I found my voice. I crawled out of my blankets and went to the edge of my campsite, and I joined my grandmother's song.

Wen day yah ho
Wen day yah ho
Wen day yah
Wen day yah
Ho, ho, ho, ho
Heya ho, heya ho
Yah yah yah

Patrol report on Yosemite Park stationery,
under "Remarks," Wawona, Cal., August 13, 1903

On August 10, I found the detachment under Sergeant Shelton, Troop K, 9th Cavalry, camped in Virginia Cañon at the mouth of the East Fork of Virginia Creek. The memoranda of scouts show that the men of this detachment have done a great deal of patrolling in Virginia, Spiller's and Matterhorn Cañons, and that with a detachment from Tuolumne Meadows Station, one scout was made to near the head of Conners creek. Four herds of sheep, about 5750 in all, had been removed from the Park since August 1. The country in the vicinity of this station is very rough and the trails are reported to be exceedingly difficult—practically nothing but sheep trails.

Very Respectfully,
J. T. Nance,
Capt., 9 Cavy,
Commanding Detachment

campfires

Being in Yosemite meant sky and mountains. So much sky, so much rock it was like the earth's bones were sticking through, jutting up like a body that's been laid to rest but keeps rising, rising, and after a time it don't remember it's dead.

But it's cold enough to long for death or at least a fire. How many times I was on patrol in that stiff McClellan saddle, my butt aching like it'd been kicked since sunup and the back of my head feeling even worse, the insides of my thighs chafed to nothing, and my back aching, my knees, my ankles, my shoulders. After riding all day, every day, all you are is pieces of what you used to be, strung together with tendons and sinew.

At least twenty-five miles every day, or so it seemed in this country, miles of up and miles of down, and hardly ever flat country in between. All day looking at the butt of another horse or mule, and someone behind you doing the same, then bedding down on cold, hard ground with just a bit of wool between you and winter, and waking up just as cold and hard as the ground you were sleeping on. And it doesn't matter if it's raining, snowing, or just blowing pine needles and dirt, it's all the same after a while, just something moving against you, most often something you can't even see cause you're blinded.

Did I mention my hands? Stiff enough to be talons a hawk or a vulture would envy. Have I complained enough, or do you want more? Yeah, this is how I'd be thinking, but no one heard it, cause if they heard Sergeant Yancy whining then they'd never find enough reasons to stop doing the same.

Eventually the sun would get tired, slumping into the west behind more mountains too distant to recall, and the horses and we got to rest. By then we'd be at a patrol post high in the Yosemite. My map showed the names of patrol posts surrounded by mountains, but not all the mountains had names. Sometimes I'd think about what that Indian woman said to me in Hetch Hetchy, that I didn't know the real name of the country, that I was lost.

After we'd get the horses settled down and convinced the mules to do the same, we ate what was available, and there ain't no hunger like the one mountains make inside you, a gnawing, emptied-out feeling like there's no measure of food could ever fill you up.

Mountains must be hungry too. Everything here is so big and so empty that it echoes like Matterhorn Canyon when those big rocks come down. God was always trying to fill it up with snow, rain, wind, and sound, but no matter how much he tried, the country was just too big.

Sometimes the silence round there could be too much of a good thing. I like quiet as much as the next man, even the stillness inside our church back in Spartanburg, but there's a limit. Yosemite was so big that things got lost inside all that silence, like a fog going through your fingers. Things got lost even when they was right in front of me and all around me. Maybe that's why trees have roots, cause they need to hold on to something. And maybe that's why we were always hearing trees, creaking cracking calling sighing, cause they don't want to lose themselves either.

Usually trees were all you heard out there. I remember a particular red fir at one campsite cause the campfire light playing over it made it look like a skinny old man with long black fingers reaching out over you, like he was wondering if he should grab hold of you or just pretend enough so you could never relax. That was one night at Reds Meadow, the tree creaking away as we sat round a fire, thinking like I been thinking, letting the fire do all the talking, until Corporal Bingham said, "Hey, Sergeant, what you say you goin to do when you leave the army?"

I was down so long in myself that his voice sounded far away and broken up by the wind. When I looked up at him it was like I was rising out of black water.

"Well, Corporal," I said, "I been thinkin bout that a long time, considerin this and that, and to be honest, I think I might try livin for a change. Cause I ain't ever done that, and I seen a lot of other folks doin it so I figure I better give it a try before I die."

I hoped that was enough to keep him quiet for a minute or so. I kind of liked the blackness I was in, just me and the fire and thinking and not saying. I kind of liked the feeling I was having just then by the fire.

Bingham just laughed down low when he heard me, sort of a complaining sound like a waterfall grumbling bout how far it had to fall through air just to feel ground again.

"But Sergeant," he said, "ain't you livin right now? No one's tellin you this or that, you in charge here right now, no officers, just me and McAllista... McAlliser... McAww, aw, damn, boy, I just can't say your name right!"

Across from him was Private McAllister, peering down into the fire like I'd been doing. Bingham couldn't do anything but talk, talk, talk, and McAllister obviously didn't want any of that. He wanted to do nothing, which is what he'd been doing ever since we got here, a whole lot of nothing, and there ain't anything wrong with that after a day's ride through a place big enough to make you feel like *you* were nothing.

"Bingham," McAllister mumbled softly, like he was drunk, "you known me a long time, long enough for you to get my name right, so if you can't say it, just say you sorry and be done wid it!"

It really quieted then, except for the fire talking. Bingham's eyes got so chilly they got frost in them, and then it melted and he began to laugh, but that laugh seemed to rise up from something cold inside him, cause I don't think he felt there was anything funny in what the private said. But what was he going to do? Bingham needed McAllister. McAllister needed Bingham. I needed both of those fools, and they needed me, cause what was all around us sure as hell didn't need any of us.

"You funny!" said Bingham finally. "You know I didn't mean anythin, I was just foolin. I mean, look at us, all sittin here like we're about to die, heads hangin down like men before the gallows, and here's the sergeant sayin he don't know what it's like to live. If this ain't livin, then what is? We got a fire to keep us warm, plenty of food, shelter. Now, what I don't have is a woman! Maybe that's what the sergeant needs."

"Bingham," I said to him, "you don't know me, you don't even know yourself. If you need a woman to feel alive, then part of you's already dead. I'm not talkin bout bein lonely, I'm talkin bout bein alone. You know how long it's been since any of us was alone, really alone out here like there was no one else anywhere, that kind of alone?

"We never got a chance to figure out who we are back at the Presidio or any other garrison, cause there's always too much going on and too many people doin it. What you need to figure out is all this . . ."

I stretched out my arms like I was trying to hold the sky. What I wanted to say was how "all this" wasn't just scenery. It was medicine. But I couldn't find what I wanted to say right then cause I was so angry. I let my arms fall.

"Look at McAllister here," is what I said. "He don't talk much, but he's thinkin all the time, so he might be lonely but he's never alone. The army tells you you're stronger when your troop is around you, that you're weak when you're by yourself. But if you're never by yourself, you can't hear yourself think, and that's what they want. They don't want you to think, just follow orders, but out here there ain't no officers givin orders. There ain't no one but us and this!"

And I stood up with my arms raised into the dark, feeling my breath going out and my heart beating fast, angry not really at Bingham but at everything I was feeling and couldn't get across to him. Maybe I couldn't even get it across to myself. Sometimes you feel what you feel but you don't know why. There was nothing wrong with what Bingham was saying, but I couldn't hear what was right in it either. I was just too mad, and the anger wouldn't let me stop talking.

"Bingham," I tried again. "There ain't no one else round us for miles and miles. These trees here, these red firs and lodgepole pines, they don't care bout your small talk, they're listenin to God all the time. If you'd listen to what they're sayin and you understood any of it, you'd see that you need more than a woman, you need all this too, all these mountains and forests and that sweet sweat comin off of them.

"Sure, a woman just makes it all better, ain't nothin wrong with a woman, but why would a woman want somebody that don't know who he is? You don't stop talkin long enough to hear your own name, Bingham, and it's a shame, cause right now somethin's talkin to you, tellin you somethin you need to hear. And I don't mean me. I mean everything round us, and you don't even hear it. Far as women go, if you really want a woman, the next time you find yourself in the company of one, you might try just bein real quiet and listenin to what she has to say. That, my brother, is how you get a woman!"

I finally stopped. I didn't really understand why I was so angry, so how could it be clear to anyone else? Bingham hadn't done or said anything different from any other time. I guess I could've gotten down on him cause here he was talking bout women, and he had a wife back in New Orleans. But plenty of soldiers had wives they never knew when they'd see again, if they ever would. So I could let that go. Maybe I was mad cause this night round this fire I'd felt something I hadn't felt in a long time, and I didn't want to spoil it with wanting this or that. There's too much wanting, and I'd had enough of not getting enough.

What I realized was how much I needed silence, needed it more than just about anything. I needed a place where I could think, slow down all the shit moving through my head, the shit that happens to anyone, the shit that makes you feel like shit. But it's the same shit you put over a field in the hope that something sweet will grow out of days and nights like shit.

I slowly sat down and took a deep breath. No one had left. Bingham was glaring into the fire, the palms of his hands colored red by the blaze as he tried to grab hold of the heat. McAllister was looking at me strangely, like I'd finally said something he found interesting.

"Let me tell you something else, Bingham." I tried to talk slow so maybe some of it would get through. "One day you're goin to forget what I've been sayin tonight, forget how you're feelin, how you're hungry for a woman, but what you'll never forget is the sound out there when you lie down on your bedroll, the sound of these mountains, the quiet. Cause it's not like an empty room, it's a different quiet, like when someone dies near you or when the sun goes down, that kind.

"And every day you been here, and every night, somethin else has been here too, and it may or may not be God, but it's holy, I tell you that, and it's what McAllister and I been listenin to all this time we been sittin round this fire. There'll come a time when this sorta quiet is hard to find except in a coffin, but we're alive now, and it's everywhere round us, and maybe if you stopped talkin now and then, you'd hear it. I know you're not listenin to me, but some part of you been listenin to these mountains ever since we got here. And one day before you die, Bingham, you goin to start payin attention."

Bingham's eyes were wide open and bright with fire. McAllister kept staring down into the smoke and flame with his hands out, raising and lowering his fingers as if he was playing the fire like an instrument, like music was coming out of it.

Bingham looked up from the fire then, into my eyes. "Sergeant," he said quietly, "Elijah, you've had your say, and now I'm gonna have mine. Those stripes don't give you the right to talk to me like I'm your boy, cause I ain't. I'm a grown man, maybe more grown than you. I feel what's out here, all right. I see the sun come up and go down every day. I feel the wind on my face, just like you, and I know these mountains are alive. You'd have to be a fool, bein out here like we been and not knowin that, and my mother didn't raise a fool.

"I see what you see and hear it too, Elijah, I just don't want to do those things alone. None of it matters if you ain't got a woman. What's the point? I could talk to God, but the conversation's a bit one-sided for my taste."

He paused, then looked at me again, considering, then grinned.

"You know, Sergeant," he went on, "there are other days to the week than Sunday. You seem to be all in love with Sunday, and I like it fine too. Where I come from Sunday meant somethin good to eat, so good it was sinful! But there are other days to the week, and nights at the end of 'em. Sunday's a fine thing, but it don't last for six days, especially not in New Orleans.

"When we get back to San Francisco, Elijah, I'm gonna introduce you to Friday night or Saturday night. Me and McAllister'll introduce you to some woman who'll make you forget what those trees are sayin to you, at least for a night. Yeah, you'll be talkin all right, talkin all night long, and she'll be talkin too, but the words don't matter when you're talkin to a woman that way. And that, Sergeant, is the kinda conversation that'll really bring you close to God!"

I just stared at him, hearing the truth in his words. There's more to any man or woman than just their thoughts and ideas. There's also a body that needs to know it's alive. I heard him, but I didn't think he heard what I was really trying to say to him, so I made one more try.

Meanwhile, McAllister just kept his seat, staring at me and then at Bingham, with a funny smile on his lips. He seemed to be enjoying this now.

"Bingham," I whispered, just louder than the crackling of the fire, "one day I'm goin to find a woman who will be my wife. You hear what I'm sayin? I'm not talkin bout a woman for Friday night or Saturday night, but for the rest of my life. And when that happens, I will be a happy man and maybe easier to get along with, but that day hasn't come. Meanwhile I'll go wherever you want in San Francisco, but that's not where I'm goin to find the woman I'm talkin bout.

"And while we're still up here, I just want you to pay attention to what's here instead of what you think you're missin. Cause it'll make you a better soldier in a way the regulations don't measure.

"Think about this." I was addressing both Bingham and McAllister now. "There ain't nothin out in this night that's goin to call any of us nigger. These red firs don't care who we are or what we are. These mountains don't even know we're here. It don't matter to the ground under us if we live or die, don't matter at all, and that's good.

"Round this fire, round any fire, none of what happened before we got here matters no more. There ain't no hate in this forest, and there ain't no love either. But there's somethin else. There's this fire warmin us, and us listenin or tryin to listen, tryin to understand, tryin to make sense of nothin at all. That's what I'm doin here, tryin to make sense of nothin at all."

And I remember the wind rose, taking my last words away into the dark, taking them so fast I don't think Bingham had a chance to hear them before they were gone, red sparks that left no trail. The wind took my voice and the look in Bingham's eyes, but it couldn't take away the light of that campfire. It's burning still, as fires often do for months, hidden below the ground, below Reds Meadow or deep inside a man's bones, smoking the marrow of McAllister and Bingham and flickering inside me, those fires still burn.

Of the Spur

The instructor explains to the troopers the use and the effect of the spur. If the horse does not obey the legs, it is necessary to employ the spur. The spur is sometimes used to chastise; when necessary, use it vigorously, and at the moment the horse commits the fault.

from *Cavalry Tactics*

horse heaven

Everyone's got a favorite place, a place that's who you are, and you can move through it, breathe the air, walk the ground, and be home in a way that you're not anyplace else. I found a place like that in Yosemite, or it found me.

It was a high meadow so close to the sky that the blue of heaven began to stain the plants below. You could see it in the high grass and flowers with the blue of the sky in their petals. Sky was so close there, maybe it was leaching its color, so after a rain the plant just pulls it from the air and gets drunk on it, waving back and forth in the breeze, giddy with indigo.

You'd be giddy too if you could walk there with snowy mountains rising round you, holding the trees in place. It was high and rocky and green and cold. Even in the sun it seemed cold and warm at the same time. Some places can hold opposite things, like putting something to your lips that's hot and cold and sweet and bitter, that's what that meadow was like. It was cold as if winter was walking out but warm as if spring was strolling in, and when they passed each other, they stopped and turned round, then spoke in the heart of it, comparing notes. It was a long conversation. You could hear their talk in the grass and in the trees and inside yourself.

Why was it so different from a thousand other meadows? I figure God's walked in all of them, but in this one he lingered. He slowed down from all his work, looked round, and said, "Now this is it!"

There's all kinds of quiet. There's the kind after a preacher prays to God in church, and the kind in Grandma Sara's room after she'd tell Death off. There's the kind round sunset when everything seems to take a deep breath and slowly let go. There's the early morning kind right before birds begin to sing. The quiet in this meadow had some of all those and more, even more variety than sound has. Out here you can school yourself on quiet, get to know all the varieties, like how Mr. Muir can tell you the name of every bird and every flower, talk about them as if they were people he knew.

If all those different kinds of quiet could be put in bottles, sealed shut, and set on a cellar shelf, that's what I'd do with this vintage in Yosemite. Then from time to time I'd open one up and drink down the quiet of that meadow, fill up with it, and no matter how angry or sad I was, I couldn't stay that way.

Yosemite taught me that silence is a sound, the best kinda sound cause it makes you listen not only to what's happening on the outside but what's really going on inside. Usually the inside was a place I didn't want to hear from too much, it'd be like feeling round the inside of a coffin to see if it would be comfortable. There would be plenty of time to get used to the feel of that. But in the silence of that meadow, I didn't mind hearing what was in my bones and my blood and my heart.

Anyway, I remember how riding into Horse Heaven would make me feel, how it would slow me down, calm me, soothe me like an ointment spread over a hurt I didn't even know I had.

I'd get off my mule, wrap the reins round his neck, and just let him go. There was always plenty to eat, so I was never afraid of him wandering off. That mule never looked happier than he was in Horse Heaven. I can still see flowers trailing from Satan's mouth, like he was puking a rainbow, and his head bobbing up and down, side to side, as he rambled round that meadow.

I didn't like it so much in the spring. Then the ground would be wet like it was remembering when it used to be a real lake, and the mosquitoes made the air hum like the strings of a banjo plucked by the Almighty himself. Then it was more like Horse Hell.

No, I mean late summer, when all the water had seeped back down into the ground, and you could lie back in the wildflowers after a long day in the saddle, and the pressure of your body would crush the purple under the red under the yellow of all those flowers, and squeeze the colors out into the air, and you could smell the flowers you couldn't see. They'd fill up your head and your lungs and someplace inside that was open and waiting.

As my eyes would close, I'd hear my mule pulling up plants, chewing noisily, the wind in the trees away over somewheres, and the droning of bees gathering pollen. I could see every blade of grass up close, a little black ant crawling up this one, a caterpillar ringed with yellow and black on that one, I could see it all up close and all far away. And me opening up to the blue, a big ring of blue bordered by pine branches, dark and green. I was right there in the center of that meadow, the center of the world.

You can see why I never took anyone else to Horse Heaven, or wrote about it in any ledger. Other soldiers and, worst of all, officers might've got curious, figured they needed to investigate. That would've ruined everything.

But even though I went there alone, I never felt alone. The grass was good company, and the flowers too. Birds were always flitting round. I noticed how a bird's song goes with what it looks like. Some birds don't stay on a note too long, as if they know it'll give way and collapse under the strain. Other birds say the same thing over and over again, like maybe it ain't getting listened to proper, so the bird's got to keep repeating what it's saying over and over till it does get heard.

It's not an easy thing to tell the truth, but birds make a song out of it, and sing it wherever they go.

The best time is the morning.

There are two sunrises in the Sierra Nevada. The second one is the one you see. It's when blackness fades in the east to a softness that ain't really a color, but then deepens to a color there ain't really a name for. Call it a distant relative of red, one that don't come round to visit very often but who's always welcome.

That cousin of red lightens to a yellow, and about then a wind often picks up, stirring the leaves and branches. You start seeing the outlines of trees that went away the night before as darkness took them. After a bit there's no doubt the sun is pulling itself up into heaven like an old man with a lamp climbing Jacob's ladder. That's the second dawn.

The first one is the one only birds see. Light has barely, barely leaked into the sky when they start up like a choir on Sunday. Bird eyes must be sharp to see it, or maybe they feel something so thrilling in that moment they can't help singing. Sometimes the whole forest echoed with what they were saying, and how long have they been saying those things?

I remember thinking maybe it was the birds who coaxed the sun out of bed and up that long stairway. The music would rise up and up, wave after wave, and the sun would follow, rising into a color that was just becoming blue, and I couldn't tell who was happier, the birds to see the sun or the sun to hear the music of those birds.

Maybe I was the happiest one, just to be there watching and listening. If you're a cavalryman and you find a heaven for horses, then you really have found paradise. I don't know, and maybe I don't want to know. Corporal Bingham taught me that thinking is good, but you can't forget to feel. When horses are tasting the wind, they're not thinking, and they never seem to worry about what they don't know.

In Yosemite, for the first time I was all right with not knowing. Usually I try to figure out something I ain't too clear on. I want to know how much it weighs, will it float, can you set it on fire, or what's it good for, but here I never looked for a reason or an answer. Some things you don't ask God. You don't say *why* to a lupine or a poppy or a shooting star, *thank you* will do just fine.

Some people call Yosemite a wilderness, but all that really means is it's a place where nothing ever stands alone but always got company, kind of like being in the military. No soldier is ever alone, cause he's got all the men in his troop. They're part of his squadron, which is part of a battalion, which is part of the Ninth Cavalry, and all those men are your family. People who will take a bullet meant for you, those people are your family. Someone who will die for you is your brother, and you're all bound to something bigger than you. You all belong to the regiment, you're all Ninth Cavalrymen, and that means something in the world.

The same thing's going on in this meadow. The grass is part of the ground, and the ground keeps the trees standing tall, and the trees hold the nests of birds, and the blue sky is beyond and between the branches of those lodgepole pines. Small things always add up to something bigger, and it never really ends. Too bad I can't see it all. Too bad I can't smell every flower. Too bad I can't hear all the music there is to hear in these woods. Too bad I'm running out of time.

That's what I always thought about in that meadow in the sky. I was running out of time. When I was there, I noticed flowers dancing in the breath of God one day, and those same flowers dull and shriveled the next. That made me think I needed to dance more, feel the wind on me, and the sun, before I went all dull and shriveled.

The place I called Horse Heaven got a real name on a map, but I'm not going to say it. You keep the whereabouts of your best fishing holes to yourself. Yeah, I went fishing in that meadow, but I was the bait at the end of the line. I was what was tossed into the high grass pushed into waves by a wind I can't feel no more. And something took the bait, took me, and pulled me up time and again into Horse Heaven.

All I got to do is think about it, and I'm there.

Everybody needs a place like that. Even Satan. Even an army mule.

Patrol report on Yosemite Park stationery,
under "Remarks," Wawona, Cal., August 13, 1903

The trail from a point on Virginia Cañon trail at the head of Smoky Jack Meadows, via mouth of Alkali Creek and McGee's Lake, to Tenaya, which is now being built and repaired by Frank C. Palmer, was examined and found to be completed to within about 3¾ miles of Lake Tenaya (about 10¼ miles of trail being completed on August 11). This trail, so far as completed, is good, and I believe the contractor has complied with the terms of his contract in the work thus far done.

Very Respectfully,
J. T. Nance,
Capt., 9 Cavy,
Commanding Detachment

꧁꧂

when blackness came
to yosemite

I'd heard from Lieutenant Resnick that the first colored soldiers
came to the Sierra in 1899. He told me he got that bit of information from the *Superintendent Report* for that year. He was reading
those reports to get a sense of what had been happening in the park
over the years.

In '99 it was just a small detachment of the Twenty-fourth Infantry, and they were only in the park for a few weeks. I guess they
didn't leave much of a mark, but it was comforting for me to know
that I wasn't the first, that others like ourselves had been here before,
though you'd never know it from the looks we used to get. By the
time the Ninth Cavalry arrived in 1903, no one should've been surprised, but I'm certain a lot of folks were.

I wonder when you really get to a place. Is it just once you've
arrived, or maybe after the animals have noticed you're there? That
don't seem to take long. When the deer and raccoons as well as the
settlers sit up and take notice, I guess you can say you're there. How
bout the black oaks in Yosemite Valley, those trees the Ahwahneechee tend and have been tending for thousands of years? Maybe
the oaks know the Indians are there in a way that the white settlers
couldn't understand. Maybe the white folks in the valley haven't
been round long enough to be noticed by those trees.

And how bout the Big Trees? Mr. Muir says that just one of those
sequoias can live for thousands of years, that the Grizzly Giant in
Mariposa Grove was alive when Jesus was walking round telling

people what they needed to hear. How does something that old know we're present, even if we was to sit in its shade every day of our life?

What I'm saying is, from the Big Trees' point of view, we're just shadows moving round and not adding up to much of anything. To those giants, the Ninth Cavalry being here is like that cloud of butterflies I saw one spring down in the canyon of the Merced. They were so beautiful, fluttering round like the sun broken up into tiny pieces, pieces that were alive and aware they weren't going to be here for a long time and they might as well spend it all dancing in the air. There were so many, like small lanterns giving light to all the places the wind took them, and the river rolled on by never noticing those butterflies.

How long do you have to be there, to be noticed by those mountains? Even Methuselah didn't live long enough to be noticed by the ground he walked on. I figured if the settlers round Yosemite didn't talk about the Ninth being there, then we were going to be forgotten. Not very long after we leave, people will be surprised that we were ever there. That's why memories are so important to me, particularly my memories of Yosemite. I'm there only in my own head, in my own heart, and in the heads and hearts of my brothers in Troops K and L and I and M. Four troops of Ninth Cavalry, two in Yosemite and two in Sequoia. Four groups of colored men. Four families sent to the mountains to take care of something that would never know it was being taken care of and probably would be just fine if every human being walked away and never came back.

But it was a wonderful time, a good time. How could it not be when we weren't in a garrison with the routines and drills of post life, and in a place nearly empty of officers? That's what I call paradise. There was an officer back in the '90s, don't recall his name, who called duty in the Sierra "the Cavalryman's Paradise." He was right.

We had to take care of ourselves, since nobody was going to do it for us. Maybe if you're in paradise, you ain't got a right to be remembered by the angels. Figure angels, cause they live forever, got a lot on their minds and don't want to be bothered whether or not Elijah Yancy bathed today or yesterday, or if he's happy or sad. But I remember a certain evening down in Wawona when we had a particular good time. And even if the ground has forgotten, and the deer don't remember, and the South Fork of the Merced never reflects on how I once stared into it wondering where all that water was heading, something happened that night that no soldier in the Ninth will ever forget.

It wasn't planned or anything. It happened on a Sunday at Camp A. E. Wood, which was park headquarters, in the southern part of Yosemite. Camp Wood was just white tents, wooden buildings, a corral, horses, and men, built on a flat on the east side of the river, a mile or so from the Wawona Hotel. Like all things army, it looked planned but really it had just been growing up here and there since '91, when the first cavalrymen were posted to Yosemite.

Work was over, dinner was over, and we were all sitting round another campfire. Actually there were several campfires spread out over a pretty good space, cause we had at least two troops of cavalry present, and all getting ready to bed down for the night. At least until someone started singing.

Usually it was a harmonica that started things off, or a banjo like the one a corporal from Troop L played. I can't remember his name, but I can remember his music well enough. But this time a man was singing, and it wasn't some popular song, it was a spiritual. And then it seemed everyone all at once remembered that it was Sunday. Maybe that was cause we were at headquarters, and headquarters meant letters and news and finding out what'd been happening in the world outside Yosemite. When we were up in the high country, away from headquarters, every day was like every other.

Anyway, that man, who was sitting at another fire fifty feet away from me, started singing "I Couldn't Hear Nobody Pray" in a fine deep voice that the still air carried over to the other campfires.

Slowly, one by one, as if on cue, the soldiers near the first man began to sing along with him. And it didn't take long for all the con-versations taking place round the other fires to quiet down as more men began to listen, then to sing or hum along. Some of them added their own harmonies, weaving their voices into whatever space they fit.

It seemed like we all remembered the music we had left behind with our families. It didn't matter whether we were from Mississippi or Alabama or Georgia or South Carolina or Louisiana or Texas, we all went to church on Sundays growing up, and we grew up singing many of the same songs.

Singing and listening to that music brought out something that had been silent in our hearts till then. There wasn't a man there who didn't ache for someone he'd left behind in those places where we were brothers and sons and husbands and fathers.

> Lord, I couldn't hear nobody pray
> Couldn't hear nobody pray
> Oh, way down yonder by myself
> And I couldn't hear nobody pray

sounded under the ponderosa pines, the cedar branches, rising up between wood and sunlight now going out slow, red as coal, and then more voices from other fires melted into the sound.

"In the valley . . ." he sang.

". . . couldn't hear nobody pray," others answered.

"On my knees . . ." he sang.

". . . couldn't hear nobody pray," came the response louder.

"With my burden . . ." he sang slow and alone.

". . . couldn't hear nobody pray," they responded, deeper.

"And my savior . . ." he sang, quieter.

". . . couldn't hear nobody pray," came the hushed response from more men.

And then a wind from nowhere picked up ashes and embers, and the voice of that soldier rose right up with them to the sky.

Lord, I couldn't hear nobody pray
Couldn't hear nobody pray
Oh, way down yonder by myself
And I couldn't hear nobody pray

By the second chorus everyone was singing, or it sure sounded that way, at least all the men sitting by me were singing, and some were crying but trying to not show their tears, acting like it was smoke that made the water flow, raking their hands cross their cheeks as they cursed the smoke. They stared into the fire, remembering and singing. I can't tell you how many soldiers went AWOL sitting right there round those campfires. They were gone, they were back home.

And it got better. A group of soldiers farther off, in a meadow on the other side of some cedars, got tired of that one and began to sing "Every Time I Feel the Spirit," while most of Troop K, the men nearest me, kept on singing "I Couldn't Hear Nobody Pray," and in the silences between the lines you could hear an echo that wasn't an echo saying:

Every time I feel the spirit
Movin in my heart
I will pray
Every time I feel the spirit
Movin in my heart
I will pray

After a third chorus the voices got quieter, and you could hear one soldier singing in a high sweet tone:

Up on the mountain
My Lord spoke
Out of his mouth came
Fire and smoke

> Down in the valley
> On my knees
> Ask the Lord have
> Mercy please

And men on both sides of the trees began the chorus again:

> Every time I feel the spirit
> Movin in my heart
> I will pray
> Every time I feel the spirit
> Movin in my heart
> I will pray

this time louder, as if to drown out the other voices singing "I Couldn't Hear Nobody Pray," but they couldn't, so you could hear both spirituals sound together, and it was beautiful hearing all those voices, all those souls finding their own path through the gathering dark.

Even the ponderosas and cedars seemed to be leaning over to hear the music, and the mountains around brought it all back, shaped different from how it went out into the world. On and on, the voices rising and falling, but building the way you see thunderheads build on snowy peaks, as if the air was trying to outdo all that granite. So were these soldiers trying to outdo one another, and it was a passion coming out, all they had and all that was taken away, coming out right there, on this side and the other.

You could see the music in the eyes across from you with fire coming up in between, you could watch the swelling of the sound in the raising and lowering of shoulders and heads, rising and falling in rhythm with what your ears could catch. I wish I could tell you true what it was like, but this is the best I can do without singing myself.

It's gone now, and the ponderosa, the cedar, the grasses below and sky above, none of them remembers that music. Like when the wind takes a spark from a campfire, and you see it fly out into the dark for a bit, and then it goes out, but before that it sure is pretty lighting up the night.

> Every time I feel the spirit
> Movin in my heart
> I will pray

sounds again through the years like time was nothing, sounding strong like that spark braving the blackness that wants to swallow it up.

> Jordan River chilly and cold
> Chills the body but not the soul
> I look around me, looks so fine
> I ask the Lord if I was blind

And then the last chorus sung loud by every soldier in camp, round every fire, brave words ringing like a farrier's hammer at the forge, a bright gift to the Sierra and to a cold river nearby called Mercy.

> Every time I feel the spirit
> Movin in my heart
> I will pray

And I know God took what we sang and held it, even though the river couldn't, even though the trees don't remember, even though the words were buried in the earth. And it can never be lost.

That was the night we really arrived in the Sierra Nevada, the night the mountains knew us, recognized us, welcomed us for the first time, and on that night we were home.

Of the Spur

In order to use the spur, it is necessary to keep steady the body, the waist, and the wrists; to cling to the horse with the thighs, and the calves of the legs; turn the point of the feet a little out; lower a little the wrists; press the spurs close behind the girths, without moving the body; replace then the wrists and the legs by degrees.

from *Cavalry Tactics*

prayers from a high country

Dear God:
      i wanna thank you for what you did
this mornin, i mean the sun
comin down slow
on Cathedral, that was mighty fine
work so early in the day,
and you were so quiet
bout it, no fuss or complainin
of the work to be done,
you just coaxed the glow
to a blaze on top
of that mountain tellin the world
below that day was comin
soon enough, i just wanna say
i appreciate the early notice
that a new day was breakin,
and how you used just a little light
to let me know that a lot more was comin
along, yeah, i appreciate you takin the time
to show me all that I was missin in the night.

dear God:
i wanna thank you for these mountains
which make it easier to talk
to you cause they so high
heaven's practically next door.

i swear i can reach up
fully into the blue of the sky
and stain my fingers
with the footprints of angels,
so maybe that's why i'm happy
cause i'm finally takin in
what i didn't even know
i was livin without,
and there's so much of it,
that i don't know what to do
with the kind of light that makes eyes
hungry, the sounds that make ears
go blind, i never knew there was such a country
called yosemite and how it would wake me
from this long sleep, wake the part of me
that needs to feel earth
or a cold wind blowin
down from places where
there are no people, i never knew
silence was a property
you could own,
but i did, once, i just simply forgot
the feel of bein naked
on a rocky spur thrust
out into space
like a prayer.

dear God:
thank you for rain
on manzanita.
i never knew water
could turn a plant
into a sunset.

leastways in the shine
after a storm
you can see twilight twistin
red into branches.

dear God:
i greatly appreciate
what you were sayin
bout that little red fir
bent double
under packed snow
as i rode through
the merced grove this past
spring cause when i reached over
and shook that tree
all the snow fell off
that fir's branches, quick
to sky the tree stood tall,
and i knew its burden woulda melted
come summer, but if you see a burden
pressin down on somethin
you just reach out then and there
cause one day it may be you
under that mountain
prayin for freedom.

dear God:
when ravens fly over
why do they sigh?
if something's botherin them
they should just speak out,
and stop all that whisperin.
i'm also gettin tired of hearin

all their squawkin bout this or that,
you see, i'm doin my best,
but bein black ain't easy
unless you a raven,
so the last thing
i need is some bird
thinkin it knows my problems
whisperin to the wind.

Patrol report on Yosemite Park stationery,
Camp A. E. Wood, June 8, 1904

I am of the opinion that a Sergeant, a corporal and six men should be stationed at Jerseydale. Their presence will prevent trouble among the inhabitants, and will prevent the herding of large numbers of cattle just over the south and west lines of the park, who are said to be driven or allowed to drift in, when no soldiers are in the vicinity. This will prevent the cutting of timber for fuel that is undoubtedly going on to some extent, among the inhabitants in wanton spitefulness of each other and to give the soldiers work.

> Respectfully submitted,
> Fred J. Herman,
> 1st Lieutenant 9th Cav.
> Com'dg Patrol

blood memory

It was hot and the old man sitting in the sand was pushing flies away with his right hand, trying to shade his eyes with the same hand. His face was lined and brown like a delta, and I wondered if it was rain or tears that did that.

His left hand was behind him in the sand, propping him up as he smiled at the little boy in the river. The river was low, and the boy who was like copper was laughing from the coldness. His little brown legs were almost buried in blue as the water went around and through them. He laughed again. The woman lying behind the old man heard that laugh and moved. She was red and brown like mahogany, if mahogany was soft enough for skin.

She reminded me of Grandma Sara. She was old too, but her hair was long and still black. She had dark oval eyes that were sunk in her face like pools in red sandstone, the kind you see in Arizona. There was something about her that made me see and feel and taste the desert, as if she had very little water in her, and even that was deep down and beyond the reach of roots. But somehow it strengthened her, gave her the grace of a flower that only needs one drop of water to bloom.

I loved her, and I didn't know her name.

Looking again at the man, I recognized how he held his shoulders and how those shoulders held him, saw how he saw, watched how he looked at the boy and the river and the sky. It was me, the me that was yet to be. It took a while for me to know myself in that place, cause that Elijah was so happy. You could see it all over him, coming off him like steam off your body when you step away from a hot fire into the darkness, clouds just sweat in a hurry to become air.

The air was heavy with joy. I could move my hands through it and taste it on my tongue. I could feel it trickling down my back, and it felt cold and hot at the same time. For him to laugh would have been too much.

I was watching myself watch my grandson who has not been born, my grandson laughing and peering shyly at an old but beautiful woman who I didn't know, but who was his grandmother.

It was my family, the family I was going to have, and I remember thinking how lucky I would be, how lucky I am right now, that this could be someday. And then I knew I wasn't alone. Looking back into the leaves and branches of the trees that crowded the river, I saw the faces of my people who had run with me through the curving paths of night in many dreams, dripping with sweat, dripping with the river that runs through us all, and they were watching the little boy and smiling too.

I was eavesdropping on my future, and they were seeing theirs too. My people who had come before, who'd been running through blackness, had eaten and drunk blackness and become blackness, had made it to this day, and they were beyond tears that happiness could be found.

It's a good day when a past that was forgotten finds a future to be remembered. And they weren't alone. Behind them, half hidden by leaves and twigs, were all the Africans who had walked out of the Atlantic Ocean in another dream, striding up a silent beach. They were here, and I heard deep within me *Yoruba* and *Fon* and *Adja* and *Bantu* and *Fulani* and *Senoufou* and *Malinke* and *Seminole* and *Fang* and *Punu* and *Kota* and *Mandinka* and *Fula* and *Wolof* and *Jola* and *Hausa* and *Mende* and *Ovimbundu* and *Bakongo* and *Kanuri* and *Tiv* and *Ewe* and *Akan* and *Ga* and *Tsalagi* and *Susu*. All those names sounding though not spoken, words coming through me, making a drum of my body. Trembling from the blows, I still could see a forehead there, an arm over here, a bit of a thigh sticking out way back there, and eyes like stars blazing in the black of the forest that surrounded us, so black even though the sun by the river was yellow and hot.

And we were all breathing hard, taking big gulps of air, as if we had just stopped running after running for days or years or centuries, and now was the first chance to slow our hearts. And that started the sweat shining down over bodies and down to our feet, water or tears flowing. What was coming off of us was real, but where did all that water come from?

There were thousands and thousands of black people, streaming with water like they'd all walked out of the sea, and it was flowing off me too, flowing in trickles and streams and little currents right down to my toes, as if I was standing under a waterfall you couldn't see. And I realized this was where the river came from, the river in the desert that the boy and the man and the woman were lying next to and swimming in and wet with. All that water was going to them, to the family that was mine and theirs too, all the people behind.

Maybe if you ran and ran for a hundred thousand years, the sweat and tears eventually would come back from the air, from the sky, and flow to you, from you, down you, making creeks, and rivers. Or if you'd been buried at the bottom of a sea you jumped into rather than be a slave, waiting for the moment to be free again, and then you stood, walked out from under the cold, and rose up onto that white beach, maybe the water would never stop coming off you.

The river was flowing from the dead and from the living, making the plants grow tall and the rocks sing loud, cooling the sky round the very hot sun that felt so good, so good that the woman turned into it fully like some kind of flower trying to find the best way to receive the light.

And I knew I would never know thirst again, and knew I would never be alone again, and it went on and on that way until I woke up. I slowly rose on one arm just the way she did, the woman in the dream, the woman who would one day be my wife, and I looked out with my eyes closed, looked for my boy's boy or my daughter's boy, I didn't know which, and I smiled, cause from somewhere close and somewhere far away there came to me his sweet laughter.

Patrol report on Yosemite Park stationery,
under "Remarks," Wawona, Cal., August 13, 1903

On August 7, a herd of sheep was found by a patrol from this station, on the Tioga road just inside the Park limits—brand of sheep, O—herder a Spaniard—owner unknown. On August 10, there was on hand at this station bout 350 lbs. of grain.

Very Respectfully,
J. T. Nance,
Capt., 9 Cavy,
Commanding Detachment

private property

I hobbled Satan so he wouldn't wander off. Bingham did the same to his mount though he didn't have to, cause his horse would stay with my mule. We were on a ridge overlooking Tuolumne Meadows. We'd been looking for a sheepherder named Emanuel cause we'd gotten reports of him and his herd of about a thousand sheep illegally grazing in the country south of Soda Springs, but we hadn't been able to find him.

These sheepherders were mostly Portuguese, Basque, Chilean, Mexican, and Indian. They knew the country better than we did. They followed the drainages of creeks and streams, cause they knew we patrolled the trails. They figured if they avoided moving along the trails they'd avoid the law, but sometimes that ain't so easy.

Since leaving South Carolina, I'd been accustomed to not taking the easy road. So me and Bingham went cross-country, looking for signs of sheep, and, well, it's not an easy thing to hide the traces of hundreds of sheep. We just looked for country that looked eaten, and when we found it way up in Lyell Canyon, we found the sheep. We also found a Mexican named Emanuel.

We could understand each other fairly well cause I'd picked up some Spanish in the Philippines. Besides, there really wasn't much to say. He knew what he'd been doing, and he knew our opinion on the matter. I remember him saying in frustration, *No es facil a trabajar en estas montañas, porque los soldades negros!* over and over again, jabbing his finger at me like a knife. *No es facil a vivir o trabajar en Yosemite! No me gusto!* And then in a whisper he said over and over, *Ah, mi familia! No hay nada, no hay nada!*

He was sitting on a small granite boulder with his head in his hands, rocking back and forth and talking more to himself than to us. He knew what we were going to do, which is why he was so upset.

The policy, started by an officer years ago, was to take any herder found illegally grazing sheep in the high country, escort him down to the western park boundary, and then take the sheep over the eastern park boundary along the crest of the Sierra. In other words, I had to take Mr. Emanuel here down into the foothills on the west side of the Sierra, while Bingham and some men stationed at the post in Tuolumne would march his sheep over the crest to the east side, outside the park.

By the time Mr. Emanuel could get back up here to look for his sheep, it would be too late. They'd be scattered far and wide by then, and the season would be over.

This policy worked really well, but it didn't say anything bout a man trying to make it on his own. It didn't say anything bout some of the sheepherders being darker than some of my men, and it didn't say anything bout how these herders weren't allowed to graze their stock down in the Central Valley on account of them being Mexican or Indian or Basque, and not white. That's why Emanuel was up on the rocky edge of sky.

Who would go to all the trouble and effort of coming up here to graze livestock if they didn't have to? It was Mr. Emanuel's livelihood, his profession, what put food on his plate and maybe his family's, but this open country was now a national park, and there was no room up here for him and his sheep. So we did the job. I separated that man from everything he owned, from his property.

Escorting Mr. Emanuel down to the foothills took a few days, cause it was a long, hard ride and there was no reason to be in a hurry. The longer we took, the better his sheep would scatter to the winds. We didn't talk. What was there to say? I felt really bad, but I had a job to do, and the rules don't take into account how a soldier might feel about enforcing them.

I had plenty of time to think on that ride, and one thing I thought about was that even though Mr. Emanuel was poor, he owned more than I did. I didn't have a house. Most of the time I lived in a tent. I didn't have a wife. I had soldiers who'd never tell me outright that they cared if I lived or died, but they'd take a bullet meant for me, and I'd do the same for them, and that made them my family. Sometimes I didn't have much hope that people would get better, but I believed tomorrow would be better than today.

When I reached into my pockets and pulled out what was there, nothing came out but my hands. All anyone saw when they looked at me was what I'd been given. They were looking at the army. My mule wasn't mine at all, or my saddle. Satan's bridle and reins and the bit in his mouth, all that was given to my care, but my name ain't on it. There was nothing but one thing in this world that belonged to me, and one thing only.

My memories. That's all I owned. No bank knew me or had anything of mine inside it. When I enlisted, when I signed that piece of paper, I became U.S. property, something listed, marked down, put down, written in, stamped on, everything you could think of shy of branding. From the time I woke up to the time I went to sleep, I was just a body with a name and a rank. Even the clothes on my back were issued to me, on loan till the day I died or my time was up. I sometimes wondered if even God could see Lucinda and Daniel's little boy hiding beneath this uniform.

But when I slept, I remembered Mama's voice, her face, her hands, her step, the sound of her walking or talking, her eyes when she was squinting in the sun, and her shadow falling on the ground.

I remembered how soft her hands felt on my face the time we came home and I was crying cause a white man had called me "nigger" and I felt "nigger" burn for the first time in my heart and my gut, and my anger was swallowing me whole until there was nothing in the world but my rage and me, so hot that if you touched me you would've burst into flame.

And my mama put her cool, damp hands on my face, and with

her voice she put out the fires inside me, and she told me that I was her child and no one's nigger, that I was beautiful, and that her day began and ended with me. And I believed her.

Well, I own that, all of it. Her voice belongs to me. Her love is still part of me. Her hands have never left my face, I can feel them still on me. This is all private property. This is what I own.

Her name was Lucinda, but I only ever called her "Ma'am." I say her name, and something deep within me answers. I own that. And my daddy so far away, his hands so far away, hands black as dirt, cracked like a creekbed at the end of summer from working that hot field, cracked with pain he rarely let me see. When he held me nothing could ever be wrong, and nothing bad could ever happen. He's still holding me, and I can still feel the grip of his arms, how hard it was to breathe, and when he let go, how the air felt rushing inside me like the first breath.

I remember all of it, and that's what I own, and if it's in me, no one can take it away, escort it to some far-off boundary and let it go. No fire can ever burn it down.

Who am I? I'm their child. They made me out of their love for each other. I'm their Elijah. I belong to them and they belong to me. We're each other's property. Folks who don't have anything only got themselves, and you can't put that in a bank, but it's yours, you own it and no one else.

Before we left Tuolumne, Mr. Emanuel had said, "It's not easy to work in these mountains because of the black soldiers! It's not easy to live and work in Yosemite! I don't like it! Ah, my family! There's nothing, there's nothing!" I could've said the same thing, and so could most of my men, except we'd take out the part about "black soldiers" and put in "sheepherders," "poachers," or "timber thieves" in its place. Otherwise, I agreed with the man, but he was wrong that there was nothing. Even Emanuel in his despair spoke of his family.

I'm poor, but it's a peculiar kind of poverty. The world just sees a poor soldier more full of pride than silver dollars, but it's not so clear that you can be rich with the people who love you. That's the kind of wealth I have. That's my currency, and it's the best kind. I spend it and spend it but my account never goes empty, it just keeps filling up every time I remember a smile or a laugh or a whisper or a cry or an embrace.

By the time I get old and eligible for a pension, I'll own so many memories, good ones and bad ones, that I probably won't need it. I'll be rich with what I've done and what's been done to me, cause wealth ain't what you have, but what has you, like how Ma'am and Sir and Grandma Sara have me, I belong to them and they to me.

So I ain't worried about death at all. By the time that darkness comes, I'll know its face, its voice, the shape of it, how it feels, and it won't be a stranger but an old dear friend, carefully removing from his pockets and gently handing over to me every single word I once spoke to God when I was trapped in pain and anger. And in the other pocket he'll have all of God's replies.

Then I'll own those too.

Manual of Arms at a Halt

The troopers are formed by the commands FRONT and HALT, as prescribed, No. 125, and are 4 inches from knee to knee. The instructor commands: Draw-Saber. 2 times. At the command, DRAW, incline slightly the head to the left, carry the right hand above the reins, engage the wrist in the sword-knot, seize the grip, disengage the blade 6 inches from the scabbard, and turn the head to the front.

from *Cavalry Tactics*

uzumati

After my journey with Mr. Emanuel, I made my way back to Camp Wood. It took a few days, but I needed the time to myself. The weather was fine, but the nights were starting to get cold. It was good to be back in the company of soldiers, good to hear a little news, good to be out of that saddle.

But once I stopped moving, I started thinking about what had happened to Mr. Emanuel. How somebody's life could change completely in an afternoon of meeting up with some soldiers in a mountain meadow. Thinking about him led to thinking about how my life had changed when I left home all those years ago, where I'd been and what I'd done since then. How meeting up with that officer who enlisted me near Fort Robinson changed everything. How my life was broken up into memories, and those memories were like pebbles, little pieces of me, scattered in a creek. Most of those pieces were caught up in the current of that creek, so they kept moving downstream, but some pieces were heavy enough that they dropped into the dark and sat there at the bottom.

I figured there must be bits of me all over. All those places where a creek slows and drifts, gets caught up round the roots of trees and sunk down in hollows, the places where too much was taken away, pieces of my life have fallen like stones dropping down to the darkness under a creek.

A few days later I made my last patrol to the edge of the sky. I was high up near Devil's Postpile, and had just ridden up from Sotcher Lake the night before. It'd been a clear night, and the moon just past full lit up everything so well, you never hungered for the day, so I just packed up and started heading out and up to the patrol cabin in Reds Meadow.

I was by myself, and wanted it that way. I figured if this was going to be my last journey through the Yosemite, then I'd do it alone. You come into this world by yourself, and you go out of it the same way. Of course, now I was riding a mule named Satan, so I wasn't completely alone.

There had been a fire through the area, which made the going a lot easier. The moon had no trouble getting past all the branches above me and finding a place to rest on the forest floor. The red firs were creaking in a wind I couldn't feel, but I could see it rock the tops of the trees back and forth, and the treetops seemed to be brushing the backs of the stars.

It was a quiet, peaceful night, the kind of night you long for when you ain't got it and you hope will never end when you do. I was getting to that place inside, the quiet place you get to when you've been in mountains a long time, so long that you feel you know them. Not just their names, which you can find on a map, but the names that are secret, and within your own silence you slowly begin to unlock, letter by letter, what God must call them in the night.

I think I was even dozing a bit, watching Satan's head rise up and down, feeling the rocking of my mule as he walked and the coolness of the summer air on my face and hands.

I should've known it wouldn't last.

I remember a kind of stiffening up in Satan. He slowed a bit, moving his head from side to side, and then with a snort he swiveled his butt upward and sideways in one motion, and just like that I was in the air. That mule bucked me off so easily, I might've been able to call it a fancy dismount if someone had been watching, but you can't lie to God, and God knew Satan better than I did. That mule was mean and spiteful, but he had a soft spot for me. We got along just fine, and that left me wondering, as I went up, over, and down to the ground, what the hell was going on.

The ground rose up faster than it had any right to and smacked me on the butt, and as I looked up I saw more stars lighting up the sky than there'd ever been before. I heard Satan bucking and dancing back down the trail, but when I looked over my shoulder all I saw was his shadow, draining away like black molasses.

Speaking of asses, mine wasn't doing too well, and as I struggled to get back up over my feet, I could feel how my legs had been left out of the plan to stand up. They were as outraged as I was and wouldn't cooperate. Eventually I was upright, standing on a steep, rocky trail in the middle of red fir forest, with moonlight clearly illuminating my bruised and scratched hands. I was thinking bout all the things you could do to a mule short of killing it, and how I was really looking forward to trying out every idea that came to me, when I saw movement up the trail about twenty feet away.

Two, no, three fairly large animals were running cross the trail, cross the very spot I probably would've been except for the disagreement with Satan over direction of travel. Peering closer, I could just make out how one of the three animals was a lot bigger than the other two. That one broke off and ran a bit toward me, fully out of the shadows into moonlight.

It was a grizzly.

And since I personally have never heard of grizzlies roaming round in herds, I figured the other two were cubs, which meant that Mama was the one taking particular interest in me. I had surprised them.

Now I was really irritated. First my mule bucks me off, probably cause it caught the scent of the bears, then it runs off, the sound of which probably spooked the bears, who likely were just trying to get away. Leaving me standing there alone, staring foolishly at my bleeding hands.

Furthermore, Lieutenant Resnick told me once that no one had seen a grizzly bear in the Sierra in nearly ten years, so I needn't worry too much about meeting one. I trusted him.

I trusted an officer. I trusted my mule.

Ain't it peculiar how the people you trust usually aren't around when you really need them? That's what I was thinking when the grizzly rose up off the ground, using her forelegs to push herself up into the air.

Now we were looking at each other eye to eye. The sow, eyes dark with glints of silver, glared at me. I slowly realized that it was moonlight reflecting in her eyes. I could feel that she was considering. I know it sounds crazy, but that's what she was doing, considering. And her cubs were still running cross the trail, but everything was happening so slow, it seemed to take forever for those cubs to cross the trail and disappear into the bushes.

Still she was staring into me with those eyes, and I could almost hear her say, "Should I kill you, or let you live? I just don't know." She seemed to sway as she thought this, at least she never fully stopped moving but was standing and walking to the side at the same time. Like she wanted to stop to consider if I needed to die, but also wanted to stay at all times with her cubs. And her cubs weren't the cute, sweet-looking black bear cubs I remember seeing before, no, they were bigger than the biggest dog I'd ever seen, and I wouldn't be calling them "cubs" if I hadn't seen Mama.

All in the same moment, and this was only seconds, mind you, she dropped down to all fours again, and there was no sound in it, no sound at all of any of them moving or running, but suddenly she was gone into the place her cubs had gone.

I was still standing there bleeding from my hands, and there was a tightness in my chest that I couldn't figure out till I realized I wasn't breathing at all. So I took a breath, lots of breaths, feeling the coldness rushing into my lungs, the ache in my busted hands, feeling a warmth spreading outward from my crotch and down my thighs.

Then I really was irritated. In less than one minute I got bucked off Satan, busted up my hands, tore up my uniform, got charged by a grizzly, and pissed on myself. It took another minute or so for me to realize that I was lucky. I could've been dead. That grizzly had me cold. But she seemed torn between staying with her cubs and taking me out. I guess she decided to run off with her cubs. But it might've been otherwise.

What bothered me most was that I got lucky only because I was bucked off here and not up there, where they ran out of the brush. If Satan hadn't dumped me on *this* cold, hard, ground, we would've been alongside those bears just as they were crossing the trail. Satan saved my life.

Mama always taught me that Jesus was my savior, and I believed her and the deacon too. How could I ever let her know that when salvation finally came, Jesus was nowhere in sight, and Satan could take credit for me being round long enough to write these words? I'll tell you one thing. Being saved by the grace of a mule hurts deeper than you can imagine.

Then I considered something else. That grizzly could've killed me but didn't. Lieutenant Resnick said that people round here had shot all those bears, that none were left. Maybe this was the last mother grizzly? Maybe she'd seen all her kind get killed one by one, the adults and their children. I'd be angry at any person I ran into if I was a bear. You hurt me and mine, I'll hurt you! But when she had a chance to do that, she let me go.

When you're in front of a grizzly bear, you're bout as close to the heart of these mountains as you can get without dying. The Ahwah-neechee call the grizzly *Uzumati*, and I got close to it, right up to the edge, and was let go. It wasn't death that had me in its grip that night, it was life. I never felt more alive than in those few seconds when Yosemite itself rose up on its haunches and looked me in the eye, and I was foolish enough to look back.

I can't forget that as long as I live.

And no, I'm not going to thank that mule. He didn't have to buck me off, he could've just stopped on the trail. There was no reason to throw me to the ground. I started getting angry again when I felt something behind me, something close. I turned and drew my Colt out of its holster, quickly raised it chest high, and nearly shot Satan in the head. Now that would've required some explaining. That mule had walked up while I was thinking, and I hadn't heard a thing.

Satan just looked at me, then lowered his head to nuzzle his left front leg. I could see the white of his teeth as he bit at whatever was irritating him. I knew the feeling.

*Patrol report on Yosemite Park stationery,
under "Remarks," Jerseydale, Cal., July 14, 1904*

To the Adjutant

Sir I have the honor to inform you that the place on the Gov.
Land is not a very suitable place to build a corral you cannot get
up there with a wagon to feed them but the place the Comdg
Officer look at is the best place. The owner was here to meet me
when I arrived and says it will cost nothing to build their. Start
cutting poles this afternoon waiting your orders will be ready to
put it up when I hear from my Comdg Officer.

Your Obedient Servant.

Sgt. Morris,

Sgt in Charge of Jersey Dale

PS please forward me some Official Envelopes.

letter from Yosemite

D ear Mama and Daddy and Grandma Sara,
I know it's been a long time since you've heard from me, and I'm
sorry bout that. I really didn't have much to say. But since I got to Yosemite,
I've been wanting to tell somebody bout it, cause it's news I really need
to share. Kind of like a neighbor's house is on fire and they don't know it,
except this is good news, being here in all this beauty and peacefulness.

It's early October, sky blue and clear. I've been out every day patrolling
between Rogers Lake and Return Canyon. The country is empty now,
but I like it that way. There are aspen leaves on the ground, and when the
wind sweeps them away they make a crackling sound like women moving
in their starched white dresses. Makes me think of being in church back
home every time the wind blows!

Mama, you'll be happy to know I'm a churchgoing man again, cause
every day feels like Sunday here. It's got that hush like when the deacon
would pause in the middle of his sermon. Not too long ago I passed some
time round the Big Trees in what they call the Mariposa Grove, down
by Wawona, and it felt like having lunch with angels. Those trees are so
tall and bigger than anything except maybe God, but peaceful, like they
don't have to prove nothing to no one. Whatever was bothering me that
day didn't seem to matter after a few minutes sitting by this one tree called
the Grizzly Giant.

Speaking of grizzlies, they do got bears here. I had a run-in with a big
grizzly bear and her cubs not too long ago. It turned out all right, but that
mama bear scared me so bad I . . . well, I'd rather not tell you about that.
It's embarrassing. She reminded me a little bit of you, Grandma Sara,

and I hope you're still around to get mad at me for saying that, but I don't know if you are.

There's been a lot worse things happened to me here, but none of that mattered too much. It's hard to tell you why, but up here in the high country feels like home to me. You can see more stars than I ever imagined could be, and they seem so close. I think they're closer cause these mountains are the highest in America, according to the Lieutenant, anyway. They so high you don't have to die to get to paradise. Here in Yosemite all you need to get to heaven is a good horse, though a mule will do just fine.

But now it's getting close to the time when us soldiers have to head back down to San Francisco. Every morning I can feel winter coming on, there's ice in my socks and shirt making them cold and stiff. I don't need a message from the Lieutenant telling me it's time to leave. Anyway, maybe you remember when I last wrote, I was still garrisoned at the Presidio, and I'd just seen President Roosevelt march through town? That was something, but I like it much better here, and I'm feeling sad bout leaving. I only ever had two real homes, back in Spartanburg with you, and here. My heart's still there with you, and it's here in Yosemite too. It's lying on some granite dome with a view of El Capitan or Yosemite Falls, and it'll never leave even if I have to.

I miss you, and I'll see you one day, you can depend on it, cause you're where I come from and where I'll go back to in some life. But Daddy, you were right bout me and South Carolina. I could never go back there and not walk on that sidewalk, not tell people what I think about them. My spirit's too big for Spartanburg, especially now. It would be like planting a giant sequoia in Mama's garden. I'm a sergeant in the Ninth Cavalry, and I've been in charge of what people do and can't do here in this national park, and that's a good kind of power to have. I can't be powerful in South Carolina, I'd just end up dead. Like that mama grizzly bear I run into. All those bears are supposed to be killed off, but apparently she never got the word. People aren't comfortable being round something so big and strong that it don't care what kind of money you got, or what fancy clothes you wear, it'll kill you and maybe eat you too! Folks in Spartanburg would think I was just as dangerous as that mama bear.

That's why I never came home. I know you understand that. But when I sleep and dream at night I'm with you. When I'm riding on some high trail or lying by a fire or sitting in the Big Trees, I'm with you. You're in my blood and every time I take a breath, you're moving in my heart. My hands are big and rough like Daddy's now. I got your eyes, Mama, and my spirit is strong like you, Grandma Sara. I got you all for company every day and every night. Yeah, I'm sort of my own homecoming walking round California, looking for a good place to throw a party.

I don't know where I'll get sent after San Francisco. They might be having some trouble down in Mexico pretty soon, the officers say. But right now I'm going to spend as much time as I can up in the high country, before it gets too cold. I wish I could show it to you. Anyway, I got to go feed the horses, but I'll write again soon enough.

Love always,
Your Elijah

Manual of Arms at a Halt

At the command, SABRE, draw quickly the sabre, raising the arm
to its full length at an angle of 45 degrees, the sabre in a straight line
with the arm; hold the sabre in this position an instant, then carry
it to the right shoulder, the back of the blade supported against the
hollow of the shoulder, the wrist upon the top of the thigh, the little
finger on the outside of the grip.

from *Cavalry Tactics*

down to the valley

Sometimes the ending you look for is not the one you get. I expected a long dusty good-bye, and I wondered how I could say good-bye to these mountains that had embraced me for nearly half a year.

It would be different from saying good-bye to a woman or someone else you love, cause you can't hold mountains in your hands like you can a woman, you can't look into mountains as if they were the eyes of someone you might never see again. And you couldn't expect the mountains to say your name over and over again or to cry.

It could never be like that, but it was, I thought, a farewell that would hurt. I was anticipating that hurt when I got word that I'd been "volunteered" to spend the winter in Yosemite Valley. I would be assisting a Mr. Harlow, who was the guardian of Yosemite Valley and the Mariposa Grove of Big Trees. Back then California controlled those lands, not the federal government. The assignment meant that I'd temporarily avoided having to leave the national park. But it still meant I had to leave the high country behind, at least for a little while, and that turned out to be hard.

The hurt began with the ride down into Yosemite Valley. I remember the jarring of the Big Oak Flat road, feeling as if both my mule and the ground were trying to buck me off, and the dust Satan kicked up covering everything behind me. Maybe even my mule was afraid of looking back and seeing all that beauty.

There was no one else on the trail that lonely afternoon. There was just the sun going down like I'd seen it thousands of times before, falling slow like it had all the time in creation to go away. One thing

Yosemite's wilderness had taught me was never be in a hurry. Don't rush, stop and consider your next move before you start down a trail you've never taken. So I pulled on the reins, eased back in the saddle, and straightened my legs till I could feel the stretch in my muscles and joints. I stopped Satan right in the middle of the cloud we'd been making out of the road and watched that cloud trail dust around us with sunlight in its wake. The road was busted up and on fire now.

The world kept moving. We seemed to be the only things that were still. Maybe this was all there ever was, this moment right there, right then. I can still feel the heat of that sun beating on me, except it was more a caress than a blow. It was like a woman holding on to someone she didn't want to let go. It didn't surprise me that such a country could give me that feeling of being held on to. I was going down to the valley, and the sun was going down, but it didn't feel like the end of anything.

Only now, looking back, do I see the beginning of the road that led up to something bigger than myself, and then down to something even bigger. Led to who I would become. On that afternoon when a man and a mule were riding down into a valley, all I felt was good-bye, but the farther we went, the more it started to become a hello.

I thought of the soldiers that would leave me behind, and how maybe it would be a good thing to not have an officer looking over my shoulder when I wasn't expecting it, at least for a few months. After all, I hadn't left the army. I was just on a special assignment. But right then, as I peered ahead into my new duty, I thought about the night that was coming, and the nights after that when I'd be on my own, and all the days and nights that would follow.

Now it's different, cause I can *remember* what came next. I can see the day after that ride into the valley and the day after that, and how all those days and nights overlap in layers, like leaves in the valley in fall after the dogwood and maple trees let go. When you put a shovel into the ground, those days and nights and years are still there, but they've become earth. Everything that once was so full of light, call-ing you to sit and drowse in it, has dropped to its own shadow, and the world is sweeter after such a rain. There in the ground, with all the dead, those days and that light still burn, and there I see the world for the first time, see how I fit, how everything fits, all bound freely as clouds are bound to sky.

Now I knew my shadow as it fell to the earth, cooled it a bit before moving on. Now I knew you can never have too much quiet in your life, if it's the quiet that finds you in mountains or forest. You can never have too much light if it's the kind that falls out of the sky at dawn or dusk. You can never have too much darkness if it's the blackness between the stars. You can put too much sugar in your coffee in the morning, but the sweetness that fills the air with every step of your mule under you as you amble through a meadow full of flowers, well, how can you have too much of that?

Before Yosemite, I knew a man needed air to breathe and food to eat and someone to love and a feeling that God was looking out for him. I thought that was it. But you also need something else that don't often get mentioned. Anyone, man, woman, or mule, needs beauty. I'm calling it beauty cause I ain't certain there's a name for what I mean, but beauty comes closest.

When I look back over my shoulder at the life I've lived, things sometimes get clearer, as if a fog had lifted. Now I see I was riding that day down into the heart of a world people spend their lives trying to find, without even knowing they're looking for it. And it was a place, a home, a heaven to me. Some folks pray for a sweet hereafter, but it's already everywhere round us, the air we take in, the light that fills us, and the darkness. It's where we hope to go at the end, and maybe where we come from at the beginning. It's the dusty trail winding down to El Capitan, into the cool shadows of black oaks, the wet meadows their roots embrace, and a river, cold and bright, that never stops singing.

I'm struggling to close things up here, but some things never stop flowing, like rivers and creeks never stop pushing logs out of the way. Flowing water doesn't want to stop. And some stories don't have endings. A period ends a sentence, makes a thought complete, but the life inside you is like water, like creeks and rivers, just getting stronger or weaker, and it doesn't end until you do.

Yosemite doesn't end until I do.

I could say that's all there is to my story, but you can't see my eyes and how they're still filled with the fire of a sun long since set, can't see how I'm still breathing in a wind that hasn't touched the earth in more than forty years. The other day my wife told me I spend too much time living in the past, but I'm thinking, where else do we live? It's all going away, and it's all coming back.

I'm Elijah Yancy, a soldier who let go of a place that became part of him but now is held captive by a place that won't let him go. I've been kidnapped by the Range of Light, stolen by the quiet of mountain paths. Somewhere my broken body is rocking a chair, my dear wife is sitting next to me, but my soul is on a mule walking down from a country that knew me long ago.

The reins are loose in my hands, cause that animal knows the path we're following. We're riding down into the deep shadows of Yosemite Valley, while all around us the sheer granite cliffs are remembering a day long forgotten, and their memories are like a fire burning on the edges of the world.

Instruction to Mount Without Saddle, and to Saddle
Manner of Vaulting

To dismount, pass the left rein of the snaffle into the right hand; place this hand on the withers; seize the mane with the left hand, raise yourself on the two wrists, pass the right leg extended over the croup of the horse, without touching him, bringing the legs together, the body straight, and come to the ground lightly on the toes, bending the knees a little.

from *Cavalry Tactics*

getting done

It would've been pretty to end like that, but not every ending is pretty. You've probably seen someone after a river or a creek got hold of them, yet they hadn't been planning on going for a swim. They're dripping with what they been through and what's been through them, they're cold and shaking, hair a mess, and they're a mess inside, too.

When something you can't forget gets hold of you, you ain't pretty at the end of it, but you know one thing that's true. You're alive, and there's beauty in that, God helped me see there's beauty in that.

Now I'm standing and shivering beside what I just been through. I'm afraid to move and joyful that I ain't got to if I don't want to. So I'm just going to sit here rocking beside myself, watching what I've been and what I'm going to be flow on past, and do nothing at all. Cause at any moment the ground under me could decide not to be ground no more, could start getting thirsty for water, and that water'll flow over me again, but different next time, always different.

Big Creek's never the same from moment to moment, and maybe I'm not either, maybe I'm just as wild and hard to figure. All I know is you got to fight to keep from getting moved in this world, you got to struggle to find silence and be still, cause it's always storming outside and inside. It's all moving, and movement is all there ever was and will be.

That little boy I used to be is still lying beside a creek, cold as hell and wondering how he survived the swim. He got my name. He got my story. He got everything I had and everything I thought I lost.

I used to think I could never be that boy again, but all it takes is to be uncertain and afraid and human. Then it's easy to lose your grip and fall into that creek, let it take you to anywhere you've been in your life.

The creek beside my family's cabin is the same water as every creek anywhere. They all flow into the same place. Each drop of water's trying to be different, but you can't fool the clouds and you can't trick a river. As for the ocean, well, it ain't got a sense of humor at all, cause it's felt too much to ever laugh again. It's either whispering or roaring, and if you listen close to that big water you can hear the voices of everything that was ever put into it coming out of it again.

Water's got a lot to say cause it's been everywhere and over everything, maybe that's why it's never quiet. But now and then it slows down, gathers in a pool to reflect, and in that place I found enough quiet to know my own soul. And when pieces of me drifted to the bottom of that stream, the biggest piece, full of darkness and light, was Yosemite.

I'm going to stop now, and if I ever have more to say bout Elijah Yancy, I might start off by singing, let the music flow in and around my words like water, cause water is the language God knows best. That's why tears are easy to understand, and sweat and blood. They're all mostly water, and what's left are just words meant to be whispered or sung.

Moving through and moving round, becoming this or that, it's all the same to rain and to snow that becomes rain, falling on the land and the sea, giving back all that was given, taking away all that's meant to be.

Big Creek singing and the Ohio River too, the Missouri, the Platte, the Pecos, the Red, the Gila, the Colorado, all singing through what was and will always be Indian country, the Tuolumne and the Merced singing through Yosemite, all that water flowing down the lush green of the Philippines, and the Big Water between here and there. All that water singing in me, all of it singing

Do Lord, oh do Lord
Do remember me
Do Lord, oh do Lord
Do remember me
Do Lord, oh do Lord
Do remember me
Goin way beyond the blue

ACKNOWLEDGMENTS

The list of those I must thank for making this book possible begins with my whole family. I want to pay tribute especially to my dad and my brother, who both went to war, and to my mother for being the real warrior. I owe my father, James O. Johnson, Jr., gratitude beyond the power of any word or gift. He served in the U.S. armed forces in this country and overseas for more than twenty years, and he was the template in many ways for Elijah Yancy. After so much war, may he finally be at peace. I'm grateful to my brother, James, for surviving Kuwait and Iraq and coming home alive in body and mind, and to my mother, Shirley Johnson, for her love, strength, quiet grace, and inexhaustible kindness. I thank my grandparents, Anna Mae Yancy and Gilbert Nathaniel Yancy, for being the best that people can be; my Aunt Marna for reminding me how acts of generosity leave a sweetness like chocolate in the hands of children; and my son, Langston, for reminding me that miracles really happen, and to never take myself too seriously.

I could never name everyone who has helped me over the years, in many different ways. So to all my family and friends who have taught and continue to teach by their example, and who supported my efforts with kindness and smiles: thank you for your support. I thank Christine, Maureen, and Robert for being such good friends at a pivotal time in my life. To all my coworkers and friends in Yosemite National Park and Yellowstone National Park, past and present, thank you for wearing the gray and green, the colors of one great family, the National Park Service.

I'm grateful to Pete Devine and Bridget Kerr for their insightful reading of the manuscript early on; to Maxine Hong Kingston for being a great mentor, a steadfast supporter, and a bright example of what it means to be a writer; and to Gary Snyder for his words of encouragement when encouragement was needed. Deepest thanks to all my teachers at the University of Michigan, who offered advice and good criticism when I was their student: Gayl Jones, George Garrett, Richard Tillinghast, and Thomas Garbaty; as well as Andrea Beauchamp of the Hopwood Room; and especially Eric S. Rabkin, who told me once that it mattered.

I wish to acknowledge these friends who made a difference in my life and passed away much too soon: Maynard Gilbert, Derwin Abston, and Alex Smith, gone but never forgotten.

I'm grateful to my editors at Sierra Club Books, Linda Gunnarson and Diana Landau, who helped a manuscript become a novel. Most of all, I'm grateful to Roxann, my wife, soulmate, and anchor, who was always the first to hear and first to respond with intelligence, clarity, and wisdom, and whose words of simple praise made it all worthwhile. You showed me that I didn't need a road map to follow my heart. Thank *you* for *Gloryland*.

ABOUT THE AUTHOR

Shelton Johnson, a native of Detroit, Michigan, currently serves as a ranger in Yosemite National Park. He has worked for the National Park Service since 1987, also serving in Great Basin National Park and Yellowstone National Park, as well as in parks in and around Washington, D.C. He served with the Peace Corps in Liberia and attended graduate school at the University of Michigan, where he won several writing awards, including a Hopwood Award in poetry. Johnson has presented his original living-history program about a buffalo soldier at venues around the country and has received many honors and awards for this work, which has also been widely covered in the media; and he is featured in the Ken Burns documentary film *The National Parks: America's Best Idea*. Johnson and his wife and son live just outside Yosemite National Park.